I AM CLEOPATRA

ALSO BY NATASHA SOLOMONS

Mr Rosenblum's List
The Novel in the Viola
The Gallery of Vanished Husbands
The Song Collector
House of Gold
I, Mona Lisa
Fair Rosaline

AS N. E. SOLOMONS

The Bone Road

I AM CLEOPATRA

A Novel

NATASHA SOLOMONS

HARPER ● PERENNIAL

NEW YORK ● LONDON ● TORONTO ● SYDNEY ● NEW DELHI ● AUCKLAND

HARPER ● PERENNIAL

Without limiting the exclusive rights of any author, contributor or the publisher of this publication, any unauthorized use of this publication to train generative artificial intelligence (AI) technologies is expressly prohibited. HarperCollins also exercise their rights under Article 4(3) of the Digital Single Market Directive 2019/790 and expressly reserve this publication from the text and data mining exception.

I AM CLEOPATRA. Copyright © 2025 by Natasha Solomons. All rights reserved. No part of this book may be used or reproduced in any manner whatsoever without written permission except in the case of brief quotations embodied in critical articles and reviews. For information in the U.S., address HarperCollins Publishers, 195 Broadway, New York, NY 10007, U.S.A. In Canada, address HarperCollins Publishers Ltd, Bay Adelaide Centre, East Tower, 22 Adelaide Street West, 41st Floor, Toronto, Ontario, M5H 4E3, Canada. In Europe, HarperCollins Publishers, Macken House, 39/40 Mayor Street Upper, Dublin 1, D01 C9W8, Ireland.

HarperCollins books may be purchased for educational, business, or sales promotional use. For information, please email the Special Markets Department in the U.S. at SPsales@harpercollins.com or in Canada at HCOrder@harpercollins.com.

hc.com

Originally published as *Cleopatra* in Great Britain in 2025 by Manilla Press. Simultaneously published in 2025 by HarperCollins Canada Ltd.

Chapter illustrations © Shutterstock

FIRST US AND CANADIAN EDITIONS

Library of Congress Cataloging-in-Publication Data has been applied for.

Library and Archives Canada Cataloguing in Publication information is available upon request.

ISBN 978-0-06-344975-6 (US pbk.)
ISBN 978-1-4434-7586-0 (Canada pbk.)

Printed in the United States of America

25 26 27 28 29 LBC 5 4 3 2 1

For my children, Luke and Lara, who to my profound relief are much better friends than the Ptolemy siblings.

'Not know me yet?'

Antony and Cleopatra, Act 3, Scene 13

1
CLEOPATRA

I want you to see me as I am. You can dislike me, love me or abhor me, but know me first. I was born a girl and a goddess. A future queen, if I should live that long. My father's court teems with enemies, some of them members of my own family. Their malevolence crawls over my skin like ants, and if foul thoughts were deeds, then, like ants, they would have crept up the legs of my crib and eaten out my eyes. And yet, I am not entirely alone. Charmian belonged to me from the very first. She was taken from the mother she does not remember and gifted to me warm and milk-fed, still coiled from the womb. A goddess needs a servant to tend her, one formed to her wants like a pebble is smoothed and shaped by the hands of the sea. The priests chose her for me on discovering the hour of her birth was mere moments after mine.

It is the will of the gods that we should always be together. As infants we slept in the same crib – for I do not like to be alone – our two bodies slotted beside each other snug as a pair of proving loaves, her fingers curled against my neck. We were suckled side-by-side from the breasts of sister slaves. As we grew, she slumbered beside me or at the foot of my bed according to my desire.

I gave her a name when my tongue was able to speak. Until then, she had none at all. For every part of her belonged to me – even her name. Charmian, giver of joy. She says the joy I saw in her was my own delight reflected back, pure and bright. She is my slave, and yet for a long time she never wished to be free. For when we love are we not all slaves content in our subjugation? And, so, in my own way, I belong to her too, chained by love.

This morning we've been in the great library since first light. The pens of the scholars scratch their sheets of papyrus like the scuffling feet of mice. None of them pays us any attention for we're here every morning with my tutor, who sets Charmian and me a text to transcribe and then quizzes us in low whispers to test our understanding. The sun noses through the high windows like a snooping schoolboy hoping to copy my work. Tapering pillars are positioned carefully away from the rows of desks so that as the sun travels across the sky inconvenient shadows aren't cast upon our jottings. The mosaics are in muted colours so as not to tug at the eye of devoted scholars. Water plays in blue fountains to cool the air and soothe the mind. The great library of the mouseion is split into sections, according to language, then topic and alphabetised. I love the patterns and the divisions of the knowledge, the system itself pleases me in the same way as a brilliantly executed painting or piece of weaving. It's a temple, dedicated to both the muses themselves and to learning. The high priest librarian stalks between the shelves in his robes, ready to offer advice or produce the stick concealed in his sleeve to rap across the knuckles of any unfortunate scholar caught breaking the rules – making a mark on a library scroll or, worst of all, smuggling in an afternoon snack. Food and water are strictly forbidden, for fear of damaging the scrolls or enticing rodents. Charmian and I delight in provoking the grand librarian. We sneak in hunks of cheese that are in actuality painted wood, carafes of wine where the contents are not liquid but glass, purely to tease him. Although I am certain he would not dare strike his stick across my knuckles.

Today I sense a restlessness amongst the scholars. I know even though no one tells me, shielding me from the truth like flapping palm fronds against the sun, that the people of Alexandria hate my father. Rome is at the root of the trouble; Rome which has been nipping at our borders for years, eyeing our wealth. Egypt might be rich, but our armies are no match for Roman legions. We've watched other countries topple, felled like timber, their treasures and peoples dragged back to Rome. Roman power is built on plunder and slaves and avarice. What they do not own, they trample on and burn. We are the last beacon of freedom amid a dark Roman sea. One day they will come for us too.

In desperation, my father purchased a reprieve from Rome in the form of a title: 'Friend and Ally of the Roman People'.

The title is a promise that they will not gobble us up for now. But the cost he had to pay was exorbitant, vast even for a Pharaoh. And, unfortunately on the earthly side of the field of reeds, god-kings have to raise taxes. The people of Egypt resent their pockets being picked by their king on behalf of Rome. Their hate is usually tepid. A grumbling antipathy that never seeps away nor heats into violence. But their animosity has now risen to scalding. Again, my father has turned to Rome, begging for their help against his own people. If he'd asked me I would have told him that it was a mistake.

A Roman envoy came at the request of my father, trying to negotiate calm amongst the people, still their resentments. It has made everything worse still. Charmian says that the unlucky Roman killed the cat by accident, running it over with the wheels of his chariot. I am not certain that he killed it at all – or if the cat even existed – and was instead merely conjured as victim in an illusionary crime to excuse the murder. The Roman was certainly accused of killing a cat – one of our divine creatures – and the crowd vowed vengeance, mad for blood. My father's pleading and interference on the Roman's behalf only incensed them further, and the unfortunate man was dragged from his house and torn apart by the mob, his head ripped from his body, eviscerated as a cat would a mouse, left in pieces upon the cobbles. It was clear to me from that moment that my father was losing any influence he had, and every day since I sense it leach further away.

If there are whispers here, then the unrest has reached the palace. And yet in other ways, the library itself seems as tranquil as ever; in the centre of the mouseion, in front of a large rectangular pool, presides Plato himself. He's sculpted gazing upwards to the opening in the temple roof, but the tilt of his head and his frown makes him appear less engaged in intense contemplation so much as worrying about inclement weather. Sighing, I read back through my translation of Aramaic into Greek. It's poetry, supposedly, but I much prefer original Greek verse, which is earthier, more elegant and funny. This Aramaic verse is desiccated as old roses. I'd prefer to be studying the treatises on rural tax matters that we spent the previous week deciphering. Charmian stifles a yawn and plonks her forehead on the desk with a groan. Giggling, I nudge her. After we've been quizzed on the awful poem, and I have answered every question correctly and Charmian none of them, the tutor sighs.

'Come. Let me walk with you back to the palace,' he says.

'Please, I want to stay here. Just for a while. You don't have to remain with us. We're fine alone,' I say.

Usually, he understands my request to be a dismissal and retreats with good wishes, but today he shakes his head.

'I will not leave you without a guard,' he says and gives a signal. Ten warriors approach.

I'm used to their presence, but Charmian and I are expert at eluding them where necessary. Perhaps it's foolish, but in our bravado we believe that if we can escape my guards, we can outwit any assassins.

'Prepare tomorrow's texts carefully,' he says.

I need no urging, while nothing could entice Charmian. Academic pursuits hold no interest for her, although I've yet to encounter a courtier she could not charm, a slave whom she could not persuade to surrender their hoarded secrets to her.

Once he has gone, Charmian and I stroll through the library, ignoring the guards who trail behind us. To my relief they keep a respectful distance. There are carved wooden desks and tables laid out at regular intervals in each of the different sections of the reading room. The stone building is vast, adorned with columns, each decorated according to the section it houses: Doric columns in the Greek, and carved, illuminated Egyptian pillars in that section. The Greek section is the largest and busiest, crammed with scholars like caged chickens at the market. The next biggest is that dedicated to the Egyptian language, and it throngs with students and priests as they pore over texts containing the secrets of religion and divine law. There are other areas devoted to foreign languages, all meticulously ordered – Latin, Aramaic, Gaulish and yet more scrolls in the language of the Troglodytes, as well as beautifully illustrated texts in the Arabian and Syrian tongues. Charmian and I slide through all of these, passing the tidy combs of scrolls in papyrus and parchment and paper stacked as in a hive. As we walk through the Greek section, I pause, retrieving a scroll from a high shelf with care. A young man looks at me in surprise, about to object to its removal, and then seeing who it is that has taken it, snaps his mouth closed. We hurry on until we reach my favourite part of the library.

It's emptier here in the 'Ship' section. We retreat behind a pillar and perch at the base. Charmian produces sweets from her tunic – we're well concealed from the eye of the priest-librarian. These scrolls aren't about ships or oceans or maritime laws but are all documents that have been confiscated over the centuries by the Pharaohs from ships sailing into the harbour. The law here stipulates that all scrolls entering the port at Alexandria must be inspected by the librarians, and if they are not versions of texts already held here, then they must be loaned to the library and copied. Of course, it's never the original that is returned to the unfortunate merchant or traveller, merely the copy. My father and his fathers before him have pilfered and hoarded knowledge from all across the world and stacked it here in these sagging and overloaded shelves.

We sit in silence for a few minutes, the only noise is our sucking on the contraband sweetmeats. The air is perfumed with rosemary and myrrh to drive away moths and other scurrilous insects, but there is also the dry scent of the papyrus scrolls themselves, ensuring that now, to me, thoughts and words have a smell, herbal and enticing. I glance towards the Greek section where the original manuscripts of Aristotle and Plato are kept. They were written by the philosophers in their own hand, their ideas flowing straight into the very papers still held here. My tutor showed us one afternoon when we'd pleased him on our weekly tests. Or, rather, I had done well enough for both Charmian and me.

Within these walls are scrolls detailing all history from the siege at Troy (the egg Helen herself hatched from is held in another part of the mouseion) to Alexander himself to even the meagre achievements of my father. These shelves contain the whole world in thought and idea and possibility. Well, all the Greek and Egyptian world, but does any other really matter? I wipe my hands on my tunic, carefully removing all trace of stickiness, and then unfurl the scroll I borrowed. Charmian leans over my shoulder to look.

It's the first Ptolemy's life story, Alexander's general, and my ancestor. Our line of Pharaohs are all descended from him. After Alexander's death, Ptolemy, his favourite general, had Alexander's body placed in a coffin of hammered gold and, in time, it was brought to the new city of Alexandria and Ptolemy became the first Pharaoh of a new dynasty, mine. I like to pour over the details of his life, the sad death of Alexander, the birth of the new city. The dead king in his golden coffin. I can read about it three hundred years later because that Ptolemy wasn't only a soldier but a storyteller, the narrator of his own life. This is my favourite scroll and I read it here so often that I know much of it off by heart. Today, I don't read more than the first few sentences, and then I lean back against the pillar.

'I think I shall be like Ptolemy, Charmian.'

'Of course you will. You'll rule and be wise and beloved.'

'Yes, I shall. But I'll also write about it like he did. I'll write my own history.'

Charmian looks at me, a little surprised but intrigued. 'I'm not writing a single word that I don't absolutely have to. But then I'm lucky. No one will be interested in me except how I reflect you. You are the palace, I'm just the mirror pool, here to make you look even more glorious.'

I laugh and say, incredulous, 'So you only get all your work wrong to make me look better?'

Charmian grins. I lean back against the pillar and continue.

'I'll write my own history. And one day it will sit in the library here, and in a thousand years people will come to the library and read my story, just as it happened. They'll see me. Know me as though they'd wandered through my court.

I won't leave it to others to translate me. I'll be like Ptolemy. I'll write every word myself.'

Charmian listens for a moment, her expression serious. Then she adds with a wry grin, 'Don't make it too long, Cleo. Maybe don't do lots of things, then you won't have to write them all down.'

I laugh and she smiles. I stretch out, yawn, certain that this library will last forever like the ideas it holds.

Charmian and I race scorpions in the palace, their feet scratching against the smooth marble floors. We whoop for joy, goading them faster, poking at them with straws. But then, to my irritation, panicked slaves appear and stop the game. 'What if you're stung, princess?' they demand. No one worries that anything might happen to Charmian.

Either way, I take no notice. Grabbing her hand, I simply lead Charmian further out into the gardens, dodging all the palace guards, and we race the insects under the lemon groves where the household slaves can't find us. I love Charmian because she fights properly, hissing at her scorpion to win, she never throws a race even though I'm her mistress and princess. We play for so long, we don't notice that darkness has stolen into the groves all around. We creep back to the palace, hoping that no one will notice, but of course they do. We're spotted in an instant, my robes are streaked with grime.

The chief of the palace guards is livid with rage.

'You were told to stay with the guards today. The entire royal staff has been hunting for you both for hours,' he says, vibrating with anger.

I want to tell him that they're pretty useless if it's taken them this long not to find us, but I don't want to make it any worse. And then, fear nudges me – perhaps the threat is more insistent than usual. I think of the cat and the Roman and the blood upon the cobbles and feel a little sick.

'Your father requires you,' he says.

I know that the punishment will be worse for having made my father wait. He will have had the slaves whipped for failing to produce me. We walk to his apartment in silence. He rarely summons me in the evening. He's wedged on his throne and when he tries to rise on seeing me, I realise that he's stuck. I hurry over to him and kneel at his feet to save him the humiliation. He places his hand on my cheek, it's moist with sweat, and he leans over, whispering in my ear.

'You are safe. I am glad you're safe.'

I am the only one of his children whom he views with real affection. His easy favourite. I amuse him with my beauty and cleverness. But my family doesn't respect love or affection, only power. And early on, my father chose it for me. I am not the oldest, but it's me who my father wants to succeed him. I know that one day, power and Egypt will come to me and not to the others. It will come, or I'll take it.

'Papa? Great Pharaoh?'

I kiss his damp palm.

'We are leaving for Rome, in the morning. I find myself in need of counsel,' he says.

I stare at him in surprise. He doesn't want counsel, he wants an army. He worries the mob will reach the palace. He's not only lost the affection of his people, he's lost control. He hopes Rome will give him soldiers to take it back. I look into his eyes, and for the first time I see he's frightened. He's running away and he's taking me with him.

The palace is in chaos all through the night as the slaves prepare for this sudden journey. My siblings are to be left behind, my oldest sisters Cleopatra Typhinia and Berenice to rule by proxy. They are not Pharaohs, but stand-ins for my father. Unlike him, I'm not convinced that they understand the difference. My father plans to return with an army provided by the Romans and slot himself back onto his throne. With Roman legions beside him, any whisper of rebellion will hush, or if it does not, the legions will rid him of dissenters. I'm uneasy about his plan. I do not like that he turns to foreigners to help him with Egypt's problems, least of all Romans. They watch our shores greedily, eyeing our riches like uninvited guests slobbering at a feast. And, I wonder at his choice of my older sisters to keep his throne warm. They care for no one but each other and, like evening is to night, they are indivisible. They hate me, any affection scorched by our father's preference for me, and I scrupulously stay out of their way.

My only solace is that in the turmoil the chief of the palace guard has forgotten to punish me for my earlier escapade in the lemon grove.

'Princess.' The head of the guard approaches, his head bowed in respect to me. My stomach turns.

He has not forgotten. To my dismay, under the watchful eye of the nursery slaves, a young guard with a thin moustache like spider's legs is ordered to punish Charmian for our misdemeanour. I watch, weeping, as she's whipped.

I can't be punished but seeing her suffer for me is a worse pain. Two slaves hold my shoulders, restraining me so I can't get in the way of the whip, and I stand there with lemon leaves in my hair, watching her accept our punishment, my winning scorpion scrabbling in a bag at my waist, tears and snot streaking my cheeks.

Afterwards they let us escape to my rooms, and she sits on the floor of my chamber, her back striped with red welts, tears easing out from under swollen lids. Another slave girl tends her wounds, wipes away the blood, applies a poultice to the bruises. I slide Charmian the bag with my winning scorpion. She accepts it, squeezes my hand and doesn't let go. Charmian is the only one who knows that in my heart, I'm just a girl with lemon leaves in her hair.

We lie in bed, side-by-side, our feet tangled together. I watch the rosy light of dawn ripen outside the window. Still, unable to sleep, I think about Rome and listen to the scorpion inside its bag in the dark, scratching, scratching.

2

CLEOPATRA

I do not want to go to Rome. In my thirteen years, I have never left Egypt and for all the dangers and skulduggery of the palace, Alexandria is home. Rome is filthy and loud in comparison, even from behind the curtain of my litter. As I am carried through the streets, the stink overwhelms me. The taste of rotting vegetables and butchery and the ever-pervasive reek of sweat and human flesh grates the back of my nose and throat. I sniff at the oil of myrrh daubed on my wrists to try and stop the bile rising in my stomach. The roads twist, narrow and dark as a vein, and I long for the wide-open streets of home. There is no ocean breeze here, only the fermenting stink of shit and piss – urns set out on every corner for all citizens and slaves alike to fill and then leave for the dyers and the laundry men until the entire place reeks of stale urine. We have been away now for more than two months and I long to go home.

The road we progress along is slammed with ox-carts lined up nose to tail and the shouting of freedmen and slaves, the slap of their whips against the bony backs of the cattle. Peeping out of the curtain, I glimpse Charmian walking beside the litter trying to keep up, stepping around the molten rounds of dung. I wave at her, and she blows me a kiss. I see a few eyes marvelling at the magnificence of the litter, its golden struts studded with a hundred varieties of polished shells and black scarabs, the thick red curtains. Most, however, grunt and swear at the inconvenience. Our train of litters and attendants are clogging the already busy street, and the muscular slaves on either side of us wield stout cudgels to keep the path clear.

There is a sudden cry above, an almost human shriek of grief. I tug the curtain aside again and, glancing upwards, I see a flock of pintail ducks, a fleet of arrows sailing towards the sun, outlines sharp as a whetted blade against the brightening sky. I marvel at the wonder of them, my heart catching. They're gone in a moment and I feel a pang on seeing them vanish. I scour the sky, hoping for another glimpse, and to my delight I'm rewarded when the birds turn and appear again for a few seconds before melting into the clouds that seem to peel apart to accept them. I notice that Charmian has stopped to stare up at the sky too, searching for the ducks. She stands in the street, quite still, the crowds surging around her like a river rushing around a rock. With concern, I see that our procession has continued some distance without her and I shout out. Startled, she races to catch up, shoving her way through the crowd which now swarms into the space left by the departing train. I reach out of the window, and her damp fingers brush mine.

The litters halt outside an austere villa set back from the road, surrounded by a lush garden. A path of bleached stone leads between sentinel rows of orange and lemon trees with myrtle bushes at their base, their purpling leaves coated with dust and crowded with butterflies. Neptune bathes in a fountain before the entrance, holding his polished trident so high that it looks as if he wishes to spear the sun. Yet, it is a villa and not a palace. I can't understand why we must walk to Cato the Roman and he won't come to us; my father Auletes is a god-king. I don't know why my father holds Cato in such high regard. He is just a senator, but supposedly renowned for his honesty, integrity and parsimony. The last of these doesn't interest me and the first two I doubt. I'm yet to meet a Roman who cared for anyone other than himself, for anything other than the interests of Rome.

As our party reaches the end of the path, a slave opens the door. The litters are set down on the floor and Charmian hands me down. We stand in a large and sunlit vestibule lined with shrines and garlanded statues of their gods around a low pool. They look small to me and badly carved with misshapen, lumpish limbs, the secret godhead missing from the sculptor's hand. They shall not dance into life at dusk. With a flurry of activity, my father emerges from behind the curtain of his litter, sweating and corpulent, and yet the moment he sees me, he smiles. Winks at me. Concern and affection nudge me. Perspiration is beaded in the fleshy folds at his wrists and in the sausages of his neck. I pity the slaves who lugged him here, and I watch as one of them vomits in the corner, exhausted from the effort. No one takes any notice. More slaves and servants crowd around my father the king, plying him with cool linen and drinks flavoured with roses and herbs, chilled from the river. I linger further back while Charmian adjusts my cloak and the jewels stitched into my hair. After a few moments, a man appears before us, his toga white like his hair, skin creased and yellow as old papyrus. He mumbles a series of compliments but his flattery is as tired as his face. My father winces but cannot voice his displeasure.

'Senator Cato is ready to receive you, great Auletes, mighty ruler of Egypt and the lands of the Nile,' concludes the man with a flourish.

If this declaration of power were true and not just breath, then we would not be here, forced to pay morning *salutatio* to a mere senator and magistrate. My father holds out his arm, and I take it. He places his slippery hand over mine. He's comforted having me at his side. I know how much he dislikes politics and manoeuvrings.

'Do you think he received the gifts we sent?' he whispers, anxious.

'Of course he did,' I reassure him. 'He will thank you for them prettily in a moment.'

Or so he ought, I think, but with these Romans nothing is certain. As I glance at my father, pale and sweaty with worry, I know that he'd prefer to be at home in the palace, eating figs and overripe cheese, his feet tap-tapping to the cheerful medley of assorted musicians. I stifle a sigh, my frustration and irritation scratching against my affection for him.

We follow the man but to my bewilderment he leads us straight through the triclinium with its sofas covered in silk and its frescoed ceilings and into a much smaller room half bathed in darkness. The smell hits me first. More shit. I hold my wrist to my nose and try to block out the stench. I cannot distinguish the man in the gloom. Then, I see him. At first I thought he was seated on a throne, and then I realise he is on the latrina, his toga hitched up around his waist, the nest of pubic hair visible at his crotch. He does not rise but grunts and there follows a wet squirt as excrement slops into the brimming bucket below. My father stands and gapes at him, unspeaking and wretched. He grips my arm, uncertain of what he ought to do. Disgust rises in my throat and mingles with rage at the insult. I hardly dare to breathe, which seems wise considering the circumstance.

'Welcome, Great Pharaoh, Ruler of the Red Lands and the Black,' says the man, who I now understand to be Cato himself. 'I am sorry to receive you like this without the honour and pomp you deserve, but I had taken a laxative before we received notice of your intention to visit us this morning Rome.'

This is clearly a lie. Our caravan of gifts would have alerted him to our plan.

'We understand and take no offence, senator,' replies my father Pharaoh, forcing himself into obsequiousness, pretending the Roman does not fib. 'It is your advice and help we require, not empty ceremony.'

'All the same,' responds Cato, 'we would have preferred to receive you properly. There is food and music at least.'

I look around and now notice a banquet has been laid out at the side of the room: bowls of honeyed figs and melon, cured meat, flagons of wine, bitter leaves spread with pomegranate seeds, dishes of oil, mounds of herbed olives and elaborate plaited loaves of bread; a large plump fish with glassy, unseeing eyes and its skin peeled back and a stuffed peacock on a roost of lemons and walnuts, the eye feathers stuck into the lemons so that the dish leers back at us like the giant Argus. The bodies of several dozen roasted quail huddle beside it. Yet the food is like a feast from the underworld, it stirs no appetite for the room is crammed with the foul and pervasive smell of Cato's bowels. The musicians cannot fit into the small room and the sound of the lyre and mournful singing filters through an open doorway. I observe that while Cato apologises for his bizarre and inadequate reception, he does not acknowledge that he ought to be the one to appear before King Auletes.

'Please, if you do not wish to eat, sit. Sit,' says Cato with a wave of his hand, as though the Pharaoh is an ordinary supplicant.

I wait expectantly for my father to admonish him for his disrespect. I exchange a look with Charmian, for she and I have witnessed lesser slights provoke the tinkle of spraying teeth and the wine-red splash of blood against the wall. Charmian winces in anticipation, but my father only blinks and swallows in astonishment, like a plump and glossy bullfrog. A moment later, at a loss for what else to do, he sits, releases my arm and perches on the edge of a small sofa. It creaks beneath his bulk.

I eye both men, my heart burdened with sorrow. I love my father and yet my affection does not blind me to his ineptitude.

'You have come for my advice,' says Cato.

I do not get to hear it, for at that moment a woman appears and inclines her head to my father – Romans will not bow even when they are not on the toilet.

'Servilia,' says Cato. 'My sister. She is here to offer hospitality to the royal princess.'

I am torn, for while I want to stay with my father, listen to the politics and the suggestions of the famed Cato, the smell is overwhelming and I long to escape. As it is, I have no choice, for my father signals me to follow Servilia.

Unwillingly, Charmian and I trail after her into the garden. Beyond the vine-strewn loggia is spread a green paradise of tranquil beauty but I observe it all with impatience. I'm a princess, a Pharaoh in waiting, but because I'm a woman, Cato the Roman has shuffled me into the garden with the children and the dogs. There are scented mulberry bushes, their leaves silver against the vivid blue of the sky. A sculpted Priapus with a distended cock lurks amongst a cluster of birches, which I assume are metamorphosed nymphs, transformed into trees as they tried to escape his ravishing. It's mystical and charming but I don't care. Irritation prickles my skin like a heat rash.

'May I offer you some wine?' says Servilia. 'Or a tour of the viridarium?'

I shake my head, impatient. I have no interest in the roses sprawling across the dusty trellis and festooning the statues of lascivious Roman gods. I want to hear Cato speak or else how can I counsel my father?

I see her give a small nod, a tiny tight smile playing at the edges of her mouth as though I am exactly as she expects: a foreign princess, spoiled, rude. I take a breath.

'I wanted to hear what my father and your brother discuss,' I say. 'I need to know what advice he offers.'

Servilia is quiet for a moment, as though still considering

me. 'My brother's advice is renowned. It doesn't mean that it's right.'

Then, I realise, it's not Cato who has concocted this plan to prise me away from my father but Servilia herself. I'm intrigued and suddenly, the heat is less irritating, the noise of the crickets less loathsome, and I look at her with interest. Her eyes are a soft blue-grey, petalled with thick lashes, but their expression is so shrewd that I'm certain they miss nothing.

'Why, madam, I think I have changed my mind. Let us walk around the viridarium. I should like to rest in the cool of the fountain,' I say.

We process slowly, Charmian trying to shade me against the barrage of the sun, but I signal to her to stop fussing. The heat of Rome is nothing to me. When we are a little distance from the villa, Servilia sends the slaves away and waits for me to do the same with Charmian.

'She stays. I would sooner remove my shadow,' I say.

Servilia nods, accepting her presence. She trails long fingers in the spray of the water; rainbows shimmer where it catches the light, colouring the mist.

'Is there advice that you would you give?' I ask.

Now she smiles, warm and open. Her teeth are white and small as seed pearls.

'I heard that you were pretty. That didn't interest me,' she says. 'I also heard that you are clever. Cleverer than your brothers and sisters.'

She doesn't include my father, but we both understand her implication. It is mere months since Charmian and I were racing scorpions in the palace, and yet it feels so long ago. I was a child then. I am no longer. Servilia does not treat me as a child but my father's daughter, a princess. Her expression darkens and grows serious as she speaks.

'My advice is this, return home and persuade great Auletes to make peace with the warring factions in your country. Do not ask Rome for an army. The price is too high.'

'My father is rich beyond thought,' I say. 'He can pay any price.'

Servilia shakes her head. 'The greed of the men in Rome is insatiable and if you converted all Egypt into cash it would not be enough for them. You will be in perpetual servility to Rome, not only your father but all his heirs.'

She shapes her advice so it pricks at me too.

'I am grateful for your insight,' I say. 'It is wise and considered, but you must understand my hesitation. Why do you give it? Excuse my bluntness, but what do you care, madam, if Egypt is reduced to rags, her gold shipped across the sea?'

Servilia looks at me, her expression grave but a smile twitching at the corners of her mouth.

'I like your cleverness,' she says.

'Don't distract me with flattery,' I say. 'I'm not a man. It won't work.'

'I'm not trying to,' she says softly. She takes a deep breath and sighs. 'Pompey wants your father to have his legions. He wants your father in his debt. He seeks to pocket Egypt and all her riches.'

'And you do not like Pompey? You do not want to see him fat on our gold?'

All humour leaves her face, her voice hardens. 'I hate Pompey. He killed my first husband. It was a coward's murder. One day, he will receive the retribution he deserves from the gods. Until that day, I will not aid the murderer of my son's father.'

I study her expression, full of loathing and rage. I believe her.

'Pray to Osiris if Mars does not hear you,' I say. 'His vengeance is swift and vicious. He'll drag Pompey down to the underworld, voiceless and alone. The prayers of Rome won't reach his soul there.'

She bows her head.

'What would you have me and my father do?' I ask.

'Sail home. Go now and seek reconciliation. There can be no happiness for you otherwise. Grasping senators will melt your crown into coins.'

'But without a Roman army, how shall my father remain king?'

'What king will he be, if he and his heirs are owned by Rome?'

I do not answer. She voices those fears that already lingered in my breast from when my father first told me that we were coming here as supplicants. He must not sell Egypt. I will not be owned by Rome. I am to be a queen, not a chattel. I only hope that he'll listen to me.

We return to the villa, and find Cato still seated upon the latrina. He's talking as we enter, pausing only for a moment. Auletes' tongue darts across his lips, quick as a gecko. Cato continues.

'The signs are against you. Did you not see the birds this morning? The ducks circled and then flew east. The augur says they shrieked as they flew. Your situation is perilous. The gods warn against helping you. Romans will not want to offer you an army now.'

Auletes' expression tightens, alarmed.

'I understand. The price is high, if I must buy against the warnings of your gods,' he says.

Fury heats inside me. I understand what my father does not, that Cato is preparing him to be bled, to gush Egypt's riches into Rome. I glance at Servilia, and she is looking at me as if to say, 'See, I told you so? Take heed.'

My father rises and steps forward as if to take Cato's hand and then, remembering what the senator is seated upon, hesitates. Cato, however, unconcerned, beckons him forward, and rising a little from his noxious throne kisses Auletes' cheek.

As we leave, Servilia places her own kiss upon my cheek, and as she does, she whispers in my ear, 'My counsel is offered in friendship. Do not let your father become a beggar king.'

I want to talk to my father after his potbellied advisors have retired to sleep. They do not like that a girl countermands them. I wait until he's in bed, and then I slide into his chamber and sit at the bottom of his bed. His skin is waxy and pale. All my life I've observed my father's mistakes, the greed and sycophancy of his advisors, their dry whisperings as much use as the shuffling of old papyrus. At home, I sit at my father's side or in the great library at Alexandria, learning how not to rule. The only time I ever really see him happy is when he picks up his wooden flute and plays. Then he sways to his own music, for once his bulk almost graceful, the childlike expression of bliss upon his face transforming his features into surprising sweetness. He ought to have been a minstrel and not a king, but such is the will of the gods. He had to rule so that his throne could pass to me.

I brush his cheek with my fingertips, and he smiles at me.

'Papa, don't sell us to Rome. It's a bloodletting.'

He looks grey but he continues to smile. 'One we can afford.'

'No. They want to reduce us to nothing so that we can be absorbed into the Roman empire, like milk into linen.'

'What would you have me do? We need the fist of Rome.'

'The money you'd pay to Rome, pay to our citizens instead. Use it to raise our own army.'

'They will not fight for me, child.'

'Then pay them until they will. The money will seep back into Egypt, like the rain from the sky always finds its way to the Nile. But, if you water Rome with our gold, then it will be their rivers that shall swell, their land that shall fatten.'

I talk for nearly an hour, and he listens. He asks questions and I try to answer as best I can. I offer him Servilia's warning and he frowns, unhappy, but does not ask how or why I came to such a view. At last he sighs and closes his eyes.

'I shall sleep on this, Cleo. But, it is true that I do not like it here. The food sickens my stomach. I should not be sorry to be travelling home.'

I kiss him good night and go to bed with my heart lighter, almost certain that I have persuaded him.

*

We are living in a villa that Pompey has lent us. He seems to expect our gratitude but it is cramped and it smells of river mud and effluence. I pine for the salt sea air, and the date palms and the wind singing through the high reeds. Rome is stuffed with great men, a forest full of lumbering oaks, but there are two taller than all the others: Pompey and Caesar. They are joined in an uneasy sharing of power, but the city is divided into factions. We tread lightly, trying to buy new friends on every side. My father wants to purchase enough senators to approve his request for Roman legions in the senate. They demur and obfuscate, pretending reluctance. My father sends emissaries to haggle. The great men of Rome have a price. Over the next weeks, we allow prominent citizens to call upon us and stuff us with compliments. The senators smile and blink and suggest to my father that they can be bought, at a price. They'll support his plea to the senate for legions in exchange for gold and cash. Auletes thanks them for their greed, which he renames as kindness. But we are already planning our journey home. I feel the relief like the bright sea air of Alexandria. I wait to see if Servilia will come again, but I do not see her face amongst the other Romans. She is the only one who snagged my interest. The others are all alike in their flattery and avarice. Their sticky compliments leave a residue on my skin like honey and I long to wash them away.

We are sitting in the garden of the villa listening to flautists play. I watch my father, shiny with happiness, when a messenger arrives. He's grey with dust and half falls from his horse. The beast itself is more than half dead, flanks hollowed out and snorting a gale. The slaves catch the man as he slumps and carry him to us, laying him on the ground at my father's feet. His lips are cracked with blood and muck. A slave pokes him with his foot, until he speaks.

'One of your daughters is dead. The other declares herself Pharaoh,' he whispers.

'Which is dead?' asks my father with a lack of grief.

'Cleopatra Typhinia. Berenice proclaims herself Pharaoh.'

My father's eyes go very wide. He is more wounded by this betrayal than he is by the news of the other Cleopatra's death.

'How did she die?' I ask.

The messenger shakes his head. 'I do not know. A sudden illness.'

A sudden illness called Berenice. I had always thought my sisters were attached to one another as twisting vines. It is now clear that one vine has strangled the other.

'Berenice sends a hundred men to Rome, to argue her case in the senate. That she is more beloved by the people than you and should be declared Pharaoh by Rome. I rode ahead but they follow quickly behind.'

I can see my father is dumb with fear.

'We must go home,' I say. 'You must punish her and reclaim your throne.'

'Without a Roman army?' he asks. 'That means death.'

'We must go back to Egypt,' I insist. 'We will buy more men as we approach. There are still some who are loyal to us and no one has love for my sister.'

'No, I need a Roman army,' he insists. 'But Cato warns me that the Roman gods are against me. There was a portent. The gods do not want us to have Roman legions.'

'For shame! He said this to raise the price. The Roman gods do not care about us one way or another. We belong to our own gods. We wield their power. You know this, Papa.'

He grunts, uncertain.

'Do not buy their legions.'

'And what of your sister's agents coming to Rome, their pockets stuffed with gold and bribes?'

'You are richer still. You are Pharaoh. And as for her men, Papa, dead men can't argue in the senate.'

I look at my father. He knows what he must do, if he wants to live. If he wants me to live. He blinks and swallows. He rubs and rubs his hands, until the skin is red and raw.

I order the slaves to prepare for our journey back to Alexandria with all haste. While my father hesitates and fumbles, I take charge. As they pack and assemble horses, I go to the temple of Isis, preparing to make an offering, taking only Charmian with me. Isis is my goddess and I am her earthly body. She is the most powerful of the women gods, the mother of the earth and magic, married to Death himself. I brush her power with my fingertips.

Charmian and I ride to the temple together in the litter. This is an indulgence that would not be tolerated at home, but here no one notices. In any case, I sense the household looks at me differently. Before I was a precious and indulged child but now I am the royal consort, my father's voice. They won't beat Charmian again as my proxy, they would not dare.

The streets are as packed as ever, and I stare through a gap in the curtain with little interest, busy with my own thoughts.

Berenice must be removed and punished. The nature of her punishment will be up to my father, but it will almost certainly be death. Anything less will suggest weakness. And, then, something intrudes upon my thoughts. I notice more litters than usual amongst the traffic. They're all the same, and in Egyptian style and colours. They're borne by Egyptian slaves. For a moment, panic flares – my sister's men are here. Then, I realise, the colours are my father's. The purple and white of our royal house. These are gifts, bribes for Romans. We pass three. Four. A dozen. A horrid suspicion grows. Then, as we stop, held up by cattle who've wandered onto the road, I notice a wall papered in flyers. Charmian sees it at the same time and has slid down from the litter in a moment and run across the street to the wall. She tears one down and carries it back to the litter, narrowly being missed by a cart piled high with dung. She presses the parchment into my hand. It's written in Latin in large letters, and I read aloud in dismay.

'To the people of Rome, support the cause of the Great Auletes, friend of Rome. Grant him Roman legions.'

My father has ignored my pleas. He is trying to buy Rome, and the price will be Egypt and a mortgage on my throne.

That night as Charmian undresses me with the help of her fellow slaves, I'm quiet, steeped in my own thoughts. I don't even murmur as she yanks at the knots in my hair or as she bathes my hands, feet, face and private parts in warm and scented water. Furious thoughts buzz around my mind like biting flies. The other slaves withdraw, leaving me alone with Charmian. Only then do I finally speak, my words hissing from my lips, globby with rage and frustration.

'He won't listen. How can someone capable of such sweetness also be such a fool? Giving him advice is like hurling drops of water into a pan of fat. It comes back at you, spitting.'

I ball my hands into fists so tightly that my nails dig into my flesh. I'm so angry that a mess of tears and anger knots in my throat, choking me.

'He might love me. But he will beggar me anyway. Not through design but folly.'

I take a breath, trying to steady myself.

'When I am queen, I will not plead like him. I shall never supplicate to a man straining upon a latrina, where his attention is divided between my country's fate and his own arsehole.'

Needing air, I stalk to the window where the lid of sky droops heavy and purple with dusk. I take deep breaths and blink away my tears. When I speak again, my voice is steady.

'And, Cato was wrong about the birds. His augur should be beaten and told to read more books so he can divine better. Pintail ducks in flight declare a woman's power. Her resolve. What my father gives away, I shall take back.'

I stare at Charmian.

'I believe you, princess,' she says.

I am shiny with anger and brimming with absolute resolve. I order her to bring me papyrus and pen and ink. I do not want this moment misunderstood by those who come later. I write for myself and so that others can know what happened. By the light of the candle, I sit and I write and write, my pen scratching in fury, as though through the act I can exorcise the rage inside me and lance my resentment with my sharpened nib.

3

SERVILIA

You know the name Cleopatra, but I doubt you've ever heard of me. I'm one of the women at the edge of the history, brushed to the side much as the slaves sweep away dust and debris. I have had two husbands and in time I grew fond of each of them. I bore them children and tended to their houses and slaves. If there was not love between us, then there was at least affection, if not heat then warmth. I was not unhappy. Many women have worse husbands and more of them. I had only two, neither unpleasant nor unkind. One could say that I was in fact fortunate and, truly, I felt that luck and gave thanks to the gods. But I am more than the men I married and the children whom I bore. And, if you listen a while, you'll understand how I am part of Cleopatra's story too. Our lives are threaded together, at first by shared love and later by death. All these things happened so long ago that almost everyone else has forgotten my part. But I'm skipping ahead – it's a habit when one gets old, everything happens at once, time is kneaded and folded in on itself like soft dough.

Let me turn the scroll back a length, to the end of Cleopatra's first visit here in Rome. I was glad to see the Egyptians go, a departing storm of chaos, money and death. For months, the entire city of Rome had been drunk on Egyptian gold. Citizens and senators walked out into the streets and held out their hands as though to catch raindrops and gold fell into their palms. Their greed triggered a kind of madness, blinding them to the murder and mutilations that followed in the Pharaoh's wake. Even weeks after the foreigners left, we were still finding corpses in Rome. It was easy enough for the citizens to turn a blind eye for none of the dead were Romans, merely Egyptians sent by Berenice, daughter of the Pharaoh, to plead her case in the senate. Berenice dispatched men to argue on her behalf but she sent scholars and politicians, not warriors, and their sharp wit was no match for the sharp swords of the thugs and mercenaries belonging to King Auletes. Not a single one of Berenice's men lived to plead a single word in Rome. Slaves discovered a dozen bodies on the road into the city, throats slit, wounds scabbed with flies. Others were stabbed or strangled and tossed into the Tiber, the corpses catching on the bridges and silting up the flow. A few of Berenice's men succeeded in reaching the city and toasted their safe arrival with wine. That toast was their last, the carafe laced with poison. Everyone whispered that it was the Pharaoh who had ordered these killings. They might have been right. But I wonder whether it was Cleopatra. They always say that poison is a woman's preferred choice.

The first time we met she was just a girl, or perhaps I ought to say woman, for she was only a little younger than I was when I married my first husband, somewhere around thirteen or fourteen. She was small and thin, but with black hair and eyes and the promise of prettiness to come. But, while everyone laughed about the fat Pharaoh, her father, few seemed to notice the clever, dark-eyed girl at his side. I did.

During her visit to Rome with her father, I watched her for a while at public gatherings over the weeks, before finally speaking to her at my brother Cato's house. Cato wished me to talk to Cleopatra. He had prepared his own speech for me to give. I listened politely, allowing him to assume that I would repeat his opinions. I was fond of my brother, but also aware of his intractability. He assumed that his opinion was so persuasive that I could never think otherwise. I allowed him to believe this – and then took my own way. I had my own reasons for wanting the Egyptians to return quickly to Alexandria, and without Roman soldiers. Pompey wanted to give Auletes his legions and be paid the wealth of Egypt in return. My hatred of Pompey was deeper than Hades, and whatever Pompey desired, I was determined he should not get.

There was a time, long ago, before Cleopatra was even born, that Rome seemed to grow tyrants like a hydra sprouts new heads; as soon as one foul oppressor was removed, another grew in his place. The worst of these hydra was Pompey. When my first husband Brutus left Rome to join the rebellion in the name of the republic, he fought against Pompey and tyranny. Sometimes now I can hardly recall

Brutus's face. Yet, I can still hear his voice, his certainty and affection when he spoke of the sanctity of the Roman republic. He never spoke of me with the same passion. Over dinner, between sips of wine, he liked to recount the legend of the first Brutus who had killed the last king of Rome, another monster. He believed he shared more than just a name with that Brutus, but blood and honour too, and it was his destiny to fell tyrants.

My husband was gone for months, and the household continued without him in much the same manner. We weren't relieved or cheered by his absence for he was no despot, but our union was one of polite companionship rather than easy or deep affection. I recognised him as a good man, decent and earnest if a little dull – a man whose anecdotes never seemed to lead to a punchline and yet were oft repeated. Mostly I was occupied with my son Brutus, and content to devote myself to him and his education. At ten, my boy was bright, interested and interesting. As a baby, I adored him and was frightened by him in equal measure. He was too small and too fragile. I hung his crib with amulets, death was black-eyed and hungry for infants, and I endlessly pressed the slaves to be careful with him. But as he grew into his busy boyhood, stout and pink-cheeked, I relaxed and enjoyed him. We were happy, the war was far off and distant, and while it was dangerous in Rome I did not fear for myself or my boy. We lived quietly, rarely ventured out, and I persuaded myself that we were safe, that nothing needed to change.

The day started warm and pleasant, no different from any other. The slaves were pinning up laundered linens amongst the lavender to be scented by the breeze as they dried.

The cook was fussing that the fish that had been delivered wasn't fresh, the sound of his complaints spilling out across the gardens. I listened to the hum of the bees in the honeysuckle outside the window as I tallied accounts. Then, the messenger arrived. He sauntered into the triclinium where I sat, with the barest effort at politeness, the slave who'd opened the door to him trailing behind, upset that he'd been unable to announce him. The visitor was bearded and dirty from some days upon the road and smelled accordingly. I did not rise and greet him, his rudeness made him forfeit such civilities.

'I am sent by Pompey,' he announced, self-satisfied and preening.

My husband was fighting against Pompey and his allies, and I could not at first understand why his enemy would send a messenger to me, at my house.

'Praise Mars, the war is done. The great Pompey is victorious,' he said, his voice hoarse. 'Your husband and his fellow rebels surrendered.'

Fear rose in my throat, bitter as gall.

'And how fares my husband?' I asked.

'Dead.'

The bees buzzed and hummed, their sound pulsing in my head.

'How did he die?'

'On the great Pompey's command. He died by the sword.'

'During the battle?'

'After. On Pompey's orders,' he repeated, his tone crowing and without an inch of pity.

'Afterwards? He had surrendered?' I asked, the villainy that had taken place now slowly clarifying.

'Yes,' said the messenger, only now displaying a touch of unease.

'Where is his body?'

'Disposed of. Burned.'

I saw now that he carried the ashes of my husband in an urn, tucked under his arm like a flowerpot. I turned from him in contempt. I would not let him see that I was saddened and disgusted. My face was not his to read.

I left the room and went outside. Brutus was playing in the garden, and I walked along the paths, calling for him. After a minute, I found him and watched as he ran towards me, his cheeks flushed with exertion. Knowing what I must do, the pain I must now inflict, my stomach filled with dread, and my mouth dried. I crouched down, and placing my hands gently on his shoulders, I explained that there was a man come from Pompey with news and he must be very brave.

'Is my father dead?' he asked, looking steadily into my eyes.

My voice caught in my throat, and it took me two attempts to answer.

'He is with his ancestors,' I replied.

Brutus made no answer and did not cry. As we made our way slowly back to the house, he remained silent. He walked beside me and I saw him straighten, discard the stick with which he'd been playing as he discarded the last vestiges of his childhood. In truth, I never saw him play again. When we reached the house, the messenger was waiting for us outside on the loggia. Roses, lavender and jasmine were strewn all about him in the beds, and the prettiness of the scene and the sweet fragrance warred with the horror that he now forced upon us. Brutus looked up and down at the messenger still clutching the pot of ashes, and he grew very still. He did not weep or shout, but asked very softly, 'That is all that remains of my father?'

'I am so very sorry, my love,' I replied, speaking before the messenger had time to heap on yet more insult and pain.

Brutus's face did not change. He only asked, 'Who has done this thing?'

'Pompey,' said the messenger quickly, before I could reply. And then, with phlegm and excitement, he began to recount the details of the murder. How Brutus's father had surrendered, realising victory was impossible. How Pompey had accepted, and then, had him murdered anyway. Perhaps on seeing how my son listened so quietly, the horror and disgust showing on his face, the man began to deflate like a pig's bladder as he told his tale. If perhaps it had sounded glorious in his mind as he rehearsed it, now it was grubby and foul.

'This was a crime. Unworthy of a Roman,' I said at last when he was done.

That night I sat with Brutus until he fell asleep. He was so quiet, but his face was painted with grief and rage. It was the face of a boy, but the expression of a man. When at last he was asleep, I quietly crept out into the garden. It was oddly bright, lit by the full-face moon. I muttered a prayer to Diana, asking her to watch over me and my son, now that we were alone. I picked handfuls of herbs that I'd tended and grown myself, then fetched a cup of wine and the best of the nuts from the larder and walked to the shrine in the midst of the garden dedicated to Mars. I placed my offering before the shrine and lit a candle.

'I ask Mars the avenger to enact vengeance upon Gnaeus

Pompey. May he suffer and bleed, be cursed and betrayed. May his corpse weep from the banks of the Styx at its lack of funeral. May Pompey be denied the rites and privileges in death that he denied my husband. Let his corpse be burned before a death mask can be cast, so that he is denied a place in his atrium with his ancestors and his spirit rove the earth, restless and without peace.'

My voice shook as I cursed and made my appeal to Mars. There was no sound in the darkness, but Diana in the guise of the moon far above watched me and bore witness.

And yet, to my surprise, I found another reason to help Cleopatra other than my hatred of Pompey. The more I watched her, the more she interested me. I realised that I did not want to see this girl beggared to Rome. Not that my words made any difference. When they left Italy, it was with four Roman legions. Four legions that would come in time to cost her the whole of Egypt. Once Rome takes an interest and a chit is opened, like a racketeer Rome will not stop until the client is bled dry.

I did as Cleopatra suggested, offering prayers not only to Mars and Diana, reminding them that they had not yet delivered me vengeance upon Pompey for my husband's death, but also adding prayers to Osiris and Isis. I did not mind which of the gods enacted my revenge. Whenever I murmured those prayers, I thought of Cleopatra. She would not have waited for the gods. Her sister Berenice died on their return to Alexandria. I do not know the manner of her death, only that she disappeared, silently sliding out of history and this world.

4

CLEOPATRA

The sacred Buchis bull and my father die on the same night. The aged bull has been sickening for a while. His perfect white flanks are hollowed, his breath rattles and his black face is speckled with grey. The priests fan him and incense drives away the flies, but even so, the bull-god dies, sloughing off his mortal form, ready for the next. A few hours later, my father joins him in the field of reeds. His face bloated and hands clawing at the air, clutching at life until the end. Yet, it says much about my father that many more people mourn for the bull than for poor Auletes. Both were living gods, but the bull was not damaged by his extravagance and bad decisions. The bull was beautiful and beloved. My father was loved only by me.

I'm winded by my grief, it's a sudden punch to my belly.

In my eighteen years, I have not felt a pain such as this. I never knew my mother. I assume she was one of the nameless slave girls who drifted through my father's bed, tumbling over each other like dry leaves. No one spoke of her. Or they didn't to me. She was no more worthy of mentioning than one of the cats which spew out litters beneath the grain stores. Only, she did not spit out kittens but a princess. Perhaps she died while birthing me, or else she was pensioned off to the countryside. I never asked. Neither her life nor, if she has passed, her death have any meaning for me. I am my father's girl.

I drift around the palace, my pain a burden I carry from room to room, unable to set down. My smile is painted on my face like one of the gaudy frescoes on the palace walls. I rule through a fog, bewildered and pierced with grief. It dissolves me like a hot knife into the butter of my heart. Charmian won't leave my side, whispering to me the next duty that I must be seen to perform. Without her reminder, I would stand lost in each room, forgetting why I am there, aware of nothing but the steady throb of my heart. She tethers me to this moment, stops me from drifting away on a tide of loss. We have been together for all of our lives, never parted for longer than a few hours. I know that no one else grieves, they only pretend in a shadow play of feeling. I watch my siblings, they burn incense and offer up prayers, but my little sister stifles a yawn, and my brothers pick their noses as the priests sing. They all three ply others with gold to recite the necessary prayers for Auletes' soul instead of saying the prayers themselves. And yet, while I'm annoyed by the hollowness of their pretence, I understand why they do not grieve. I was always his favourite.

We are a family of living gods. We are the divine brought

to earth like lightning. Our people recognise us as such, fall to their knees and tremble with awe and fear and deafen us with their prayers. We certainly behave as gods – my father murdered my older sister Berenice, and my younger brother's allies come up with schemes to kill me. These are the acts of wrathful gods, not ordinary men. Only my little sister Arsinoe now regards me with anything approaching affection. She hasn't tried to murder me, and in our family that is as close as we can get to love. I comforted her when she cried as a baby, and gave her my amulet to teethe upon, the tiny dents she made in the pliant gold more precious to me than any of the inlaid jewels. She is Clytemnestra to my Helen, and even if we weren't hatched from the same egg, we are still sister goddesses. Yet we are mortal deities. My father died. I bleed and I piss and even the nipping flies ignore my orders to leave me alone. I command neither fire to spring from the rocks, nor water from the clouds.

Even though I'm the only soul who truly grieves for my father, the royal palace is brimming with courtiers performing rituals of mourning in rooms that feel strangely empty without the largeness of my father's presence, his laughter. Arsinoe and my littlest brother, Ptolemy but always known as Tol, are secluded in the nursery with the priests, praying for his soul. Along the hall my other brother Ptolemy wails and screams in a wild performance of grief. I long to slap him. My hands twitch at my sides. His charade is entirely unnecessary. Everyone knows that my father and his eldest son loathed each other. My father was corpulent and incompetent, and despite his geniality and good humour, he loathed the expression of the worst parts of himself in his eldest son. Despite his aversion, my father had little choice but to declare Ptolemy and I must rule together after his death. The Ptolemies always rule in sibling pairs, our blood unthinned by interlopers and unthreatened by the interest of rival houses. A family united in power. But we two are united only in our loathing of one another.

One afternoon we are married in a farce of love. My slaves dress me in silks and bauble me with jewels and then the priests lead me into the temple, where my younger brother waits, sulking. He doesn't look at me. His detested sister-bride. At least he doesn't have his midday meal smeared upon his robes or his face. His nursemaids have cleaned him for our wedding. The priests call out our names and those of our ancestors in song. My sister strews flowers upon the altars, and little Tol leads a procession of holy animals: crocodiles, herons, tame jackals. The animals relieve themselves on the mosaic floors, so the air is thick with the smell of flowers, incense and dung. The heat swells and drips. I glance at my brother-husband, he's abandoned any pretence of interest and is squashing a column of ants with his toe.

Afterwards we walk out together, keeping a careful distance from one another. We cannot bear for even our fingers to touch. Ptolemy. The young Pharaoh who is now my husband, at least in name. Our courts have always been rivals, his ruled by his eunuch generals, Pothinus and Achillas. They haunt the clear skies of the court like locust clouds. If they could have caused my death by wishing it, then I'd have been sealed inside my tomb long ago.

Our enmity is old and entrenched: their power flows from my brother Ptolemy, mere tributaries fed by his spring.

Pothinus is even fatter than my brother, a plucked and hairless boar, glossy and nicely basted ready for the oven. Achillas is similarly smooth, but he is all angles, and his brown eyes are thatched by thick black eyebrows. He has no other hair on his body, and so I wonder whether he has a slave glue on his eyebrows every morning. The two men are Ptolemy's creatures, his advisors, his generals, tutors and the conjurers of his nastiest whims. And, they have longed for my death or downfall since my girlhood. They are malevolence clarified into flesh. They were castrated as boys, moulded and created to serve my brother and not be governed by their own needs. They have no desire other than power, cannot lust for man or woman, can neither marry nor father any children. Their incomplete state binds them to my brother. He is the only family they can ever have, their legacy can flow only through him.

These two jackals hunger for my flesh and I cannot tell whether this desire has now transformed into active scheming. As I walk the halls with my new husband, followed by our competing trains of slaves and guards, I wonder if death lurks amongst their smiling faces, ready to slide a dagger into the pliant flesh between my ribs.

As we parade through the palace, a flotilla of thousands of butterflies is released, fluttering around us as we pass. The insects settle on me like colourful curls of ash, landing upon my eyebrows and hair, pinned to my robes like living bejewelled brooches, but there are too many and I long to flick them away. The courtiers sing and shout, pretending Ptolemy and I are lovers, and shower us with good wishes. Their compliments and happy hopes curdle as they reach my ears. I know it's hollow and I cannot see how this union can possibly last. Ptolemy and I are supposed to be Isis and Osiris: queen of the earth and magic and creator of life, and her lord of death. One cannot exist without the other; they are a perfect pair, day and night. But Ptolemy is no Osiris. We might be a family of divinities but my brother is a terracotta god, hollow and fragile. He has no thoughts of his own, and his skull reverberates with the grisly ambitions of Achillas and Pothinus. When he speaks, I hear their words spew from his mouth. They have schooled him in how to be selfish and decadent and cruel, nurturing his aversion towards me. The tender plant of dislike has flourished into a thriving hatred.

At the end of the hall, abruptly he turns from me, and retreats to his suite of rooms without a word. I release a breath I didn't know I was holding, the happiest I've been for days simply to see him go. His presence is a noxious cloud that pollutes the air of any room he haunts.

I understand the danger I'm in. I'm trapped between my brother's presence and my father's absence. One presses against me, a pain squeezing my skull; while I feel the hole my father has left as a hollow space in my chest. He can't protect me any longer. I'm tight and thrumming with fear. Restless, I lie awake listening to the steady breathing of Charmian on the mattress at my feet. I resent her peace but I can't bear to wake her. A little before dawn, I slide into an uneasy sleep and dream I'm dragged down into the underworld, where Anubis waits for me, his curved blade in his fist. I scream and writhe as with a sigh, he slices open my chest and pulls my organs out, first my lungs and then my still-beating heart, which he places in waiting canopic jars. I call out, telling him to stop, I'm alive. But he shakes his head.

'You are steeped in death, my love,' he says. His breath smells of grave dirt. He licks my cheek with his cold jackal tongue. 'You are mine.'

And, with a scalloped needle, he stitches me back together with black thread. My heart and lungs are missing, there's a bloody void in my chest. I wake sweating and breathless and for a minute I'm terrified that I can't breathe because my lungs are still down in the underworld. Charmian holds me, dabs my forehead with cool water. I gasp and inhale a gulp of cool, bright air.

'I am too much in death,' I tell her.

I have been warned by the god himself. I must cling more fiercely to life or I will join my ghost heart in the underworld and the next time Anubis will not allow me back up.

I try harder to attend the business of the court. I prick my finger with a pin every time I feel myself drift into melancholy. I can't let my grief make me careless. So each morning as I wake, Charmian whispers to me that my father is dead and I am queen, for I must not forget. It is dangerous even for a moment. The others sense the shift in me, the sudden sharpening. Everyone waits, a breath yet to be exhaled. They don't know what kind of queen I shall be. I don't know yet either. I wear power like a robe of stars. It dazzles and yet I discard it as I sleep. I tell stories and jokes, try to charm them. My father thought I was funny. But now when I tell a joke, everyone else laughs before I've finished, they daren't wait to see if it's amusing.

I long to be alone but courtiers watch me as I eat, shit and sleep. They argue for the privilege of emptying my bedpan. Even as I think in silence, my eyes closed, I can still hear the tick and hurry of their minds, feel the prickle of their gaze upon my skin.

My brother's half of the court longs for me to fail with the fervour with which they might pine for a distant lover. They don't like that a woman has power, that my brother is merely my consort, and it is me who rules. They consider my father's faith in my abilities an aberration, a perversion of the natural order. I know that they don't believe that I am the true Pharaoh, and they want to see me subjugated to my brother or, better still, dead.

Ptolemy and I sit upon twin thrones in one of the palace halls. The walls and ceilings are gilded with so much gold that it's like being inside the sun. The gold is mosaiced with jewels depicting jackals whose black fur is inlaid obsidian with bloody rubies for eyes, and they squabble upon grassy emeralds while the desert sky above is made from fat beads of turquoise. The scent of oil of roses and bay leaves perfumes the air. I'm used to these marvels. I hardly notice. It surprised me as a child to venture beyond the palace bounds and see that there was another world, one wounded, grubby and stinking and not beautiful. I did not know before then that this was beauty as I had nothing ugly and broken to compare it to. Before I'd thought this radiance and delight was the whole world.

The kingdom I have inherited from my father is a tangled ball of thread, and it falls to me to try and unknot it.

Our wealth is the Nile. She feeds us with her tears, spilling into the fields, but this year she denies us. The sun parches the fields, and the crops wither like my father in his tomb. I feel the wings of the Roman crows gathering, demanding to be fed. I glance at Ptolemy. He's slumped in his throne beside me, sucking on a date stone. Resentment bubbles in my chest. He wants the power and riches but he has no interest in the tedium and responsibility of rule.

We have sat here for hours, listening as slaves bring us meat and nuts and fruit and pour goblets of wine. Yet nothing can distract from the boredom of a day of petitions. The sun has begun its descent towards the underworld but Ptolemy and I are still sitting in the grand chamber, listening, or rather I am listening as he fidgets and makes faces. Despite the duck-down cushions, my backside aches. I long to shake out my stiffening limbs and walk. The light moves across the walls, shadows stroking the inlaid gods. As the evening stretches, I notice a man lingering at the back of the room. He allows others to take his place, never pushing forward to voice his motion, listening with careful attention to the other requests. He is simply dressed in pale robes, and yet I can see the fabric is the finest cotton, his bearing absolutely upright, exuding self-confidence. I watch him, keeping track of him as he moves around the room, as I would a wasp. I have my slaves write down all the items and I pay attention, even as my head thrums with heat and boredom. I glance at Ptolemy and see that now he's fast asleep, head lolling, cheeks pinkly flushed. Sleeping, he looks almost sweet, his face the flower that belies the sting of the bee concealed within. He doesn't need to pay attention for Achillas and Pothinus act on his behalf. A farmer pleads for leniency. The floods are low this year and he cannot pay the tax I demand. I pause, considering. The treasury is rapidly emptying, a flagon sprung a leak, and without the bounty of the Nile, we cannot sell grain for gold. Yet, this early in my reign, I wish to be benevolent.

'We grant you mercy, for this year. But, next year, the outstanding debt must be paid with interest. My slave will work out the rate.'

He bows, relieved. Then, for the hundredth time today, Achillas and Pothinus clear their throats. It's a dry sound like the crumpling of papyrus. I should order a slave to mix them a tincture to cure coughs. Achillas steps forward, his voice sticky with condescension.

'Queen Cleopatra is wise. Her goodness flows from her womanhood.'

I flinch. They wield my sex as a weapon and would use it to slit my throat if they could. Whatever I say, they slide forward to offer contradiction. The farmer freezes, a hare spotted by the wolf.

'Do you still own property?' asks Achillas.

The farmer hesitates. 'Some.'

'Don't be so modest. You're a man of some considerable means. I have here a list of holdings.'

Achillas reels off a summary, including dozens of farms and vineyards, villas and scores of slaves.

'Have I missed anything?'

The farmer swallows, shakes his head.

Achillas smiles, but his voice is hard, seasoned with cruelty.

'Sell what you need. Then pay our Pharaoh Ptolemy. And his oh-so-kind-hearted queen.'

He pronounces kind-hearted as though it's a shameful weakness, a liability of womanhood. It's also a lie, my generosity wasn't kindness but pragmatism. I understand my need for friends. I'll buy them a bushel at a time if I must.

The unfortunate farmer blanches, considering the cost to him of selling his property and stock. 'I must sell at a fraction of the value. This year is lean. One doesn't sell a cow at market until she's fattened.'

He looks to me, bewildered by the conflicting decrees. Who does he obey? I am queen, and yet the eunuch speaks with the voice of my brother-husband. I have little interest in this actual farmer, but, it's clear that the court is paralysed. Whatever decree I issue, my brother's proxies contradict. They do not care for this farmer or the coins he can deposit in our treasury, they seek to undermine me, sow chaos and discontent, which they hope to reap and convert into their own power. I glance at Ptolemy: he's still asleep.

The farmer scuttles out, comforted by his sons. Only now does the stranger step forward. The last of all the petitioners. He's stayed throughout this endless day, watching the manoeuvrings of the court, the stalling and side-swiping. I can see him storing it all up in his mind, scraps ready to be mashed together and fed to his superiors.

'Welcome, Roman,' I say. I know who he is, and why he has come.

'We pay tribute, great queen and Pharaoh, Cleopatra, and your brother-husband, King Ptolemy. I bring you gifts in tribute.'

I glance with little interest at the offerings in trunks that slaves have now dragged into the hall. The slaves themselves are part of the gift. One of them catches my eye. He's the largest man I've ever seen, tall and lean, with muscles like an ox while every inch of his brown skin is covered in tattoos. The Roman diplomat smiles. He has too many teeth.

'This slave is Apollodorus the Sicilian. A gift for you, great queen.'

The slave stands still, hands clasped behind his back. His black eyes are shrewd and I do not trust him. A Roman slave is still a Roman. There are already enough spies watching me.

'We hope you enjoy our tributes,' continues the diplomat.

I bite my lip. He does not pay tribute. He wants payment. This is the way of the Romans, they know of no other. My father's corpse is not yet dry, and already the scavengers are here to peck away at the remains. This is Year One of Cleopatra. My father died and Egypt is reborn anew with me. A new Pharaoh, and a new world, and yet I am haunted by the old. It will not leave me be. My father's choices seem to take form and reach up as if from the grave to snatch at me, choke me. I think of Cato's warning issued from the latrina. Years ago against his advice, my father sold us to Rome, and now I must find a way to pay.

I still can't sleep and now I'm afraid to dream. What if Anubis still waits for me? I pace my rooms, drinking cup after cup of sweet wine. Charmian stays awake with me watching, her face tight with concern. She doesn't offer advice, only the comfort of her presence. I'm crushed between Rome and the eunuchs, one is the wheel and the other the road. I must find a way to escape. I chew my finger. Rome is as unavoidable as nightfall, its shadow reaching across the world with black fingers. I cannot fend off Rome until I have escaped the plotting of my brother and his cronies. This fight to survive until tomorrow has been my whole life. I don't know anything other than this. I turn to Charmian.

'They think I'm weak. I am the one to be kicked to death or drowned in the river.'

Charmian flinches.

'I must show them that they're wrong. It's me who's strong. My friends aren't here in Alexandria, but they do exist. I have to show them so they dare not strike against me.'

Charmian doesn't answer. She takes my hand and I sit beside her, my head resting against hers.

I lean back against the wall and close my eyes. The heat radiates through the brick. I am damp and sweating and a little drunk. From outside I hear laughter. I glance through the window and see my sister and smallest brother, Tol, playing in the fountains. They splash and shriek with laughter. Evidently they were too hot to sleep, and their slaves have permitted them outside to cool down in the waters.

I watch them with a mixture of affection and envy.

'You remember when this was us?' I say.

'Of course,' she says. 'But for you it was never like this. Not really. You were never free.'

I stifle a laugh at the irony of the slave telling the queen that she was never free, but it's true. Ever since I was conscious of my first thought, I knew that I must be prepared to rule. And yet, now, in this moment I rattle. I feel the emptiness in my chest. Is there more than the fight to survive and the constant echo of death, crooning to me, always ready, always waiting?

What would it be like to play chase around the fountain without fear? I'm irritated with myself for even allowing such a useless thought. For me there's nothing else but this.

Turning away from the window, I rise and lay out offerings for the gods upon the alters in my chamber. Grain and gold for Isis, my protector and own goddess. Yet, I do not neglect either Osiris or Anubis. The death gods have marked me. I must appease them. I give them milk and cooked meats and carved statues and ply them with prayers. Charmian prepares me a sleeping draught and settles me onto the bed.

'Don't leave me,' I say, suddenly frightened, clinging to her hand.

'I'm here,' she whispers, and kisses my cheek, but already I'm falling to where she cannot follow.

I am with my father. He sits at the head of a feast in the underworld; the table is heaped with food, all of it rotten. Here is the grain and meat and milk I offered, only down here it moulders and the milk is rancid and sour, the meat green, the nuts and fruit withered and thick with flies. My father eats, regardless. Flies swarm in the black hole of his mouth. He looks so sad. His fat has sloughed away, his skin sags around his face and dangles in curtains from his arms. I reach for him, but he shakes his head. If I touch him or I eat from this rotting feast, then I cannot return. He points with a thin finger, and I see Anubis sits in the corner on a bed of golden straw playing with a pure white calf with a black heart-shaped face. The animal is radiant, its coat glows like a lit star. Its little horns are polished metal and tipped with gold. To my relief, Anubis is so busy with the beautiful calf he hasn't noticed me.

In my dream I understand. The calf will become the new Buchis bull, I am witnessing the birth of a god. Through the new god, there is new power and life. My father continues to stare at me as he eats the skeleton of a mouse, its bones snapping between his teeth. His face is bright with love. I shall not see him again, not until I join him in the field of reeds. I must leave him behind before Anubis spots me if I want to be free. I raise my hand in farewell. He only stares, crunches his mouse.

I wake to find Charmian kneeling over me, her nose almost touching mine. Her expression is tight with fear.

'You were crying out,' she says. 'I couldn't wake you.'

I tug her towards me and plant a kiss on each cheek.

'We're going on a journey.'

5

CLEOPATRA

We sail along the Nile in the royal barge, gold cast upon green as fallen leaves upon the surface of the water. The wind plumps the sails and we rush forward, cutting through the waves. The Nile is crowded with golden ships, the sky stuffed with purple sails. Menelaus' fleet when it set out for Troy to fight for Helen was not as splendid as ours nor as blessed. Every one of my ships is gilded, some are shaped in the form of swans and fish, and it appears as though with my divine magic I have caused gold to float upon the waters, reversing the laws of nature. As I stand at the prow with the wind in my face, I laugh in delight. This is the first time I've felt free since my father died. My ships can outrun them all – the poisonous hate of my brother and his eunuchs, the spit and snarling whispers of the court. Here, there are only friends and the gods.

I want them all to see my power, witness my ships and the men who love me. Dusk falls and the river is a black ribbon spooling in the dark. But the golden boats are lit with a galaxy of candles and the light rivals the moon and stars. The hundreds of boats become a thousand in reflection, doubled and wobbling in the waters. I wonder that Artemis doesn't descend to remonstrate that we've stolen her glory. But then, this is a holy procession, each vessel a floating temple, our voyage a prayer and supplication.

My royal barge is the tip of the armada. It's the most splendid of all the crafts, its purple sails shot through with silver thread. Three hundred oarsmen pull the boat through the water, their oars burnished with silver so that they catch in the moonlight like snags of lightning. Slave girls play flutes to set the rhythm of the oars, so as the galley slaves row, we are pulled through the water in a steady dance. Priests burn incense, perfuming the very winds that fill the sails. The heady scent and snatches of music coil around us, mingling with the breeze. However, amid the sweet fragrance I inhale the sharp stink of cow shit for my barge bears the brand-new mortal god, the Buchis bull. While he is a god, powerful and glorious, his earthly excrement comes in thick spurts, cutting through the perfumed night air, coating the deck. Slaves sweep it away as fast as it slides out of him, but still the muck falls, spattering the beast-god's tail and besmirching his perfect white flanks. The slaves clean him, scrubbing and washing under the close direction of the priests. Two dozen priests are gathered here on my barge, all of them tending the new calf. A net of silk is cast over his eyes so that the biting river flies and mosquitos don't plague him. They feed him handfuls of the tenderest, sweetest grass, which is converted into more squirting greenish shit at dizzying speed.

Apollodorus the Sicilian is busy trying to prove his worth. I still don't trust him, but I can see him oozing charm before Charmian. She laughs and throws back her head as he leans in. He whispers something in her ear, and she turns to him, face raised upwards, sunlit. A splinter of something catches in my belly. I inhale sharply, as though a bee has stung my foot. She has never looked at someone else before with that easy, open joy. Only me.

Apollodorus sees me watching and our eyes meet for a moment, and then he bows. I trust him even less. He would take her from me, if he could. I can have him killed at once. No one would question it, not for a moment. And yet, I do not want to kill him or send him back to Rome. Charmian would never reproach me aloud, but I would see her anguish and resentment. Everyone else's affection for me is bought, Charmian's was gifted to me long ago and I will not spoil it. She'll soon tire of this pretty Sicilian, I tell myself. There were probably other boys before, I just didn't notice them. Even as I say this, I know it isn't true.

Turning away from them both and trying to escape the smell of the bull, I leave my pavilion and move to the very edge of the deck. Fresh, cool air stirs my hair and below the water swirls and foams. I'm adorned in my crown of plumes, the shining sun disc set into my hair bracketed by a pair of gilded horns. My neck aches with the weight and yet I can see the delight in the faces of the crowd gathered on the shore as we pass. They're all here to witness the new god beneath the new moon. We sail as close to the bank of the river as we dare, the shore thick with people. They reach out to touch us, skim the boat with their fingertips. As they see me in my crown, they holler in ecstasy, as overjoyed to glimpse me as they are the bull-god. They had faith I existed, but to see me, in flesh and crown, is to see earthed magic. I am their Cleopatra. I feel their excitement and their love. It lands on my skin like fine spring rain. Leaving Apollodorus, Charmian comes to join me, kneeling beside me, and I squeeze her hand.

'I can hear the laughter of gods,' I say.

My heart is pounding against my ribs. The screams and fervour of the crowd are a thunderclap. The air is thick with music, bonfires glow along the shore and I can see people dancing. I pull Charmian to her feet and we dance together, laughing and waving at the throng. Apollodorus stands at a little distance, aware of my distrust. But, caught in the thrill, I gesture to him to join us. Let him report to Rome how I am adored and worshipped.

'All the gods are here,' I shout over the din. 'Diana and Bastet and Neith.'

They are the goddesses of power and the dark, their names and shapes change and shift like the waters of the river, but their force is eternal and unstoppable. Apollodorus stumbles as the boat lurches and Charmian steadies him. His cheeks are glossy with excitement.

'They love you for coming, great queen and Pharaoh. This Buchis bull is especially blessed for he is carried on the vessel of a goddess,' he says.

His expression is bright with pleasure. He is difficult to dislike, especially in this moment when I am giddy, thrumming with their love. My foolish brother worships only the Greek gods. I accept them all. He condescends to the Egyptian gods as well as the people. He risks the wrath of both.

I am as young as this tender moon, and so is my reign. This fresh moon is in her own celestial boat at the beginning of her monthly voyage across the sky. We will celebrate every night as she sails, her plump pale face growing skinny and then fattening again, while we feast and dance. She sails above and we below, all of us journeying towards the city of Memphis, the moon herself leading our flotilla, tugging us along in her wake.

My head aches. I lean over the side and am sick into the water. Charmian holds back my hair, but her face is as pale as mine. She smells sourly of stale sweat. Kohl is smudged beneath her eyes. I just want to curl up in bed. The rhythm of the barge upon the tide is wretched and relentless, and with each shudder of the boat another wave of nausea rises in my throat. I don't want to drink or feast or dance or wave at the crowds again tonight but I know that I must. New faces line the banks each evening as we sail and for them, the celebration is fresh, the spectacle already clarifying into a story that they will tell and retell to their grandchildren. For me, however, every day and night is the same, tumbling over each other. The shores are lined with a crowd buzzing with veneration, but I can't tell the new faces from the old; they're identical, shiny with ecstasy. I wonder if the gods tire of their feasting and our worship. I suppose they do. Boredom drives them to meddle with the lives of mortals. I long to sleep at night and to see Ra high in the sky, a polished gold plate spinning against the blue. I don't. I wave and smile and dance and my head throbs. I fall asleep at dawn and then rise again at dusk, the taste of vomit and wine souring my mouth.

I wake up cross, and damp with sweat. Mosquito bites mar the tender flesh on my arms and legs. Charmian soothes them with herbs and oil, and begins to dress me once more for the evening's celebration. I've lost all count of the days. They fall from the trees in a glut like overripe fruit. Apollodorus approaches and stands at a little distance waiting, hesitant, holding something behind his back. I sigh, irritated. I am too tired to be bothered with the trickery of Roman spies.

'Leave. You are not wanted. If I desire your presence, I shall order it,' I snap.

He bows low but to my astonishment, he does not leave.

'Do you disobey your queen? Or do you ignore my command, because you are no Egyptian?' I say, my voice low in anger.

I can have him cast into the Nile and drowned in a moment. Apollodorus studies me intently, and then kneels, proffering me a flask.

'Drink and recover, goddess,' he says.

His voice is gentle. For a moment I wonder if the flask contains poison. But the Romans don't want me dead – at least not yet; they want me to pay them first. I take it and sip. The liquid is so cold it burns my throat. I feel the chill spreading out like cold fingers across my body, reaching up and cooling the pain at the base of my skull. I feel a little better. No longer so tired, nor as irritable. I say nothing, but he smiles. He can tell. If it wasn't for Charmian, I would almost like him. Not as she does, of course. I have no desire for his body or his arms or his brown eyes.

I wish that I could set aside my godhead for a single night and sleep unwatched. I'd like to sit with Charmian and perhaps even Apollodorus and talk of ordinary things. I realise that I don't know what ordinary things would be. I feel a tug of sadness. Apollodorus still stands there, waiting. Charmian looks at him with such tenderness that irritation flares again within me, igniting into real anger.

'Go! Leave me and this ship. Return to your true masters,' I tell him. 'I don't trust you, Roman.'

He frowns, his expression sad. 'I am not Roman. I'm yours, goddess. One day, you will understand the truth of this.' He stands and begins to walk away. 'I shall return to you, and when I do, you won't ask me to leave your side again.'

I don't reply, but through half-closed lids, I notice that Charmian's mouth is pursed, tight with displeasure. I understand that she has grown too fond of the Sicilian and is angry that I have sent him away. I can't remember her ever being angry with me before. Now, her eyes are shiny with tears and she pinches the flesh of her arm, refusing to meet my eye. I'm torn between resentment – she should only ever want me – and guilt. It is unfamiliar and unpleasant, and I try to shove it away, but the feeling pops up like a bubble that will not burst. I do not like it.

The next night, I decide that it's time for me to undertake another expedition, but this time I must travel alone. Iras helps me to dress Charmian. Iras is one of my favourite slaves, a girl of fifteen who has served me since she could proffer a goblet of wine without spilling it. She's small and scrawny, her wrist bones like those of a thrush. Together, Iras and I dress Charmian in my own costume: at first she's unsure, skinny and stooped beneath the weight of the headpiece, jewels and robes. But then, Iras paints her face and I make her follow me around the deck, head erect, stepping in my own footsteps, and as the lights of the shimmering sun disc headpiece glint in her hair, she is enough like me that no one will dare offer an objection. For this one night she may wield my godhead by proxy. The people will never know and I hope the other gods will forgive me.

With the help of Iras, I slide from the royal barge into a small wooden boat. I almost miss Apollodorus, for it's another slave who rows me. It's taking too long, and I know that Apollodorus with his colossal strength would have reached the shore in half the time. I wear Charmian's simple linen tunic, and only a thin gold serpent twisting around the top of my arm hints that I am no ordinary slave.

Behind me on the water, the nightly celebrations continue. The moon is thinning, we're halfway through her monthly voyage. The royal barge glows like a white star and a brazier shoots a column of crimson rain upwards into the dark. Above the music of the flutes and drums, I can hear the bellow of the little bull. As we reach the shore, a priest is waiting. If he knows who I am, he says nothing, only helps me out of the small boat.

It's a relief to walk on dry land after weeks upon the barge, but the ground shudders and heaves with each step and I stumble. The priest grabs my elbow to steady me. I'm surprised at his touch. No man would ordinarily dare, but tonight, in this moment, I have shed Cleopatra, so I allow it to pass. We move unnoticed through the crowds. Behind me, my stand-in drifts upon the water, absorbing their adoration like parched ground soaks up rain.

We walk quickly away from the river. The streets are empty. There are stalls stuffed with trinkets and mummified animals for tourists and pilgrims. Tonight, this far from the river there is little business to be had amongst the travellers as they all throng to witness the armada. Seeing me pass, a stallholder rouses himself, suddenly alert and eager for a customer, and shoves a tiny mummified frog towards me.

'Excellent price. He will bring your family good fortune.'

I frown at him. I don't want his knockdown fortune or cut-price luck. He's persistent, now he's spotted me – a tourist after hours; he's determined to press for a sale and reaches for another bundle, thrusting it towards me. 'Rat? Or perhaps crocodile?'

The crocodile must be a juvenile for it's tiny, shrivelled to nothing within its bandages. I don't want any of these cheap trinkets of death and shove them away more forcefully as the priest hisses at the vendor to leave us be.

We hurry on through the evening, eventually reaching the start of the Sarapion Way. It's a wide, straight road stretching through the lonely sands of the desert. It leads to the temples and is lined on either side by hundreds of carved statues of sphinx, who eye us with disinterest as we pass. The night is cool and strewn with stars, and the rimless eye of the moon surveys us, curious. The moon is still bright enough that the sphinx cast long shadows against the sands. There are no other travellers at this hour and the stillness is that of death. The road marks the transition between the mortal world and the realm of the dead. As we walk, I can see the final journeys of the countless souls filing along this path – the last Buchis bull borne by his priests and attendants and thousands of mourners, noisy with grief under the silent gaze of the sphinx.

I'm relieved when we reach the first of the temples. There are dozens of them huddled together – a village of the gods. The great ones – Isis, Osiris, Ra, Horus – have grand and magnificent palaces devoted to them, carved and adorned with paintings, but even the lesser divinities have their allotted shrines. Memphis is a city of temples, but more of it is laid out beneath the earth than above, an underground metropolis of the dead. As we approach, the smell of incense mingles with the fires that burn all night. It's late but the temple complex is still busy, death must be tended and fed – and it's thronging with priests and slaves, while the air is pierced with the barking of dogs and the mewing of puppies. The priest takes a torch and beckons for me to follow as he enters a large temple dedicated to Osiris and Anubis. I trail him inside, and glancing upwards, see that the interior is covered in elegant carvings and a library of hieroglyphs. He walks quickly past the alters heaped with offerings of fruit and wine, past statues and painted reliefs to an entranceway that leads to a tunnel, a black yawning maw. I hesitate, watching as he disappears into the darkness. I don't have to go. I don't have to follow him. But a voice inside me whispers that I do, I must. Taking a deep breath, I pursue him down, down into the dark, into the labyrinthine tunnel of catacombs. The only light is the flame from the torch in his hands, and I experience a sharp snarl of fear. Will I find my way back into the light and the return journey across the Sarapion Way? I remind myself that it's in order to find my way back I make this journey.

The stench of death and dry earth grows stronger as we descend, and the silence reverberates around us. Neither of us speak. The only sound is our footsteps upon the sandstone floor. I can't tell how long we walk for. There is only darkness in front and darkness behind. There's no time, just the beat of our feet, and the small yolk of light that spills from his torch. Suddenly he stops, so abruptly that I nearly walk into him.

'We're here,' says the priest.

For a moment, I'm not sure what he means, and then as he holds up his torch, I realise that we're standing in a chamber carved into the rock. He uses his torch to light several more in sconces set into the walls. Craning my neck, I observe that the ceiling is high, whether hollowed by hands or part of a natural cave, I can't tell. Although the walls are plain and unadorned, they're lined with wooden shelves that stretch up and up towards the roof. Upon each shelf is wrapped a small mummified body. There are thousands and thousands of them, all neatly rolled and stacked. This room is stuffed with death, the priest and I the only living things.

'As the queen ordered,' he says. 'All in the image of Anubis.'

Inside the wrappings the bodies are all dogs and jackals and foxes. A gift to Osiris and Anubis, the jackal god who prowls the underworld. Anubis prefers sacrifices that look like him. The farms above us are filled with breeding dogs, all future offerings. I have paid for all of these bodies – thousands upon thousands of canine lives in exchange for mine. Many are tiny puppies that never opened their eyes, but slid straight from birth into the ready arms of death. The stillness in the chamber is absolute. A moth flutters around a torch flame, getting too close and singeing its wing. I'm desperate to leave. I have too much life in me to be here, I can feel the blood fizzing in my veins. I want to shout and clap and dance, disturb the unnatural stillness. Every nerve tells me to run and escape outside and inhale cool, fresh air. But, if I run, I'm as likely to run further in and down than find my way out. And, I need to linger long enough to offer my prayers and spells. Anubis must know that these sacrifices are from me and release his claim upon me.

I murmur my prayers and retrieve from the folds of my dress a pomegranate. I split it and place the offering on a small, low shrine, bloody seeds spilling out and staining my fingertips. I dismiss the priest and order him to retreat along the tunnel – I don't need him to be my intermediary.

'I'll summon you when I need you to take me back,' I say.

Alone, I talk to the gods myself. I pray but I do not plead. I demand their favour. These gods sneer at supplicants. I pick up a torch from one of the scones and hesitate. There is no sign that they have heard me. Only stillness. Turning away from the chamber, I walk back through the tunnel past the waiting priest, and unlike Orpheus during his ascent from hell, I don't look back.

I return to the royal barge as dawn reaches across the sky. Iras helps me clamber aboard. I retreat straight to my pavilion, where the painted Cleopatra sleeps, small beneath her borrowed robes. I don't wake her but slide into bed beside her, wrap my arms around her slim waist. In a few hours I shall be myself again, but not yet.

We finish the last night of celebrations with relief. I can dance and drink no more. I could weep with relief as Charmian and Iras remove the golden disc from my head. I'm light, weightless, released from the trappings of divinity. Even the bull seems tired, exhausted by the adulation. Tomorrow, I shall begin my return journey towards Alexandria. It is time for the bull and I to part. He will continue onto Thebes where his temple is prepared and live out his mortal portion in gentle delight. I must go back to court and take my position amongst the snakes and liars. I have missed no one, except for my sister. I worry about how she fares in my absence, lest my brother's thugs – bored without a focus for their hate – turn their eye upon her. Perhaps I was mistaken in not bringing her with me. Guilt and fear nudge at me, and I lie awake for a while, listening to water slap against the hull, until at last the motion rocks me to sleep.

I'm woken at dawn by shouting. I scramble to my feet, annoyed, and hurry to the port bow, trying to see what has caused the commotion. My view is blocked by sailors jostling and yelling, my private guards hollering back in return, and it takes a moment for them to realise that I am standing here amongst them. With swooping apologies they part, and I walk to the side of the boat and see a small fishing boat bobbing in the waters. A hundred of my bowmen have trained their arrows upon him.

'Are you such poor shots that it will take all one hundred of you to hit him?' I say.

All the bows but one lower.

The man in the boat raises his hand in greeting. If I hadn't seen him myself, I would know it was him by Charmian's sudden smile.

'Lower your bow,' I say to the last archer. 'Or you will pierce two hearts at once, and one of them, at least, I love.'

Charmian blushes and murmurs her thanks.

'Don't. I may still have him killed later and risk your heart.'

Nimbly, Apollodorus tethers his boat to our barge and climbs aboard, swinging himself up the rope ladder cast over the side. Within a few minutes he stands before me, his clothes bleached from the sun. There's thick stubble on his face.

'Don't go back to Alexandria. Turn around. They pursue you,' he says.

I stare at him. 'Ptolemy?'

He nods. 'Your brother and his vipers have taken the city and the palace. He sails towards you with a fleet, while his armies lie in wait upon the road.'

Is this a trick? Does Apollodorus try to scare me, to force me to turn around, to trick me into retreat? He looks across at Charmian and his expression is bright with affection. His loyalty towards me I might still doubt but I don't believe he would allow anything to hurt her. I'm not foolish enough to trust his love for a woman over his love of Rome. I turn to my generals.

'Send out scouts. See if what he says is true. Keep him here until they return.'

Apollodorus surrenders peaceably to my guards. He knows that if it is discovered that he lies, then he will be put to death.

Either he is very confident that they will find him to be telling the truth, or he has made peace with his Roman gods.

Until the scouts return there's nothing to do but wait. The sun rises. We wave farewell to the bull, who continues on his way. I order our ships around a bend in the river where we are safer, half hidden and more easily defended. Charmian offers me food. I wave it away. Her gaze is constantly upon where Apollodorus sits in the corner, his wrists bound. I catch her watching him, her face tight with anxiety. He winks at her and she smiles. I look away. I like him and I should be sad to see him die, but I hope he is lying. The alternative is far worse. A heron fishes from the side of the boat. The sun starts to sink into the river. The scouts return. I can see from their faces that Apollodorus tells the truth.

My courtiers turn to me, faces pale and wide with fear. Everyone wants to know what we are to do.

'We leave the river at once. He expects to find us on the water. We must retreat into the desert. Her sands and heat will hide us.'

I instruct my generals to raise an army. These soldiers with my fleet will not be enough to fight a war.

I take a knife and cut Apollodorus's bonds myself.

'Shall I go with them, my queen?' he asks. 'I will speak eloquently in your name and raise ten score of men to fight for you.'

'No,' I reply. 'You will stay with me. At my side.'

Charmian takes my hand, kisses it. I don't squeeze it back for this decision was not made for her. He's proved his loyalty to me. And it is that I reward; I do not indulge her affection.

I huddle in the first boat to leave the royal barge, Charmian and Iras crouched beside me. Apollodorus rows us himself, with smooth, strong strokes. In a few hours, the desert will swallow us and allow us to hide and gather ourselves. Then, I will return to Alexandria and remove the monster squatting on my throne. I listen to the slap of the oars and I understand that Anubis has released me. If I hadn't gone into the temple and appeased him, he would have let me sail into my brother's trap, and the tender arms of death.

6

CLEOPATRA

I detest having my monthly bleed out here in the desert. The great sand sea is not the place to be reminded that I'm a woman as well as a Pharaoh. My thighs are chafing with sweat and blood. Charmian washes me with scented rose water, but a minute later I'm sticky again. The smell of the rose water mingles with that of blood.

We are all damp with sweat and tiny, oozing bites from the sandflies. They nip me through the silk of my robes and along my scalp. I long to scratch at them with my nails but I can't. They're watching. They're always watching and goddesses don't scratch at bites. I wonder how Isis herself could stand it – that's a detail her priests never mention. Another fly lands on my lip, tickling and buzzing, and I flick it away. I wouldn't mind the insects, if it wasn't for the cramping in my belly. Wordlessly, Charmian tries to dab my forehead with a damp cloth but I wave her away. No one must see my discomfort. She's dressed me in the darkest of robes despite the heat so if the rag between my legs leaks no one can see the stain. Queens must hide their weakness. The pain is so sharp that nausea bubbles in my throat and my ears hum. I want to lie back amongst the cushions and cry a little to myself and then sink into sleep, but I can't. I hold so many lives in my cupped hands. I swallow, hard, gulping the burning air.

The dust is in my eyes and nose, coating my hair and lips and my teeth. I can taste only grit and sand. The sun squats low over the dunes, a red-rimmed eye blinded by yet more dust. Everything hums with heat. The world outside the tent shimmers, unsteady. Each breath I take is hot and dry. I lean against the cushions but even they are warm as though heated by a previous feverish body. The slave fans me but he's only stirring the air like a pot of stew and raindrops of his sweat patter onto the cushion beside me. Apollodorus curses the slave in Greek, Egyptian and then again in Latin for good measure and orders him to leave. The slave cringes away.

Charmian sits at my feet, chin resting in her hands. I want to reach out for her, brush her cheek, smooth the lacquer of her hair, but I don't. If I die here, they'll kill her too. I will win this fight for I am Egypt. My blood is the Nile. When it dries between my legs, it turns back into her mud.

We linger in the sands, waiting. Waiting. The sun rises and sets. The desert cicadas buzz and tick in my ears without pause, invading my thoughts. My tent might be woven silk while carpets and silks shield me from the hostile sun, but nothing can hide that my brother and his generals have driven me into exile. I worry for my little sister and smallest brother. Ptolemy has no affection for them. To him they are not siblings but rivals. They are so young, skulls still soft, too easy to kill. I should be there to protect them. Guilt nips at me alongside the flies and my anger pulses as a second heartbeat. I am the rightful Pharaoh and the queen, my father's true heir. My grief for my father has faded like a bruise, only sore when I press down on it.

While I observed my father and learned how not to rule, Ptolemy gleaned nothing except how to complain, cheat and steal. Even now, he listens to his tutors and advisors and takes their flattery as truth. They do not love him, only the power his name bestows. He's too lazy to learn. That is how I shall win. I may bleed, I may have fewer men in my army but I listen and I am clever.

Ours is not the only grubby war being fought. The whispers from Rome blow across the desert and reach us even here. They say that Rome itself is at war, the snake nipping at its own tail. My father's old patron Pompey has fled across the seas, his ship chased by Caesar. There are rumours that Pompey makes for Egypt and Alexandria, ready to call in my father's debt in exchange for soldiers and gold. In this matter alone, I do not envy my brother for to help Pompey will be to make an enemy of Caesar and it is not yet clear whom the gods favour. I have no love for Pompey, but I know little of Caesar. At least being stuck here, with dwindling supplies and men, neither general will be seeking my aid. Not until I've won.

From beneath the floating walls of the tent, I observe the men in my camp. My followers are ordinary Egyptians, the freedmen and farmers, merchants and riverboat men. I talk to them in their own tongue and worship their gods. I've gained their loyalty and love by speaking to them in their language, seeing the world through their words. I'm the first in my family to become truly Egyptian, but my brother is like all the other kings in my family, he doesn't bother with the people and their words or their ways. He's indolent and speaks only Greek for he believes the peasants are wretches – no better than ants. He doesn't understand. A colony of ants can strip the flesh from a bull in hours, leaving only bones. Alone, a single ant is nothing, easily squashed with the ridge of a thumbnail, but together, they're a black tide.

Now my men crouch in scraps of shade, too hot to talk. Too hot to fight, either with each other or for me. There are thousands of them, a river of men against the sand. Only the camels are nonchalant, chewing, coughing. We should not be here, far out in the desert with all these men. They are already starting to die. Our worst enemy here is the heat, relentless and never tiring, more vicious than my brother's army. Horses and men drop silently into the sand. The bodies are dragged further off to dry out in the sun. I can smell death in the air, sweet and rotten. I know where the bodies lie from the path of the carrion birds. They point to the dead with dark wings, black scribbles across the sky pointing to my failure. We need to leave this place. We win or we die.

'Any word from our spies?' I ask Charmian, even though I know the answer.

'Not yet, my queen.'

'I'll send out riders to look for them,' says Apollodorus and I nod.

The sky is a lid pushing down. The tents provide only the barest shelter from the glare of the sun. Time stills and slurs, slowed by the heat. My advisors come in and squabble with one another over battle plans. It's all pretend. They are as boys pushing stones around the dust. My brother's army blocks our way into Alexandria. His vagabond army of pirates, thieves, disgraced slaves and thugs. If we run at them, we'll dash ourselves to death as little ships upon the rocks. Each night at dusk, a few of my men slink away, bleeding into the black desert and escaping across the sand. We've been forced into a cramped retreat, where we lurk and slowly fade. My brother is not much more than a nasty and sulky child himself, a god-king whose too-big helmet slips down over his forehead, blinding him. He may not have the freedmen and farmers, but his supporters are the rich. He speaks only in bribes, but that's enough to buy him an army. We are stranded here, unable to reach Alexandria, while he strolls barefoot through my palace, plucking fruit from my trees, sleeping in my royal chamber. I refuse to die here. I'm like water and I'll find my way through the rockface. I'm only waiting until I can see the fissure. It's there. I know it. I can sense it just beyond my fingertips. I pray to Isis. She'll show me the way. I am her creature.

They bring figs and wine to my tent. I don't eat them. Everything here tastes only of dust, it's like consuming food from the underworld, only fit for the dead.

As the veil of dusk begins to fall, the fire of the sun is doused at last. Noise swells in the camp. Men rouse from their lethargy and begin to squabble and drink and prepare food. But the sound is more than evening chatter. Something stirs.

'Come,' I say to Charmian, rising and moving to the entrance of the tent. 'The spies are returned.'

My guards rouse themselves and surge forward with sudden shouts. The intruder is stopped a little distance from my tent. Flanked by soldiers, I march outside. In the gathering dark, I observe a rider on a pale horse, its eyes black with flies. The rider waits, poised and still, trying to calm his horse, which is tossing its head and kicking up sand. A dozen spears are aimed at him and a dagger hovers at the horse's throat. Shielding my eyes from the last of the fading rays, I study him closely but don't recognise him. He's not one of my spies.

Then, in the sinking light, I notice the symbol on the golden standard he holds. It's a vast red eagle, wings outstretched. Apollodorus sees it at the same moment and shouts at the soldiers to lower their weapons. This rider is not one of my spies nor one of my brother's men. He carries the standard of Rome.

'I come from Caesar,' cries the horseman. 'I bring a message for Queen Cleopatra.'

I tell Apollodorus to order the slaves not to announce me, and I slip into the tent and observe the messenger unseen as he reclines on cushions, drinks one flask of sweet wine, then another in desperate gulps so it spills in a trail down his chin. His face and hair are grey from the desert, his eyes veined and red, he is desiccated from the heat. The wine stains his lips so they are bloody against his pallor. Sensing me, he glances up, and seeing me, he startles and now, frantic, struggles to rise, not wanting to be seated in the presence of a queen.

I AM CLEOPATRA

He scrambles to his feet but sways so much that I'm worried he'll fall before he delivers his missive. Apollodorus steadies him, gripping his arm.

'You've drunk our wine, stranger. Now speak,' I command.

The messenger bows his head. 'Caesar desires peace. He insists this war between you and your brother must cease. You are to appear at the palace.'

'In Alexandria?' snaps Apollodorus, incredulous. He flexes his arms. They are inked all across the muscles in twisting designs, just visible against the darkness of his skin. The bones crack. The messenger nods, cautious.

'Yes. Caesar resides in the royal palace now.'

'And Pompey? Where is he?' I ask.

'Dead.'

'Killed by Caesar?' I ask.

'Murdered, by your brother.'

I stare at him. My brother has made Caesar the most powerful man in Rome. He must have hoped that murdering Caesar's enemy would win him Caesar's favour. And yet the messenger does not express gratitude towards my brother. He has not come here alone to kill me. I must try to understand why he is here, pretending friendship from Caesar. Everything has shifted in a moment. Before, Caesar was one of two men scrapping for an empire. But now Caesar's spoils include most of the world. His power is not as boundless as that of the gods, but it is close. And it is he who has the power to restore the living goddess Cleopatra to her throne.

'Your brother asked great Caesar's help in ruling Egypt,' says the messenger.

I laugh aloud. My brother will have done no such thing.

Caesar has decided that with Egypt weak and fighting itself, he will insinuate himself and plunder us. He thinks that he will install either my brother or me to rule by proxy when he returns to Rome. I am no Roman puppet. I will persuade him of my value, but not from out here in the desert.

'Do not laugh, great queen. What I say is true. Caesar wishes to help. He takes neither your brother's part nor yours. He's impartial and seeks only peace.'

Apollodorus snorts. 'Impartial? Yet asks the queen to come to Alexandria? Her brother's spies will kill her at once. That's certainly one way to end the war.'

The messenger shifts from foot to foot, uneasy, and turns to me again. 'I'm ordered to request Your Majesty's presence.'

Apollodorus's temper flares. 'Then where are all the Roman soldiers to protect her and offer her safe passage? Or perhaps they're waiting just beyond the dunes?'

The messenger is silent. There is clearly no escort. Apollodorus snorts again.

Irritation prickles along my skin. Incredulous and angry, I turn to the messenger. 'You come into the desert and offer only death. Death we have here in abundance. It lies in the sky's furnace, beneath each rock and in the buzzing of the flies. Or is that really Caesar's true offer? How he wishes to end this unhappy war?'

The messenger wipes a hand across his forehead, smearing the dirt into a paste. When he speaks again, his voice whines like the endless buzzing of the flies.

'Queen and Pharaoh. Caesar desires only peace and for this conflict to end. Your father's will declared that you and your brother were to rule together. Joint Pharaohs. As a friend of Egypt, Caesar wants to see that your father's wishes are carried out.'

I am silent for a moment, considering. None of these messengers ever speaks the truth for they do not carry it. They are given false missives full of dissemblance and manoeuvres. I must seek the truth from within the lies; it hides there like a nightingale concealed amongst the trees. Caesar is a Roman. They're all greedy for Egyptian grain and gold. They grasp and grope us with sweaty, pinching fingers until our skin is mottled with bruises. Of course Caesar wants peace. War is expensive. I try not to picture my vast grain warehouses, emptying like the tide and not refilled with the turn. Yet I don't understand why Caesar doesn't simply have me killed. Why doesn't he send a legion out into the desert and cut us down, let us bleed out into the sand? It would be quick and efficient and I'd appreciated Caesar to be a man of ruthless expediency. My death would finish this war and I know better than anyone the weakness of my own position, and yet Caesar does not declare Ptolemy his choice. I know my brother well. He is the worm that rots the fruit. What has my brother done to offend the great man of Rome?

Dismissing the messenger, I give orders for him to be shown to a tent to rest, given food and slaves to tend to him. I sit for a moment, turning these thoughts in my mind like meat on a spit. A slave appears, whispers to Apollodorus, who slides out of the tent. I don't know how I managed before Apollodorus came to me. By now, I trust him absolutely and cannot imagine being parted from him or Charmian. I swallow, lick a layer of grime from my lip. I look at Charmian, who rests her chin on my knee.

'Is it a trick, my love?' I ask. 'To lure me to the palace and have my brother's spies murder me as I try to enter? That way Caesar is not blamed for my death.'

Charmian gazes up at me, her eyes wide with fear. 'It's almost certainly a trick. Do not go.'

Fear has never stopped me doing anything. Self-preservation is sensible, but not fear for its own sake.

'It doesn't seem like Caesar's taking my brother's part,' I say slowly. 'My brother is a snot-nosed and vicious little fool but it usually takes time for people to hate him. He wears a silken cloak around his viciousness. Pompey's murder with which he sought to ingratiate himself to Caesar seems to have had the opposite effect.'

'It did indeed. A grotesque miscalculation. Do you want to hear how?' asks Apollodorus, his voice treacly with glee.

I hadn't noticed him slip back inside my tent, for a big man he moves with remarkable stealth, but as I watch him I can see he's so pleased about something that he's hopping from foot to foot like a child who needs to make water. I nearly laugh.

He walks quickly to my side, and now I see that two of my spies stand beside him, returned at last. I watch with interest. Apollodorus pokes the first man in the ribs, and he folds, like a snapped reed.

'Speak.'

The man gasps and straightens. 'I've come from the palace, where it is true Caesar now resides. He rules instead of your brother. Ptolemy sulks and scuffs around his rooms like a kicked dog.'

Apollodorus gives him another prod, hard.

I AM CLEOPATRA

'Tell the queen how Ptolemy the fool offended Caesar.'

'Caesar came to Egypt seeking his enemy, the Roman Pompey. He chased him to Alexandria but the winds favoured Pompey's ships and that man arrived first. He sent word to your brother, who waited for him on the shore. Your brother, traitor and sneak, agreed to help Pompey and give him gold and grain to feed and pay his troops, to lend him an army to beat Caesar. It was all a lie. He sent a boat to bring Pompey from his ship to the shore and apologised that it was too small for Pompey's bodyguards. The moment they were out of reach of Pompey's ship and its arrows, your brother's men stabbed Pompey to death, a whetted blade in the back that nicked his heart. The waters churned red from his blood.'

I close my eyes and imagine the scene. My brother, his plump body wrapped in purple robes that flap in the sea air, the scream of the gulls echoing the unfortunate Pompey's death cries. Ptolemy's advisors would have dripped this idea into his ear, like beads of oil to loosen wax. But its sneakiness and barbarity would have appealed to him. He'd have needed little persuasion.

Apollodorus's face is grim, his mouth a narrow line. He gives the spy a nudge, gentler this time.

'Go on.'

The man swallows, his angular Adam's apple sliding up and down like the shuttle on a loom.

'They laid the great Pompey at your brother's feet, dead and cut like a fish, the gaping wounds like gills. His blood turning the white sand black, so much viscera that it took the turn of two tides to wash them all away. They say some of the rocks are still stained red.'

I can picture my brother on the shore, his robes dark with seawater and blood, face shiny with delight. The stink of salt and seaweed and flesh.

I glance at the messenger, who clears his throat with a sound like the scraping of a chair.

'But, the weather is hot. They knew the body would soon sour and smell. And it wasn't known how far behind Caesar was. So, your brother ordered Pompey's head to be cut from the rest of his corpse. Then he had it pickled in brine.'

That I know, with absolute certainty, is an order that came from my brother himself. He takes fierce delight in acts of pain or desecration. He's imaginative in his cruelties, delighting in suffering. I like to read. Ptolemy prefers to pull the legs off locusts.

Another thought stirs within me. A face from years before – Servilia. Her vengeance on behalf of her son has finally been served. His horrible death was fitting. His murder devious and horrid. Does she yet know? I wonder which of the gods – Roman or Egyptian – enacted her revenge. I say none of this aloud. I only ask, 'And was Caesar delighted by this bloody gift? I suspect not, or his messenger would not be stuffing anchovies and pomegranates into his mouth. Instead we'd be feeding the carrion birds with our own flesh, killed by Caesar's men.'

The messenger shrugs, shifts. 'Indeed, my queen. When Caesar arrived a few days later, carried by sweetening winds, he was met on the beach by your brother himself. The very place where Pompey had been cut down. Your brother offered him Pompey's head on a platter as though it were a fattened boar. He thought to flatter Caesar with the defeat of his enemy. Your brother thought he'd be overcome with gratitude and pleasure. But Caesar wept.'

'Real tears?' I wonder, puzzled at the display of grief. The murder was sneaky and shameful and yet it leaves Caesar with no rival, either in Rome or in the world. But I also understand that men like Caesar prefer to make the kill themselves, to watch the life leach away from their enemy's eyes and know they themselves have done it. I am more used to having others act as my sword. I only order killings out of expediency and take no delight in the act. This does not make me soft or tender-hearted but careful. Bloodlust does not tug at my arm. Still, Caesar's tears puzzle me. I had not considered him to be a man of feeling, only of ambition and want.

'Apparently his tears were real indeed,' says Apollodorus. 'Pompey was his enemy but he was also a Roman. Once, he had been Caesar's friend. He was a worthy adversary and your brother murdered him with deceit. There was no honour in his death. Your brother dishonoured Pompey and himself with his treachery.'

I am quiet for a moment, considering. I sense the fissure in the rock; the possibility of victory. My friends watch me, they wait. I speak slowly.

'My brother has insulted Rome. He's a fool who pulled the head off a Roman general as he used to pull the wings off flies. But he did not understand the consequence.' I pause, thinking. My gaze rests on Charmian. 'I do not believe that Caesar wishes to kill me,' I say slowly. 'But he does not yet wish to help me either. I must persuade him.'

★

We sit alone in my great tent. Just me, Apollodorus and Charmian while a trio of trusted slaves play music just outside so that the sound from their lutes floating out into the night air masks our conversation. There are spies everywhere, always. I set my girls to guard the area outside the tent, Iras in charge as silently they scour the desert for prying eyes and ears. No one notices my girls in the shadows. They are better watchers than the bulky soldiers, who are loud and brimful of swagger and too easily avoided. Charmian lies in Apollodorus's arms. When it is only us three, I do not mind their affection for one another. I know that their love for me is beyond reproach. He places a kiss upon Charmian's forehead but looks at me, his face tight with worry. I smile at my friends, hoping that my fear is hidden, like a dagger beneath my mantle. I must pretend bravery for their sakes.

As Apollodorus strokes Charmian's arm, an idea forms in my mind. It is not what I want for myself, but I know what I must do.

'I know other rumours about the mighty Caesar,' I say, forcing a smile. 'He has a weakness for royal women. He likes to conquer them. I must let myself be taken. Then, perhaps I can conquer Caesar in turn.'

I speak with bravado I do not feel. I can hear the tremor in my own voice. Charmian shakes Apollodorus off, and he sits up, a scowl upon his face. Both of my friends know that I have never been to bed with a man. No man has ever glimpsed me naked or touched more than my hand while paying homage. I reach for wine and shrug, pretending courage. Apollodorus frowns, saying nothing while Charmian folds her arms, face tight with concern.

'My queen—'

'Peace. It is the only way. We've been waiting for fortune's wheel to turn.' I try to make my voice sound bright, full of certainty. 'We must fight with the weapons we have. Caesar likes queens the way other men like to swallow oysters or join in duck hunts. My brother is vicious and he might have Alexandria and the larger army but I have something he does not.'

This war may turn not on the point of a sword, but a soft surrender of my body and my most private self. I try to swallow but find I cannot; my mouth is dry as if filled with dust choking me. My friends eye me with concern. Charmian and Apollodorus lie together almost every night, but it is a shared decision. Though they are slaves, they are free in this, to choose each other.

'I must be brought to Caesar.'

They know I speak the truth and there's no other way, but they're frightened for me. I'm glad they're scared. They can hold my terrors for me, and I can pretend to be unafraid.

'Yes, my queen,' says Apollodorus. He bends and kisses me on the forehead. No one is supposed to touch me – especially without invitation – yet the tenderness of his gesture moves me. The ball in my throat swells and my eyes itch with tears. I cannot cry. I cannot. I dig my nails into the pads of my palms. I am Cleopatra, father-loving daughter, earth-bound goddess, Pharaoh and Queen of the Red lands and the Black. I am unafraid. I fear neither Caesar nor death.

The problem of smuggling me into the palace remains. If any of my brother's allies glimpse me, then my death will be swift and brutal. I trust only Apollodorus and Charmian. We've been sitting for hours puzzling, with the night spread thickly around us. The sky is salted with stars.

'There can be no guards,' I say. 'No soldiers at all. They'll only bring attention.'

Apollodorus looks unhappy but he doesn't argue. He knows I'm right.

'But how to hide you?' he asks for the hundredth time.

I have no answer. Refreshments are set before us but none of us wants to eat. I toy with the peel of a lemon, wrap it round an olive, seal it up again. An idea stirs.

'You can carry me?' I ask. 'Even for some distance?'

Apollodorus laughs, twitches the bulbous muscles on his arms so the ink writhes and moves. 'Of course.'

'If I'm hidden inside a box, can you still lift me?' I gesture to a carved rosewood chest, engraved with silver and gold. It's large enough for me to fit inside if I curl up.

Apollodorus nods, but I can see from his expression that he's dubious. The box is large and bulky and will add to the weight for Apollodorus. Inside, it will be hot and cramped. When I emerge in Caesar's presence, I need to look enticing and not half-addled from heat and stuffiness. The box won't do.

'What else do slaves carry?'

'Trays of food, jugs of beer,' says Charmian.

'I can't hide in a jug. I'm not a water spirit.'

At that moment, Iras opens the flap of the tent and allows in a slave.

'Set it down and leave,' she orders.

The slave carries on her head a laundry bag, full of fresh linens for my bed. She puts it down and hurries back out.

All three of us stare at the large sack.

'Is it possible?' I ask.

Charmian is the first to move, going quickly to the laundry bag and tossing out the sheets and opening it wide.

'My queen,' she says.

I step in. It's wide enough but not sufficiently tall if I stand. I crouch and Charmian pulls tight the cord.

'Shall I?' asks Apollodorus.

I'm starting to tell him that of course he needs to try and lift me, but my voice is muffled and he's already picking me up. I feel myself hoisted onto his shoulders, draped across them. I'm uncomfortable and feel more than a bit ridiculous squashed on my perch. His shoulders are hard and the bones dig into my hip. Yet, there's no other choice. This is how I must be brought to Caesar, not in triumph on the back of elephants, not in my golden barge nor in a chariot pulled by tigers, but concealed in a laundry bag, like an olive hidden in a lemon skin.

7

CLEOPATRA

We travel across the desert the next night when it's cooler. We're dressed as common travellers, and I borrow one of Charmian's tunics to wear. Apollodorus's hand twitches constantly upon the long curved blade hidden at his hip. No one in the camp sees us leave, we slide out into the dark, absorbed as rain drops into the sea. I have Iras dress in my robes and jewels and stay in my tent with the slave girls and issue orders for none to enter – Cleopatra is busy considering her reply to Caesar. If there are spies, the trick won't last long but it should be enough to grant us a head start across the desert. We travel swiftly, Apollodorus on one camel, and Charmian and I sharing another. Her arms are fastened around my waist, her chin rests on my shoulder.

We skirt to the west, keeping clear of the spreading camp

of Ptolemy's army. They block the way for my soldiers, as a dyke keeps back the pressing body of water, but we are only a few drops and we shall seep through.

Dawn reaches out across the sky with long red fingers. The sea glints in the distance, smooth and grey, and beyond it, Alexandria. Low cloud shrouds my city, making it appear insubstantial – a city in a dream. I long to stop and rest, but we can't. Every minute we linger is a minute more in which rumours I am here could chase us down. Apollodorus alternately cajoles the camels and hisses at them, lashing their backs with sticks. Neither approach has any appreciable effect on the camels, but it seems to calm Apollodorus. The last star slides behind the curtain of sky, veiled till dusk. The sun rises fully above the dunes, the world blinks awake, and already there's a whisper of heat against my skin.

The sun floats high, gold inlaid into lapis blue. We haven't paused and I'm saddle-sore. My arms hurt from gripping the reins and the dust is everywhere – in my eyes, my ears, rubbed into my hair. Deep in my belly, I ache, still bleeding, the rag between my legs is sodden and chafing. Apollodorus sings in Latin of the olive groves and clear seas of his childhood home in Sicily, his voice deep and low. Charmian smiles a small private smile of deep pleasure as she murmurs the words. I understand that he has sung this song to her before.

At last, we approach the coast and I see the curve of the bay spread out below, the deep blue waters vanishing into the vivid blue of the sky. Tiny sails like gull wings speckle the water. Suddenly we dip too low, the sea vanishes and we pass through groves of marsh reed, the desert sand liquifying into mud. The camels trudge on, coughing and grunting, feet spattered. I'm relieved that it's cooler in the shade, but only for a short while for the swamps are thick with mosquitos. I choke on them like smoke.

With relief, we emerge through the reeds and out onto the shore. The sand is sieved smooth, ghostly white. Apollodorus slides off his camel and halts us, putting a finger to his lips. I watch as he jogs along the beach, making sure we're alone. He returns, satisfied, and lifts first me and then Charmian from the camel. He kisses her lightly on the lips as he sets her down. For a moment I stagger, hardly able to stand. Everything hurts. My thighs, my back and my eyes are red raw, I blink and blink but my lids grate against my eyes. I crave sleep like a parched man weeps for water. I'm also aware that I smell very strongly of camel. I know little of Caesar's precise desires but I'm confident that this is not one of them.

Apollodorus takes a dozen paces up the beach and deliberately turns his back, granting us privacy, squatting in the sand and pulling out a short knife and beginning to whittle a piece of driftwood. My skin is filthy, streaked with grime and dust, and the waves are foaming around my feet and legs. Charmian and I pad out together near the breakwater and submerge ourselves in the waves. It's surprisingly cool, and I lose my breath for a moment and then duck below the surface, floating there as the sea rinses the desert and my failures from my skin. My hair floats out like seaweed and my hands look strange in the water-light, as though they're not mine at all. The salt stings my eyes and I dip down and hold my breath until my chest burns. I shall emerge reborn, the deaths that cling to me like burrs wash away, and as I stand in the waves, clean and slick with salt, I am Isis and Venus hatching from the sea, ready to win victory through Caesar's heart.

I stand upon a cloth on the shore, naked, while Charmian douses me in fresh water, rinsing the salt from my bare skin and my hair. Taking oils from a bag, she rubs me with them, all along my legs, my belly, arms and back. She washes between my legs with oils scented with frankincense and takes a blade and shaves away all my hair. She gives me a rolled-up ball of cotton to slide inside myself. I open my legs and push it all the way up inside; it grates. Caesar must not know I'm bleeding. I know what men believe: that our monthly blood will sap their strength. He must believe the blood is merely evidence of my virginity. If he realises this is my monthly flow, then I risk his wrath and not his protection. Charmian presses another piece of folded cotton into my hand and a stoppered flask.

'Here's more water. And oil of roses so you can wash yourself again before you're brought to him.'

I swallow hard, say nothing.

I sit naked on the cloth while she plaits and fastens my hair, scenting it with oils; her nimble fingers tug and weave. She traces kohl beneath my eyes and ochre on my lips. She has prepared me thousands of times, with twenty slaves to assist her, and yet here it is just us. My courtiers today are the darting fishes in the surf, the skinny-legged heron, the red crabs watching shyly from the rocks. I prefer my gullwing court. Finally, Charmian dresses me in a white dress embroidered with gold and silver thread and fastens golden amulets upon my arms, a pair of twisting serpents with emerald eyes, ruby bracelets on my wrist and last of all places the white diadem against my forehead, tying the pale ribbon at the back of my head. No other woman in all the world may wear this diadem, for I am a Greek queen as well as an Egyptian one. Caesar must know at once who has been smuggled into his chamber.

Apollodorus grunts – it is time. Charmian will wait here until we send for her. He kisses her and strokes her cheek. I take no leave of her and do not kiss her goodbye. I can't bear the possibility that I might not see her again. If I think about it too much, I won't be able to do what must be done. I feel her standing alone beside the surf as we walk away, watching us until we disappear.

We row across the Bay of Alexandria under the curtain of dusk. The sail is lowered to make it harder to spot the little boat and I sit at the prow on a coil of rope, concealed beneath a blanket. Neither of us speak. My mind is full of the task to be performed and endured. The harbour is scoured by customs men, looking to seize smuggled goods rather than smuggled queens, but the risk to me is the same should our boat be searched. We chose darkness but there is no true darkness in the harbour, for the massive tower of the Pharos lighthouse presides over the mouth of the bay, a vast white monument needling the sky, taller than the pyramids of Giza. The pyramids crown the desert while the lighthouse governs the waters with fire. The crimson furnace at the top blazes out across the waves, scattering the darkness. Yet tonight I don't feel pride in its brilliance, only frustration that the light it spreads is so clear that we are forced to cling to the edges of the shadows, hoping we're not spotted. My breath still catches as we approach Pharos Island. On the top of the lighthouse I see the vast golden statue of Alexander the Great as Helios burnishing bright in the reflected light of the fire, never dimming.

As we near the shore I ease myself into the laundry bag, but the boat is rocking, and I grab the side to stop myself from falling. Charmian has stitched together a longer bag, woven from hessian, and I stand upright to draw it up over my head. When it's closed I can see only a little through the small gap at the gathering at the neck. My heart is pounding in time to the water slapping against the wood of the hull and my mind bubbles with doubts. I hope the audacity of my scheme will appeal to Caesar. That he will find it enticing and bold and not ridiculous. It is too late now to change course. I hear Apollodorus jump out and drag the boat up onto the slipway. It judders and I fall, unable to steady myself.

'One day they'll weave stories about tonight, and they will not say that we hesitated or that we were afraid. They won't know,' I say, wanting to reassure myself as much as him.

A moment later I'm hoisted up, and I'm slung across Apollodorus's shoulders. It's undignified and uncomfortable. I do not want to die like this if they discover me. The ignominy of being stabbed or strangled in a bag and then tossed into the waters to sink and rot.

There's been rioting all through the docks and I see shops and stalls smashed, the smouldering ruins of carts. They loathe the presence of the Romans in our city and the civil war has thrown daily life into chaos. A layer of dust and smoke coats the city, tangling with the smell of fish guts and rotting seaweed. Where are all the Roman legionaries here to instil order?

Apollodorus walks quickly but not too fast – he must not seem afraid. I feel the crackle in the air. Peeping through the mouth of the bag, I see in the distance the vast outer stone walls of the palace. They stretch on and on, smooth and high and as unscalable as a cliff face. Then, for the first time, I observe a scattering of Roman soldiers. To my dismay they're outnumbered by a company of soldiers belonging to my brother.

As we approach the palace I hear running footsteps, and then realise it's the fierce pattering of my own heart. Apollodorus avoids the grand entryway and takes the route to the rear entrance. It's apparent that they're not expecting us to try and sneak in, for there is no increase in guards. This is typical of my brother and his arrogant advisors – they're so certain in their own triumph and cleverness that they do not consider the possibility that I might find my way here. I'm relieved at their stupidity.

I feel Apollodorus stop, shuffle forward. We are in a queue of slaves waiting to enter the palace gates. We can hide amongst them, wolves in a pack of dogs. The waiting slaves are impatient, calling out to the soldiers to hurry up and let them inside, their burdens are heavy. It's late and the soldiers, bored or tired, wave us in. I feel sick with excitement and fear. I'm back in the palace, my palace, my home. Although, this is a part of it that I have never seen and do not know. The palace is the size of a town, and these are the slave quarters, the kitchens and stores, places that as princess I did not visit. This labyrinthine under-palace of windowless stone tunnels is as foreign to me as the far reaches of Rome.

Then, after a time, I inhale the familiar perfume of savoury incense, myrrh, cedar and rosewood. We're approaching the royal suites of rooms. Legionaries mingle with Egyptian guards. There's a bustle of Roman soldiers, the clatter of swords at their hip. Apollodorus falls into step behind them, hoping that they will bring him closer to Caesar. There are dozens of sumptuous royal suites he could be in – we could search all night and not find him.

We follow in the trail of the Romans. They talk loudly with the swagger and confidence of Caesar's men. They lead us outside, through the lemon and olive groves. The evening cicadas click and the wind stirs the branches, a melodic accompaniment to the music of the fountains. Perfumed water rushes through a series of rills and miniature waterfalls. I inhale deeply the citrus and herbal scent of home, my gardens. Apollodorus trails them at a little distance. I hear their feet on the gravel. I guess where we're heading, to the grand guest villa in the palace grounds. It's a careful, strategic choice. Safely concealed within the solid palace walls, but separate enough that Caesar can place his own guards at every entrance. I guess this is where the great Roman is quartered for there are more soldiers here than in any other part of Alexandria, thronging like bees around the entrance to the hive. The small group we have followed march up to a large set of ornate doors inlaid with silver and rubies and are waved inside. Apollodorus trails after them, trying to be concealed in their wake. The guard halts him, grabbing his arm.

'What are you doing here, slave?' demands one.

Apollodorus pats me in the sack. 'Clean linens. A request came, asking for more.'

I feel the guard hesitate. He looks at Apollodorus, who slouches and stoops, making himself smaller. Time hums in my ears.

'Go on then, slave,' he says.

Apollodorus lumbers forward, careful not to seem too eager. No one is in a hurry of excitement to deliver linen. He steps into the largest chamber. There's a bustle and hum of noise, and the musicians are packed into a corner. I unknot the mouth of the sack and peek. After the dust and barren filth of the desert, I notice perhaps for the first time the opulence of the room. The floor is lined with woven carpets from Persia and the skins of panthers and leopards, while the walls are inlaid with mosaics of ivory, tortoiseshell, bloody garnets and gold. The glister of precious metals is so great it's like standing amongst the stars. Amongst the crowd, I can't see Caesar at first. Then, I notice a man in a plain white toga edged with purple, seated in a wooden chair behind a desk covered with papers. I've seen a thousand images of Caesar, he floods the world with coins and statues bearing his likeness. There's a minted army of Caesars spreading out across his conquered lands. And yet, even without having glimpsed so much as a dented coin, I'd know this to be him. There's a space around him that no one dares to penetrate. The undisputed ruler of Rome and all its territories. He's the sun, an embodiment of Helios or Ra, and all eyes are upon him. All faces in the room tilt towards him, like a field of flowers, turning their faces towards celestial light. And yet as an individual, he's unremarkable. He is not beautiful or tall, nor surprisingly short. He's neither young, nor so old. He is power, and yet he's wholly ordinary. His hair is drawn back high over his forehead, thinning and speckled with grey. I watch as a slave pours him a drink – water, I observe, not wine.

We linger just inside the doorway. No one notices us. I had not considered this possibility. That I would be brought into the great man's presence and be ignored. Whenever I have entered rooms in this palace before, there were columns of guards and slaves and musicians to announce the glory of my presence. At this moment, I lie draped across Apollodorus's shoulders in a sack, hoping I am not too sweaty or bleeding. It would be clear to anyone glancing in our direction that Apollodorus does not really carry linen, but no one is interested in us. A slave with a burden is not worth attention.

'Are you ready, my queen?' he asks, not bothering to lower his voice amid the bustle and din.

'I am,' I reply.

Apollodorus strides forward and, to my surprise, he grabs a plate off the table and hurls it down upon the hard floor. It's pure silver and the metallic sound rings out with a burst of noise as it clatters and rolls across the floor, piercing the chatter like captured thunder. Everyone stops, startled into silence, glancing around instinctively. Without hesitation, Apollodorus marches across the room to Caesar and kneeling, sets me down before him. Caesar's guards rush to his side, swords raised, but Caesar halts them with a finger, curious. My heart rises into my throat, but I will myself to be calm. I am no prisoner. I am Queen of Egypt and I have tricked my way back into my palace through courage and cunning. I ease my way free from the sack, wriggling out, first my head, then shoulders, emerging like Venus from the waves, or a butterfly from its woolly cocoon, until I stand before him. They stare. The silence vibrates.

I do not smile. I do not flinch. My skin is soaked with oil of roses and gleams in the torch light, some drops have stained the hem of my linen dress. The gold serpentine amulets on my arms and wrists catch in the torch light, sending reflections spinning across the walls. Around my forehead is tied the white diadem. I could be naked, unadorned with any jewels, but Caesar would know me to be queen and Cleopatra by the diadem knotted in my hair.

Caesar stares at me, thin-lipped, eyebrows raised. He still says nothing. I can tell he's surprised, even amazed. He is a man who can buy anything. Even me. I need his protection in exchange for myself. He's seen too much of human nature and there is no novelty left, I am not even his first foreign queen. Death, conquest and the sunrise mean little to him any longer. And yet, I can sense that by my daring I've roused him from boredom, stirred him as if from a deep sleep. He summoned me here but did not really expect that I would arrive or not like this. It was more likely that I would be presented to him in pieces, hacked up and bloody as a joint of meat. Later, I will present him with treasures from my vaults, golden flutes and jewels and animal skins and silver vases and painted statues so lifelike they look as if they will walk behind him back to Rome, but this moment, the surprise of my arrival and the reprieve I offer from world-weariness is my true gift. I meet his gaze, unafraid and resolute. He will not cow me. His eyes are very dark, deep-set and intelligent, and I feel them measure me, he's intrigued. That's not enough for what I need; I must make him want me. Not only for his bed, but as queen and Pharaoh.

8

CLEOPATRA

The doors to the guest palace are locked and barred, sentries placed at every exit. None may enter or leave for Caesar does not want news of my arrival seeping out to my brother. He says it's for my protection, but I sense that he also wants time to consider me, to decide which dice to call: mine or Ptolemy's. He plays my friend, but really is yet to choose.

'Bring the banquet quickly. We must have wine enough to drink Cleopatra's health,' he declares.

Goblets are passed around and the assembled Roman citizens drink to me, and again I see that Caesar only sips to toast and then discards his wine for water.

The feast is laid out on the finest silver and gold plates. It's a barbed compliment. The plates are mine and the food is grown in my fields, the slaughtered beasts fattened on my grass and grain, trout fished in my rivers and prepared in my kitchens by slaves who belong to me. Yet, he orders it all in my honour, as though it is his gift. And with bitterness, I understand that at present it is, for I am nothing without his strength. This hollow honour serves as a reminder of the precariousness of my position. I command nothing at this moment, not even myself. I'm here without a single servant, save Apollodorus, as a guest in my guest's quarters. As I study Caesar, I can tell that he is choosing to remind me of my vulnerability and display his power through lamb dressed with pomegranate, spiced eels and honeyed dormice instead of at the point of a sword. I feel it just as sharply, but I voice no objection. I don't dare. Not yet.

He consumes nothing but already he looks ready to eat me, I am a morsel for a monarch. I swallow, force a smile. I wish I was taller and wasn't forced to glance upwards to meet his eye. I raise myself upon the balls of my feet. It's late and the slender moon is high and bright outside the window.

'Queen Cleopatra. We are pleased to find you here.' He speaks to me in my native Greek.

I answer him in his own Latin with a smile. 'I understood that Caesar must be obeyed. But if you did not expect me to come, perhaps that isn't true after all.'

He smiles. 'It is true.'

'Then it must also be true that I was expected, if no one surprises Caesar.'

'I am not surprised. Pleased.'

It's evident from his expression that he is both. He is staring at me without blinking. I long to edge away from him. But I can't, mustn't. I recollect the million Gauls that he boasted of killing. A vast number of dead that my brother marvelled at, as others would an exquisitely decorated vase. And yet, I do not fear Caesar's hurting me. He is careful. It's written in the leanness of his physique while surrounded by epicurean delicacies. His sobriety while being pressed with cups of wine. He is a man who always looks before he treads and I'm sure that for him, murder is expedient and I'm safe for so long as my life and body are useful to him as tools of politics and pleasure. I smile, try to look pleased and ignore the hurry of my heart.

'You are fairer in flesh than we had hoped,' he says.

'Ah, so you hoped for me,' I reply, smiling.

'And me? Am I as you expected?'

I have to be careful. I cannot tell him that he's more handsome than I'd imagined for he'll know it to be a lie and that will traduce me in his opinion. Yet, I must still flatter him. I glance up at him through the lashes that Charmian has skilfully curled and thickened with kohl.

'Now we see you, our fears are purged. For you are kinder, more benevolent than we dared dream,' I say.

'You dreamed of us?' he asks, his voice soft.

'Caesar is the noblest prince in the world. Any woman with spirit would dream of such a jewel. If you did not exist then we would be forced to conjure you in thought, if not in flesh.'

My words are thickly spread with honey and I hope not over-sweetened for Caesar, but he seems amused and gives a slight smile as he replies. 'Caesar would be a beast without a heart not to be moved by Cleopatra. Your plight touches us. And your words stir pity within our breast.'

'My plight, my lord? I am the noble Queen of Egypt.

Pharaoh of the Red Lands and Black. I want no pity,' I say, my voice rising with indignation.

We both know my declaration of power to be absurd. It's true that I am a queen but I am a queen forced to conceal herself in a laundry bag. My treasuries are stuffed yet I cannot touch their gold. My fields are ripe but I cannot reap their harvests. I have an army packed with loyal men, but lodged so far away that I cannot command them. Yet in the game of princes I must pretend that I already control and own that which I seek. Caesar does not laugh nor contradict me, for in my position he would do the same. He only says, 'It is good fortune indeed that you are here. And we hope our good fortune will grow further.'

It's clear by the eagerness of his expression precisely where and in what regard he wants his fortune to grow. I offer him my palm. 'Is it true you can read fortunes? Tell me, pray, what will be mine tonight?'

He kisses my hand with dry lips, then keeps hold of it, his fingertips caressing my knuckles. Instinctively, I long to yank it away but I don't. I feel as if I'm willingly holding my hand in the fire.

'Come, let us have our fortunes told tonight. Fetch the soothsayer,' declares Caesar. 'Let us hear what she has to say about the meeting of Caesar and Cleopatra. Shall we yet knit together our kingdoms and our hearts?'

A few minutes pass while the soothsayer is found and then brought before us. She bows first to Caesar and then to me. I already dislike her for acknowledging a mere consul before a queen, although grudgingly I concede that perhaps in the circumstance she can do little else. She's a young woman, not a priest as I'm used to. She's too thin, her bony wrists jutting out of her tunic like twigs that could be snapped. Her eyes are as dark as polished chestnuts and dart around the room, half afraid as though she already dreads the fortune she must reveal. She squats and pulls out a squab pigeon from her tunic, produces a short blade and slits the bird throat to belly. It dies without a sound.

'You must pull the entrails,' she instructs, holding out the bird to me.

I shove my fingers into the warmth of the pigeon and pull out warm, sticky viscera.

'Now give them to Caesar to cast upon the flames.'

He scoops the bloody mess from my hands and marches over to the fireplace, hurls it on the embers then cleans his fingers on a linen proffered by a slave.

The soothsayer watches the entrails flare and spit and for a moment the room fills with the smell and hiss of burning meat. There is a nervous unease amongst the watchers as to what fate will be revealed by the flames. They do not want me for Caesar as companion, plaything or ally. I have no friends here. They would not have cared if I had not made it alive to Caesar. They consider this a petty war between siblings, and that one Pharaoh is enough and each option as bad as the other. The Roman war is over, Caesar untouchable, and now they want to raid our treasuries and hurry back to Rome, pockets sagging with loot. I can read the thoughts upon their faces as easily as I can the books in the great library. They display their resentments and secrets like feathers in their hats. Caesar I cannot read beyond his simple desire for me. He has learned to mask his thoughts behind a placid, weary smile.

So long as Caesar prefers me to my brother, what they think doesn't matter. I turn to the auger with open arms.

'Give me a good fortune,' I say.

'I cannot give, I only see,' she replies.

'Then see a good fortune for me.'

'You shall be fairer in his eyes than yet you are.'

Relief pulses through me, warm and fluid. It is his affection which will make me more beautiful. Caesar will love me or at least dote upon me. I hope this affection will persuade him to lend me his armies. The risk and danger I undertook in coming here will be rewarded. Caesar studies me with increased interest. The soothsayer closes her eyes and breathes the acrid smoke in deeply. I wonder that she doesn't choke.

'And this union shall be fruitful. But the fruit will outlive the tree,' she says.

My relief is undercut by instant disquiet. Perhaps I ought to rejoice in the prospect of bearing Caesar's child, but he is still a stranger to me. There is no bond between us yet. And after any affection fades, he will slit me, gut me like the pigeon if it better suits his interests than bedding me. Most of all I don't like that the soothsayer blends her prophecy of birth with death. All that Caesar's supporters will hear is that the soothsayer foretold his death and they will remember my presence in that moment, my part in the prophecy. To me it feels dangerous and inauspicious. Yet, Caesar himself appears unperturbed by the mention of our prospective children or his own demise. He shrugs. 'May it be so that all children outlive their parents.'

I long to ply the soothsayer with more questions but I bite my tongue. It is dangerous to ask when you are not already certain of the answer. For now, I must trust in fate and in Caesar. He takes my hand again. There is still a rind of blood beneath his nails.

'Come, Cleopatra. We are two lions, I the elder and more terrible. And you, what kind are you?'

With this question, he leans forward and takes my chin in his fingers and kisses me. His lips are dry and warm, and his tongue prods at my teeth. I have no choice but to open my mouth. He tastes sour like wine left out too long in the sun.

He pulls away at last and I see that much of the crowd has withdrawn to another room, and yet half a dozen people as well as several slaves remain. Caesar is entirely unconcerned by the audience. He lives always in company and no longer notices them. This is true for me too, and yet those present are not my friends, nor are they my slaves, and for this, the moment that is to come, I do not desire spectators. I cannot ask them to leave. I cannot show I am afraid.

'Rare Egyptian,' he says softly.

A slave steps forward and unfastens the sword and belt from Caesar's person. Another moves to me and waits for me to give her permission to remove my dress. I hesitate only for a moment. I nod and raise my arms. She pulls the simple linen over my head. I stand before him, naked and resolute, wearing nothing but jewels and the diadem upon my forehead. He waits. Looks at me, my bare skin a mere document to be assessed and appraised. He does not touch me or speak. I do not cover myself for I am Egypt. I am unashamed. Out of the corner of my eye, I see Apollodorus turn and face the wall. He will not witness my debasement. The kindness of his gesture touches me, and a knot of tears catches in my throat like a fishbone. I swallow it down, hard. I don't want Caesar to know what this surrender costs me.

'Come,' he says, not without gentleness. 'I am stirred by Cleopatra. Come, my queen, I shall teach you about desire.'

I step towards him. I hope I do not bleed. I hope that if I do, he will not be angry.

He kisses me again and I force myself to respond. My fists are clenched by my sides and deliberately, I uncurl them. My shoulders are set, stiff, but Caesar doesn't seem disturbed. He reaches up and tugs hard at the braids of my hair, forcing back my head and exposing my throat. He inhales the scent of my skin and, leaning closer, whispers to me low, in Latin and then more slowly in Greek. His breath tickles my ear, hot, damp, sour. I try to answer him, to croon back tender nothings as is expected, but I can't. My lips and body won't obey me. I conjure the image of Charmian instead. The two of us on the beach. The cool waters over my head. The slap of the waves against my skin. I am not here. Caesar lifts me and lays me down on the bed. He looms above me for a moment, looking down at my body, and I long to cover myself with my hands, but queens aren't embarrassed or shy. His expression reveals a faint trace of satisfaction, I wonder if he has the same expression when surveying the ruins of a vanquished army. A knot catches again in my throat. I swallow and see instead of Caesar the sky above the beach, the swirl of the clouds against the blue sky. He nudges my legs open. Without meaning to, I stiffen and resist. He chuckles, and nudges them again, more forcefully this time. I must allow this invasion. I open my legs. I will myself to look at him, steadfast. He smiles. I don't smile in return. I'm deep beneath the water, exhaling bubbles that sail upwards to the surface. I feel his teeth rasp at the tender skin on my shoulder and throat. I make no sound at all. I can't for I'm underwater and no sound is possible here. He thrusts into me, again and again, grunting. It hurts, but only a little. His sighs are the lapping of the waves. He thinks he takes me, but I'm not here at all. He cannot reach me.

I wake to find that Caesar has already risen. I glimpse him through the open doorway already at his desk, reading papers while supplicants buzz around him. And yet, as I turn, I see that I'm not alone in the bed. To my amazement, I see Charmian beside me, her face close to mine, her breath upon my cheek. For a moment, I think she is still part of my imagination, that I only conjure her, such is the force of my need for her. Then I reach out and pinch her cheek, it's warm and soft between my fingers.

'How are you here? How dare you risk coming? I did not order it,' I whisper, joy warring with reproach.

'Apollodorus sent for me. I travelled with a dozen of your private guards and Iras. Caesar has given orders that they be allowed into the palace.'

'You brought Iras too?'

Charmian laughs. 'You did not think she would be left behind? We are yours.'

I'm relieved to have Charmian and Iras as well as my own guard here. Caesar's soldiers will only protect me so long as our interests are allied, and I'm too happy to see Charmian to scold her any further. I let her embrace me, and inhale the familiar scent of her hair, her skin. Standing, she dismisses the other slaves, and shoulders the massive door shut, shielding us from Caesar's gaze so that to my relief, we are alone.

'How are you? Was he gentle?' she says, her expression tight with worry.

I understand that she asks me not as a slave, but as my friend and as a woman. I try to tell her, but I can't. I know that she lies with Apollodorus, but it is not the same. She chooses to sleep in his arms when she is not my bedfellow. She gives her body to him willingly and with enthusiasm – judging by the noises and laughter I hear – and also with tenderness, even love. My gift to Caesar of my body was given in lieu of the gold I cannot yet offer, the jewels and grain that are no longer in my power to give. And yet, even if I had given him all the riches in Egypt, I know that he would have asked for me too.

She stares at me, her eyes big with worry, and I force a smile. I don't want to talk to Charmian about what it cost me. There is no time for how I feel, not now. There is no room for Cleopatra the woman. I must not think about Caesar fucking me, but lock the thought tight away, a viper in a jewel box. For tonight, I must please him again, if he wishes. And tomorrow. I kiss Charmian's cheek and say nothing; she grips my hand.

'I'm sorry,' she says.

'Don't. Not another word,' I reply.

A moment later, Iras enters, carrying in jugs of warm water. She kneels at my feet, and presses her lips against my hand. I am no longer quite so friendless. The two slaves set out clean linens and I climb out of bed and squat over the basin. There is blood smeared on my thighs and I wash it away, turning the water red. Charmian tries to wash me, but I shake my head. I want to cleanse myself. I don't want her to see. This is mine. I scrub and scrub for I need to sluice Caesar out of me, rinse his smell from me, and I scratch at my wet skin with my nails, reddening it. The soothsayer says that one day I will bear his child, but today, this minute, I want to be clean and free of him. His scent lingers on my skin. Beneath the smell of sweat and his pleasures, there is the sharp stench of age. He is powerfully built and yet there is loose skin covering the muscles on his arms, his bald pate is mottled and flakes. He wants me not only for my name as Egypt and as a foil for my brother: I can feel that it is my youth and spring brightness that tugs at him, as if he hopes that through proximity to my vitality, he can pause the turn and creak of the earth. I must make him believe that it is possible.

I reach inside myself and slowly pull out the bloodied cloth. The basin fills with beads of dark blood that marble the water.

'Did he notice?' whispers Charmian, glancing over her shoulder even though there is only Iras here.

I shake my head.

Iras hands her dry linens and the two slaves pat me dry. There are red and black bruises blooming all over the fleshy tops of my arms and on my thighs from his amorous pinches. I hate that he has marked me as if I'm a slave and not a queen. He was not unkind and was gentle enough, his grip on my skin was during the service of passion, but I did not want him for myself or my own desires. I wanted him only for Egypt. I sensed his weariness even as he moved within me and as he whispered to me I heard the echo of other well-worn sighs. We both pretend to each other; we lie together and lie with our sighings. I feign desire and he that the pleasures I offer him are new.

A sudden eruption of noise outside the windows disturbs my reverie. Iras runs to the windows and slams the shutters closed. From the gardens there are enraged shouts and then the sound of a scuffle. A pot is hurled and breaks against a wall with a rain of shards. I hear cursing in a colourful blend of Latin, Greek and Egyptian strong enough to make a maiden blush. Yells and cries float in through the shutters. Iras is rigid with fright beside the window and Charmian unfastens an ornamental dagger from the wall and stands beside me, the jewelled hilt glinting. I don't know how deft she is with a knife, but I know she will use it without hesitation to protect me.

There's a bang and Apollodorus shoves open the door to the room, and on his signal my personal guards race to where I'm standing wrapped only in a sheet and surround me, swords and shields raised. I'm relieved to see them and realise that they must have been stationed outside my chamber for some time to get here so fast. Charmian quickly straightens the silken diadem around my forehead. If I'm about to die, then it will be as queen. Iras comes to stand with us and on Charmian's signal is about to help me into my dress, when I recognise a petulant voice yelling amongst the cacophony: Ptolemy. My brother. My husband. My enemy. I stay Charmian's hand. I want him to find me naked, there is power in my nudity and I want it to be clear out of whose bed I have just tumbled. The yells continue and I flinch in disgust – my brother's shouts are shrill and loathsome. He has never known how to act with the dignity befitting a king.

'Let me in, you fools! You loathsome fucks. Where's my bitch whore of a sister?'

There is hammering on the outer doors.

'Let him in. His tutors too. But not his soldiers,' commands Caesar from the adjoining room, his voice now that of the general.

There is the slap of running footsteps on tile and more shouting. Then the doors to my chamber swing open and, apparently not expecting them to be unlocked, Ptolemy half falls inside, sprawling on the ground. He's hauled to his feet by his commanders, the eunuchs Pothinus and Achillas. The pair grimace when they see me, as though I'm a rotten, dead thing brought reeking into the palace. Ptolemy straightens, standing flanked between them, and I see that his crown is on crooked, as though he's only trying it on, a pretend boy-king. I stand absolutely still and naked while Charmian combs my damp hair. Achillas stares at me with unconcealed distaste, his lip curls. I meet his eye and he looks away. My feet are bare, and I am not yet decked in my jewels. Only the diadem marks me out as queen but it doesn't matter. I hold up my arms and allow Charmian to tug the linen dress over my head, then step forward to greet Ptolemy, who recoils from my outstretched hand as if he's just gulped curdled milk.

'Hello, cunt,' he says.

'Brother, dearest. My love for you is as fathomless as the sea. It's always an honour and a delight to be in your presence.'

'You whored yourself to him. How dare you? Caesar is mine.'

I want to laugh at the absurdity of his remark, as if Caesar is a child's rattle to be tussled over between two infants.

Caesar himself joins us and his presence withers Ptolemy's next retort. Ptolemy falls at Caesar's feet, prostrating himself before him and touching his feet.

'Do not listen to her. She's a serpent. She slithered out of the Nile.'

Caesar stares at him with distaste, repulsed by the display. As he grovels before him, Ptolemy's crown falls off entirely and rolls to land before Caesar's feet, only the white diadem beneath remains on his forehead. Caesar looks at the crown with antipathy, with a similar expression I imagine to the one when he beheld Pompey's severed head. I wait to see if the Roman will hand the crown back to my brother. He doesn't. He carefully steps around it. Ptolemy's imps lurk behind him, faces rigid with dismay. Achillas stoops to retrieve the crown and tries to place it on Ptolemy's head, but the boy moves away oblivious so that the eunuch is forced to try again, chasing him with the crown until at last he gives up the attempt and clutches it to his chest. It's a moment of pathetic ignominy but Ptolemy hardly seems to notice. His voice quivers with rage.

'I invited you into my palace, great Caesar, as my honoured guest. Have I not treated you with loyalty and respect? And then, you collude with her? I am betrayed.'

He is pale with anger and stamps his foot in a display of petulance.

'I am friend to you both,' replies Caesar evenly.

'Yes, but better friend to her,' hisses Ptolemy.

Caesar ignores his peevish innuendo as he would a child. He won't be riled.

'Your father willed you to rule together. It's the duty of Rome to see his wishes upheld.'

As he says these words, I realise that I haven't won Caesar yet. I may have lain in his arms, but he isn't declaring for me alone. However, I observe ruefully to myself, ruling with my brother in Alexandria is a stronger position than the one in which I found myself yesterday when I commanded only sand and a ragtag army. I've ruled with Ptolemy before. And over him. I will get what I want in the end.

Ptolemy however is furious. He went to bed believing himself sole Pharaoh, certain I was driven out and defeated. And now Caesar is telling him to share his crown with me. Ptolemy never could share toys or slaves. He would rather the spinning top or ball was broken in two than surrender it, the slave torn apart.

Caesar is also lying. Or at least speaking a convenient half-truth: he does not care what my father wanted – Rome desires only what is best for Rome. He uses my father's will as a shield and ruse. I must persuade Caesar that it is better for Rome and him for me to rule alone, that while I am clever and useful, my brother is reckless and vicious, his advisors indifferent to the command of Rome. I shall make my desires Caesar's. I can see Ptolemy's eunuchs squawking in his ears. I hope they are urging a pretence of restraint and civility. Actually I don't. Let him be feckless and cruel. I want Caesar to see him for what he is.

I'm fortunate then because Ptolemy is all fire and heat and idiocy. He shrugs them off and, turning, marches from the room. He strides across the gardens, scattering the slaves tending the roses like playing counters on a board, and rushes to one of the open curved guard towers that peer out over the city. Caesar signals for soldiers to pursue him. I hurry after, worried as to what Ptolemy is intending. Charmian and Apollodorus run alongside me, and Caesar joins us, only a little behind, his guards swarming behind Ptolemy. As we approach, my brother throws open one of the lookout windows of the tower and leans out. There is a roar from the crowd gathered below like the swell of surf in a storm. My stomach lurches. I realise that he or his eunuchs have been planning this from the moment they realised I'd snuck into the palace. It's all laid out. I turn to Caesar, my heart beating fast.

'Tell your guards to stand back,' I tell him. 'If the crowd see Ptolemy manhandled by a Roman, they'll detest you more than they do already. You'll be doing what he wants – he needs them to riot. He wants them to storm the palace.'

Caesar doesn't hesitate. He knows I'm right and commands the guards, who fall back out of sight.

With a smug smile, Ptolemy approaches a stool which I realise has been carefully placed there for this very moment. I worry for the safety of the stool, for my brother is like the other Ptolemies: fat as an overstuffed partridge, the filling oozing out. He does not understand the restraint of any appetite – for food, flesh or violence. I'm certain that his eunuchs have summoned this crowd and paid for it. The seething mass below are all Ptolemy's supporters. Caesar hisses orders to his men, who start to crawl to Ptolemy on their bellies, below the view of the window and out of sight of the crowd. But they're not fast enough for before they can reach him, Ptolemy stands on the stool and climbs onto the sill of the window so the crowd can all see him.

'I am betrayed. Egypt is betrayed! The Roman chooses a

whore to rule over you and not Ptolemy's son. Rome does not care a jot for you.'

With that, he rips the white diadem from his forehead, showing his debasement at the hands of Rome, and hurls it into the crowd. They roar and scream. The cries are so loud that I almost put my hands over my ears. These are his people, his paid-for friends. The gods know, he's plied them with enough gold to love him. He holds up his hands, and wobbles precariously. Then, to my astonishment, Ptolemy jumps and falls. I think for a moment, with a lurch of my heart, he's choosing death over defeat but as I run to the window and look out, I see that he's been caught by the crowd. I'm astonished they can support his bulk, and I worry briefly for those he landed upon. But they don't seem to care. They don't see a corpulent and vicious tyrant, but the protector of their own corruptions. They cradle him rapturously, screaming blessings, and then, on spotting me at the window, spray curses upon me and Rome. A cup is hurled towards my head. It misses, shattering on the wall beside me, but is followed quickly by other, fouler objects. I hurriedly withdraw. I am not loved here. My friends are elsewhere. The Alexandrians will use my lying with Caesar as an excuse to hate me even more. Those loyal to me will be grateful, and understand that I lie with him for Egypt, for them, to purchase Rome's favour. They will love me more, knowing that I offer myself to him, that we might yet be free.

'Go out there, get him back. Bring him here,' yells Caesar. 'That boy wants bloodshed.'

'Send my guards to fetch him back,' I say. 'He must be captured by fellow Egyptians or Rome will never be forgiven.'

Caesar absorbs the truth of this, then turns to his commander.

'Flavius, conceal yourself amongst them in Egyptian garb. Take a dozen men with you similarly attired, and then take with you a company of the queen's guard. Roman or Egyptian, they are under your command.'

The soldiers depart apace, and we all stand listening to the screams of the crowd for a moment, then Caesar turns abruptly and returns to the guest palace. The eunuchs cower, simpering apologies. Caesar pays them no attention. If I know that they're behind Ptolemy's escapade then Caesar does too. They want a mob to attack the palace, burn it, kill us all. The problem is that they might manage it. I've only been in Alexandria for less than a day, and even I've noticed the lack of Roman soldiers.

Caesar strides back into the palace, leaving me and Charmian and Apollodorus alone.

'Come,' I say, leading them back towards the olive groves.

We walk amongst the trees, dusty silver in the morning light. I am silent for a long minute as I think what I ought to do. They both watch me, waiting.

'Caesar is cautious. He lacks his usual strength,' I say.

'His legions are missing. He only has four with him,' says Apollodorus. 'There are more being sent from Rome. But, until they arrive, he is exposed.'

'Then, we must help him in this moment of vulnerability. Show him our loyalty now, so that when his strength is restored, it's us that he favours,' I say. 'Apollodorus, send for our men in the desert. Tell them to come closer to the city.

As close as the generals dare. Have them ready, should they be needed.'

Now I am back in the city, I understand Caesar stays in the palace to rest his men and assert his dominance over Egypt, but also because he's trapped until more legions arrive to relieve him.

'Pompey is defeated but Caesar cannot cement his victory,' I say. 'The Alexandrians hate Caesar even more than they loathe me. Given a chance, they'd kill us both.'

'I shall never let that happen, my Pharaoh and queen,' says Apollodorus.

I kiss his cheek and squeeze Charmian's hand, and she tries to smile, but she can't manage it. I'm relieved to have my two friends with me. But, even with Caesar here, I'm afraid.

9
CLEOPATRA

The guards scour the city for Ptolemy, but his allies Achillas and Pothinus remain in the palace. I wonder that they don't leave, slink out into the night to keep guard over their prince, but they choose to stay here to watch us. We're enemies walled up together, scheming for death. I was safer in the desert, where I only needed to fear the heat and the black cobras sliding on their bellies outside my tent through the dark.

In the palace the air hums with fear like a rush of bees. In fact, even the bees themselves seem unsettled, swarming from their hives in the gardens and hanging in a writhing black knot on the gatepost to the temple as servants try to drive them back into their hives with smoking heaps of dung. Everyone watches and suspects everyone else of dissembling.

The eunuchs are the poison from whence the sickness flows like pus from a wound. They mouth allegiance to Caesar and pretend that Ptolemy is inflaming the city according to his own whim, but we all know this is a lie. We perform in an absurd pageant where they snivel apologies to Caesar, and we pretend to believe them, while they sneer and conspire behind our backs. They have my brother well hidden in the city, the bellows to the rioters' flames, as they remain here listening, watching, plotting, waiting to murder us.

As we lie in bed, I warn Caesar that their viciousness is sneaky. 'They came for your old friend and foe Pompey with a knife, but their methods are not always so direct. They will poison you with kisses. I've seen the ash that tarnishes their souls. Their consciences were removed with their testicles.'

He studies my face carefully and listens but does not reply. I can only hope he pays heed to my warnings.

'When will your legions arrive?' I ask.

'That's the will of the gods,' he replies. 'We must pray for favourable winds.'

'My army is coming closer. They'll wait beyond the confines of the city. They will join your legions,' I say.

He brushes my knuckles against his lips.

In the morning, when I wake he is gone. I sit in bed alone, until Charmian knocks on the door calling my name, and a moment later it flies open and two children come tearing in. My sister Arsinoe stops short, hanging back, suddenly shy. I almost don't recognise her, she's grown tall in the months since I left, a sapling sprouted, long and lean. But then she smiles, and it's the same lopsided grin I know and love. I hold my arms open. She hurls herself into them. A moment later, the boy lands on my bed, flinging his arms around me. My youngest brother, Tol. He smells of soap and honey. I'm touched by the warmth of his greeting. He grins at me, and worms his tongue through the gap in his teeth.

'I lost a tooth,' he says proudly. 'I didn't cry.'

'Yes, you did,' says Arsinoe. 'You cried like the baby you are.'

With that, Tol jumps to his feet and yanks my sister's braid until she yelps and slaps him hard across his cheek, leaving a crimson star. I grab her wrists and slide in between them both, dodging the raining blows.

'Peace! Both of you. We have other enemies, there's no need to fight with one another.'

They eye each other with hostility across the battleground of the bed. Arsinoe sighs and slumps onto the cushions.

'I missed you, Cleo. I was afraid.'

I pull her close, feel the downy softness of her skin. I shouldn't have left her here.

'I'm so sorry, my darling. I'm here now. I won't let anything happen,' I murmur into her hair.

I hope this is true. I can hardly protect myself.

'I don't need you. You left me,' she says, defiant and brimming with reproach and shoving me away. 'I have Thoth.'

For a moment, I think she's talking about the god himself and then she gives a low whistle and there's the sound of wings beating against air and a large falcon sweeps across the ceiling as if one of the frescoed birds has sprung to life and then dives onto her outstretched arm, which I now notice is sheathed with a stout leather wristband, studded with golden rivets. From its perch on her arm, the falcon stares at me with flat ambivalence but imperiously permits Arsinoe to stroke his feathers as she feeds him scraps of meat from a little bag at her waist. Tol squats on his heels and studies them both, frowning.

'I want a bird to hunt with. I'm a boy, it isn't fair.'

'Your being a boy has nothing to do with it. You must show you're enough of a man, as your sister is enough of a woman to have a bird. I will bring you a falcon, but you must train it properly, like your sister has.'

'Really?' He stares at me, shiny with delight, big-eyed.

Laughing at his happiness, I nod. I will find the best falcon trainers in Egypt to coach him. I had not realised the simple joy to be found in pleasing these children.

'We can only hunt with him in the palace grounds. It's boring,' Arsinoe grumbles. 'We used to hunt in the desert and in the fields.'

I want to laugh that the civil war is a mere inconvenience to them, an interruption to their games. Yet, I am glad. My childhood was so brief and theirs will be too. I must ensure it isn't brutal.

'Then, it's good that the palace grounds are large,' I say. 'And perhaps, you must learn to hunt him along the corridors. Set free a mouse for him to chase and devour.'

Arsinoe frowns. 'I'm forbidden. He terrifies the slaves and the courtiers when he flies above their heads.'

I smile and shrug. 'Then, let them be terrified. You are a princess. You must learn to be pitiless.'

Arsinoe grins at me, thrilled. Even though I long to linger with the children, have sport with Arsinoe's falcon, I need to send out my other birds to listen. I send them back with their slaves to their lessons, while I dispatch Charmian, Iras and Apollodorus to attend to the muttering of the slaves and servants in the palace. They will hear the rustle of more whispers than any Roman, and I can only hope that they will uncover any scheme to kill us.

'I have spies everywhere. From the kitchen porters to the eunuchs' own slaves,' Apollodorus says. 'Achillas and Pothinus are feared but not loved. My best spy is the palace barber, a man who doesn't speak – dumb since birth – but he hears everything and those whose beards he trims often mistake his silence for a simple nature.'

I know of the man. He tends to the eunuchs' bodies every day, keeping them smooth. I'm intrigued. I'd thought they were hairless through nature, but it seems it's partly the barber's doing. I pity him his task – although I suppose that at least he does not have to pluck their balls.

Already the grain and fruit that enters the palace is mouldy, while the meat is green and rotting. At dinner in the hall surveyed by the shining gods we're served wizened food on golden platters. Caesar loses his temper and confronts Pothinus. 'Are you incapable of finding fresh food in all of Egypt? Is this simple task beyond your power?'

Pothinus bows and snivels, smirking. We know he controls the grain warehouses and all routes into the palace.

'Oh great and worthy Caesar, I fear that you must learn to like it. This is the only food we poor Egyptians have. And it is being given to you and your four thousand legionaries without cost. And we Alexandrians have a saying: a man who does not pay must accept with grace what is given.'

Caesar hears both the slur and the threat – he has few legionaries with him, and the eunuch general knows it. Caesar has enough only to protect his position in the palace, not to control the wealth of Egypt or the port. He doesn't reply and reins in his temper. But his anger is cold and palpable, I hear it like a hornet buzz. Pothinus will pay dearly for his easy insults later. Caesar is a wounded beast whose might will return with the thousands more legionaries sailing towards us from Italy.

To me, the question is who will kill whom first between Caesar or Pothinus. Caesar clearly wonders the same as he has two slaves test his food and won't allow me to eat from the same dishes as him in case they are poisoned – 'They shall not murder us both with a single bite.' I'm more afraid that we'll die from consuming rotting, foul food rather than any drops of venom. Iras tastes mine. I watch her with terror and would rather not eat at all if it were possible. I have never had less appetite.

Caesar and I no longer sleep at night, even surrounded by guards it's too dangerous. Instead we rest at odd hours, the rags of time. I see assassins and cut-throats hiding in every shadow, and they steal out from the underworld to pursue me through my dreams. Perhaps that is why Caesar hardly seems to sleep at all, napping on a sofa, his hand always on the sword at his hip, eyelids fluttering. The strange restless cycle of sleeping in snatches during the day and sitting awake through the night makes the days flow together in a dreamlike state. Sometimes I'm not entirely sure if I'm waking or sleeping, I seem to exist in a weird half-light, a liminal place between dawn and dusk. Caesar however is used to this peculiar existence, it's his campaign practice, and while he's many things: consul, senator, general, most of all he's a soldier. This is merely a campaign directed and fought from a palace instead of a mountainside, river bank or ditch. I can see him hunker down inside himself, find comfort in the ritual, where for me there is only strangeness. The unease binds us together. I begin to find that I do not dislike him for a bedfellow. He is clever and amusing and hides his viciousness beneath his skin. I know it is there, but I show him no fear. He doesn't want that from me. The assassins who want to harm us are the mere pickpockets of death, filchers of the occasional soul, while Caesar is a true ally of Osiris. He has peopled the underworld with battalions of souls for the death gods to weigh.

Caesar has a shrine to Venus placed in the corner of the room where we pretend to sleep, but next to it I have one for Isis and Osiris carried in and adorned with flowers and offerings of gold and myrrh and blood. Caesar makes no objection, and we blend our gods and our blessings. Privately, I trust in my own gods for Rome's Venus is too tender, while Isis is a sorcerer married to death himself, whom she resurrects with her own magic. And yet on the altar side-by-side I can see Venus and Isis are sister-gods. Perhaps the brew Isis uses to resurrect her brother-husband is bound with love.

Caesar and I are united by our shared danger and stranded here in the palace now become an island we cannot leave, we turn to one another. After we have lain together we rest naked beside one another and he strokes the outline of my lips and cheek with an idle finger. Instead of murmuring sweet nothings, he asks me about the grain stores and the number of ships in the Egyptian navy, the position of my troops and the reliability of my spies. I tell him everything where our interests are allied, but I am silent or deflect where there are details that he doesn't need to know. Sensing my holding back, he studies me with intent, but asks no further, knowing why I will not tell him.

I am never safe, not even as I lie in Caesar's arms. There are many kinds of poison, some are dispensed through words not herbs. In the morning a slave announces that Achillas wishes to speak to us, and Caesar waves him inside. The dictator's personal guards slide in behind the eunuch. Caesar and I sit together on the sofa, his arms are around me, and I'm sprawled half across him in a state of undress as we quietly discuss the position of the scant Roman troops – not for us the empty nothings of ordinary lovers. We fall silent as Achillas enters and stands in the doorway, his face dripping with feigned concern. A slave is by his side holding a poultice on a tray.

'I took the liberty of preparing this strengthening mixture myself. You smear it across your belly and it will nourish the child,' says the eunuch with a bow.

Caesar glances at me with surprise, wondering if I am already with child and haven't told him.

'My womb is empty,' I say to Caesar, ignoring the eunuch.

Achillas feigns wonder and pretends consolation. 'We all heard what the soothsayer foretold. It will happen with another moon.'

The slave steps forward and holds out her tray. I take no notice of her. Achillas knows I would never touch food nor any other potion he's prepared and so this is not an attempt to poison me through my mouth or skin. But there is harm intended, I'm certain.

'Or perhaps the time was not yet fruitful when you began lying together,' he says.

His words are a liberty and intrusion, even though a queen's body is never her own. But there is something else in his tone – a note of triumph. He knows something. I glance again at the slave's tray, and notice that beside the mortar holding the poultice are tiny folded pieces of cloth, round and edged with gold. They look dirty, despite having been washed, and then I realise the stain isn't dirt but blood. My blood. These are exactly like the cloths I slid inside myself to absorb my monthly courses when I first lay with Caesar. Perhaps they are the same – I don't know how Achillas found them. It does not matter, for I understand his intention is to rattle me, he seeks to set Caesar against me. I conceal my unease and glance at Caesar, who just looks impatient at the interruption.

'Too much blood can impede the flowering of the child. Perhaps this was the cause of the queen's empty womb,' says Achillas, looking at me. 'Did you bleed profusely when you first lay with Caesar?'

The blood that now flows is to my cheeks for I'm angry and a little afraid. Before I can speak, Caesar snaps at him. 'Enough! For a eunuch you are well informed on the getting of children. Yet, your information is all reading and no experience.'

'It's indeed fortunate that I like to read,' says Achillas, unruffled.

Soon after, he leaves the room with a pert little bow, accompanied by the slave who sets down her tray upon the table and scurries out behind him.

Caesar and I talk some more, discussing how best to guard the harbour, and the rapid emptying of the palace food stores. Yet, he does not touch me again, no longer casually drapes his arm about my shoulder nor brushes my cheek with his knuckles. Slaves bring us food, and then, after we've eaten, I wait for Caesar to kiss me and signal that he wants to lie with me. Instead he remains seated on the sofa, at a little distance from me – never has an arm's breadth of fabric felt so wide. He's quiet for a while, the only sound is the tap-tapping of his fingers on the seat. At last he clears his throat and says, 'I've heard all sorts of stories travelling. From Cyprus to Athens the world is full of fears and hopes. One learns which hold some truth and clever magic, and which to disregard. Kiss a mule to cure your cold. Caesar does not kiss an ass.'

I make myself smile at his joke.

Caesar continues. 'But I would not let my soldiers march for three days after the augur saw a flock of sparrows fly to our left.'

'An ill omen indeed,' I agree.

'And if a woman lies with a man when she's bleeding it can be fatal to the man. Or, it can be if the sun and moon are in conjunction.'

I don't answer or look at him. Does he believe that I put him in danger when we first lay together? From his voice, I can't tell if he supposes this to be true or is recollecting some rustic belief that he disregards. He's unreadable – an engraved tomb rubbed clean by time and sand. But what is clear to me is that Achillas and his insinuations are a danger to me and my relationship with Caesar.

For a day and a night, Caesar is absent from my bed and I'm needled with worry. My life and my power rests on his favour. I require his partiality and resent it all at once. I'm careful, however. I mustn't seem too eager or contrite. I light candles to Isis and – in deference to him – to Venus, his family goddess. The politics of Rome and Egypt has contracted to this bed, the desires and whims of one man. While I wait, I call Charmian and Apollodorus, and ask them to bring the children to me. They come in the evening, landing on top of me as is their wont, talking over one another in their eagerness to tell me what they've learned in the day's lessons. Dusk begins to fall as we talk, and the door to the chamber opens. Caesar stands in the doorway. I don't acknowledge him, but pretend to listen only to the children, even though in truth I can no longer attend to a word either of them is saying. Seeing me occupied, he comes into the room, dismisses his guards and quietly sits on a sofa, watching us. He likes children and surveys us with indulgence. He says nothing, only watches as we talk. Tol tears around the room with a toy horse in one fist and a soldier in the other. Arsinoe holds out her wrist for her falcon, but it perches imperiously on the horn of a sculpture of Isis, and ignores her for a minute before returning to her glove.

'You need to train him to come to you quicker,' I say, as the bird flies again, squitting messily on a sculpture of Artemis.

'Fortunately the goddess of the hunt won't take offence. She's indulgent towards all her hunters, even the winged ones. But, I was more careful with my training.'

'You had a falcon, Cleo?' asks Arsinoe.

'When I was a girl. He was a gift from Charmian.'

As we talk, Caesar leans back, listening. I stretch out and fiddle with Arsinoe's braids, twisting them between my fingertips.

'Charmian bought the falcon from a market stall, trading him for one of the tiny golden vipers pinned in her ear, unable to bear the noise of him screaming in his cage. He called to the sky he couldn't touch.'

'Did you love him?' asks Arsinoe.

'From the moment Charmian gave him to me, scraggy and hooded.'

'I love Thoth,' says Arsinoe, staring with reverence at her bird.

I remember how I removed my falcon's hood for the first time, how, like a lover, I drank in the bill sharp as a knife blade, the yellow talons bright as sunshine, the berry-black eyes. I owned many creatures and people, and yet the loyalty of my falcon I had to earn. I turn to Arsinoe.

'I spent many months coaxing my bird. Just as you teach Thoth. I trained him to fly and to return to me, to land on my glove as I held out a scrap of crocodile meat. In time, all his kills belonged to me.'

'Thoth won't give them up to me,' says Arsinoe, and I can tell she's reluctantly impressed at my skill.

'Not yet. Patience. Practice.'

'What did he look like?'

'He was smaller than Thoth here. He had stippled feathers like the sand marked by the retreating tide. He slept on a golden perch above my bed. I had no need of a cage, you see, as he would never leave me. I never chained him.'

'Never?'

I shake my head and Arsinoe stares at me with big eyes, and even Tol has stopped jumping around and sits listening. Caesar smiles at us from across the room. It's a strangely familial scene. I carry on.

'He slept next to me in his hood. I had a new one made and decorated with the white and red crown of Horus. He'd claw and nip at anyone who reached for him other than me. They say that birds are stupid—'

'People are stupid,' says Arsinoe, indignant.

'Indeed. For they say birds lack the loyalty of dogs or the cleverness of a cat, but my falcon was loyal and clever.'

'Like mine.'

'Of course. Little Horus sensed my moods. If I felt irritable or low, he would fly to my shoulder and rest there, and if that failed, he would hunt for a mouse or snake, and instead of consuming his prize, drop it on my lap.'

'Yuck,' says Tol, wrinkling his nose.

'But a gift is precious when it means something to the giver. They feel its loss but give it anyway. That is a true gift. And my falcon's bloody offerings meant more to me than any jewelled presents given by supplicants at court.'

'You trained him well. Your bird was a good servant,' said Arsinoe.

I shrug and continue. 'I didn't think of him as my bird but as my friend. Everywhere we went, little Horus followed.

Even our father was charmed by him. He used to wonder aloud if he was indeed the manifestation of Horus himself. People began to bring the falcon offerings of small animals as sacrifices, in hope of good fortune in return.'

I glance at Charmian, then carry on with my story.

'Charmian says this is where the trouble started – that Ptolemy and his eunuchs could not stomach that a bird was being held in higher regard than them. Their hatred festered like an untreated sore in the heat. Little Horus hated them too. He would ignore any morsel they proffered, no matter how succulent. And, when flying back to my glove, he would skim the top of Pothinus's bald head with his talons, forcing the eunuch to duck, and if he was too slow, Little Horus would slice open his scalp, shrieking with triumph. The entire court laughed to watch the eunuch squirm and shout and bleed.'

The two children giggle as they picture the scene.

'Oh, I wish I could have seen,' says Arsinoe. 'It sounds so funny.'

'It was, but humiliating your enemies can be dangerous.'

The children wriggle closer to me, even the falcon seems alert and listening.

'You see, one morning after a year, I woke to find him missing from his perch. As I looked up, I couldn't see his hooded face, only the empty gold branch. I scrambled out of bed and found him collapsed on the floor. He was in a puddle of blood, his hood cut from his head.'

Arsinoe gasps in horror, reaches for her own bird.

'As I picked him up, he twitched in my hands, his glorious talons snatching at the air. Blood foamed in his beak. As he writhed, he'd plucked out his own eye with his toe.'

The children recoil.

'I held him tight, kissed the soft feathers on the top of his head and then I wrung his neck.'

I can sense Caesar's approval. That I did not flinch from what needed to be done.

'He went limp. I sat with him in my lap, his blood and spray of shit spattering my dress. He was surprisingly light in death, as though Anubis had taken his substance along with his life. He had no visible wound, other than his missing eye and that he'd mutilated himself.'

'What killed him?' asked Arsinoe, her voice hushed.

'Well, I searched around the room and noticed his bowl of water. It was red and brackish. At first, I thought it was stained with his blood. But then, when I sniffed it, the water smelled strange and bitter.'

'Did you cry?' asked Tol.

'No, of course not. I was a princess.'

Arsinoe nods gravely. As I've been talking, two slaves have come in, and they linger, waiting to lead the children off for their meal. I gesture to the slaves to take them.

'Go, both of you. Eat, we'll talk more tomorrow.'

Muttering with reluctance, they trail out after the slaves. Caesar comes and sits beside me, our knees still not quite touching.

'You did not weep for your bird? I wept for Pompey. My enemy and my friend. It's not feeble to cry.'

'You are a man. And not any man, you are Caesar. You and I have different eyes upon us.' I try to smile but find I cannot. 'So, no, I shed no tears. I buried my bird and swore revenge. I knew they had killed him, Pothinus and Achillas.

They had not done it because the bird humiliated them nor out of jealousy. They had done it simply because I loved the bird and to destroy it gave them pleasure.'

Charmian watches me steadily and says nothing.

Caesar pulls me closer and kisses me. I'm flushed with relief at his affection, and then, to my surprise, desire. He notices, pleased.

'Come here, madam, I shall ply you with kisses,' he says.

Tonight I unfurl like a new leaf in the warmth of his curiosity, the fervour of his interest. I'm relieved that Achillas's insinuations have not damaged me too heavily in Caesar's eyes. He asks endless questions, not about the campaign, but rather about my girlhood. I find myself recounting my childhood and confiding stories about my father, whom I know Caesar viewed with scorn, but he does not snigger when I describe how I cared for him. My eyes get hot when I talk about how I made my father laugh, and Caesar takes my hand with something not unlike tenderness and presses it to his lips. I could almost be tricked into believing his attention, kindness. Caesar does not love me, for this thing between us is not love, and yet somehow I sense that I am already precious to him. I fascinate him like a puzzle box or new species of hunting dog he has not glimpsed before and is reluctant to surrender to its kennel master. He wants to keep me close and play with me, ply me with sweet wine and questions.

Outside the palace the rioters are busy. The night air is full of the stink of burning wood and plaster, the shouts and smoke carried on the wind instead of salt and the scent of the sea. I live on pins, and yet with him here beside me, the threat of war and the chaos seems strangely distant, as though we are on a ship, watching the world burn from the prow.

He sprinkles kisses and caresses all along the soft skin of my wrists to my ear, and tickles behind my knees with his tongue and smiles to see me gasp.

'I am your friend,' I whisper. 'I am Rome's friend.'

'I know,' he answers, sliding his hands into my hair. 'My sweet queen. Venus herself would blush to see a bride so lovely.'

I don't want to be plied with compliments and fattened with sweet nothings. Those empty words are for other women. My fortune is tied to his like a child to its nursemaid's apron strings. I begrudge it and yet for now there is no other way.

'I am Egypt's daughter. Her only Pharaoh and queen. Tell me, I am her only one. Her only child.'

'Most lovely goddess,' he murmurs, leaning in closer and kissing me again, not hearing the sharpness in my voice. I long to shove away his mouth. I don't want more kisses, however tender, I want only to draw from his lips promises and assurances of my position, how I shall rule alone, that he does not support Ptolemy's claim, but he slides his tongue into my mouth to stop my questions.

Although I find that I do like him, much more than I expected, I never forget for a moment even amid my new unforced joys how crucial it is that he likes me, prefers me to my brother. I must draw out his affection and fascination for me like blood from a wound. Everything I have depends on his regard for me. As I lick a trail from his lips to his naval and attend to his pleasures, my skin prickles with resentment.

I find myself considering his other lovers. I know there

have been countless women. We are connected, unknowingly, slave girls, Roman matrons, foreigners, senators' wives and queens; we are almost bedfellows. Do the other women feel like me? This need to offer themselves in exchange for his favour? I wonder how it must be to have a choice, to have the power to select my lover, not out of design or necessity but simply desire or love.

10

SERVILIA

When I met the Princess Cleopatra in Rome, of course I did not think how one day we would share a lover. That Caesar was the fulcrum point between us. I knew he was in Egypt, I did not know at first that he was with her. Over the years, when Caesar embarked upon campaigns away from Rome, he would disappear again and again into silence. Sometimes I would receive a letter with news, mostly the letters just served to tell me that he was alive when he had written it. I was used to silence and hated it all at once. We shared so many last kisses. He'd left Rome once more, this time to chase Pompey around the world. Months bled into a year, and I received no letter or news at all, and I did not know if I missed a dead man and this separation was to be forever. Then at last a ship arrived. It did not bring me Caesar but the news I'd been longing for since the death of my first husband. Pompey was dead. Caesar lived.

They might have made me wait – for gods do not keep to mortal time – but Mars and Diana enacted my revenge in the end. When I heard the news of Pompey's grisly demise, I made offerings to them in gratitude. At last, he had suffered as he deserved. I liked the grubby and foul manner of his demise. It was underhand, brutal, and fitting. It might have been decades since he'd had my first husband murdered, but my hatred of Pompey had not mellowed. I'd tended it carefully, keeping it cruel and sharp.

Perhaps it was the news about Pompey that made me think back to those early days with Caesar – it was Pompey's murder of my first husband that sent me into Caesar's arms – or maybe it was simply that Caesar was still gone from Rome and I missed him. Whatever the reason, I found myself thinking about him and our first days together, my mind straying back to those first months after my husband's murder. It was a period of grief, confusion and new-found love. My loss sharpening my new love for Caesar, like the fresh scent of the earth after rain.

The ship bringing news of Pompey brought gossip too; whispers that he was living in the palace with the Egyptian queen. I was used to his lovers by then, but only a fool doesn't notice when her lover takes a queen as his mistress. The rumours in Rome were full of scorn and innuendo, but I did not join in their denigration of Cleopatra. I knew she was shrewd, her mind more captivating than her beauty. And I was aware that it was a women's mind which kept Caesar's attention once he wearied of her physical charms.

Caesar and I had met many times over the years, and I always felt the tug of him. Rather than becoming lovers at once, we'd become friends. My family often describe me as quiet – I never think of myself so, for it is always loud in my mind – but I was certainly never quiet with Julius. I stored up the little happenings of my day, sweet morsels of amusement to feed him when we next met. At parties and gatherings, he sought me out the moment he spotted me, and before accepting an invitation, I know that he would check first whether I too would be in attendance.

As soon as we found one another, there was no room for anyone else in our conversation. We talked about the works we had read and admired and those we scoffed at and I would recite snatches of the latest speeches by famed senators, aping their manners and exaggerating their age and pomposity, sometimes pretending to fall asleep mid-rendition, until he snorted wine. I found him funny, although I noticed that he rarely seemed to amuse other people. At social occasions I watched for him, impatient, hungry for his presence, and if he wasn't there, I felt a sudden snag of disappointment and was then unable to attend to the chatter of others. I had no appetite for anyone else. I did not know then that these were the seeds of love.

We enjoyed a friendship bolstered with longing. After my husband died, when the initial keenness of grief and shock faded, I found myself thinking again of Caesar. He came to see me some months after the news of my husband's death. My son, Brutus, and I remained at home in mourning, the death masks of our ancestors shrouded or turned to the walls. It was a profound sorrow and insult that his father's face was not amongst them – another ignominy we placed at Pompey's feet. Brutus, now fatherless, went daily to my brother Cato's house, where Cato was beginning to teach him rhetoric and the politics of Rome. I could have taught him myself, but I thought it prudent to encourage uncle and nephew to form a close bond. And, Brutus seemed to find it a relief to walk to Cato's house accompanied by one or more slaves and spend the morning studying there. He appeared to enjoy his company – which surprised me at first. Brutus, although his spirits were depressed by the recent death of his father, had a joyful, irascible streak – quick to temper and to laughter. I have no memory of my brother Cato ever laughing. He hardly smiled, merely bared his teeth in a grimace. He was a man who scowled with pleasure, even at a joke.

The day of Caesar's visit to me, Brutus was already with his uncle. He'd left, still a little pale, quieter than he'd once been, but children have a natural buoyancy, and I could tell by his fidgeting that he was excited to spend time with Cato. I wondered if my brother revealed a softer aspect to his character with his nephew. I doubted it. As I considered these questions, the slave announced Caesar. At once my heart raced inside my chest, a hare pursued by hounds. I reprimanded myself for such silliness. Although every morning I wondered whether this might be the day that he appeared, now seeing him in the flesh standing before me in the tablinum made the blood swish in my ears, and heat rise in my cheeks.

Yet, the man who stood before me was different from the one I'd first known. The smart youth in his nifty toga was gone, along with any hint of boyishness. This was a man, mature and self-assured. His beard was shaved off, his hair cropped short and I saw the first hint of a bald patch on the crown. He'd broadened too, the arms that held me were muscled, the skin latticed with new scars. Glancing up at him, I felt almost shy, although as a grown woman, already a widow, I should have no such girlish affectations. He saw my shyness and smiled, gratified. It had now been some years since we had met, although my interest in him had never wavered. As he walked slowly towards me and then after the briefest hesitation took my hands in his, secreting a kiss in each palm, I realised that neither had his. We stared at each other in wonder and wordless delight.

'I am sorry for your husband. He did not deserve such an end,' said Julius at last.

I found that I could not speak.

'And as you grieve for him, then I am sorry for you too,' he continued.

I swallowed and forced myself to reply. 'I grieve for the father of my son. For my son I feel the loss most piteously.'

Julius drew me closer, and held me in his arms, whispering words of consolation and regret. I inhaled the warmth of him, the solidity, the faint tang of salt and leather. I had forgotten the scent of his skin. We stood there for some time in one another's arms, his chin resting on my head. Time slowed and swelled, the beat between the chirping of the cicadas seemed to lengthen and pause. I wanted to stay here always, breathing in the scent of him, feeling his warmth, the tightness of his arms around me, the comfort of his words.

'I have been away too long,' he said, running a finger along my cheek. 'We are not as we were.'

'No. And yet, I am still Servilia and you are still Caesar.'

He pulled me closer, and gently bit my ear lobe, hard enough that I cried out in pain and desire, and then to my surprise released me. He looked down at me, his expression half amused as though deciding what to do next.

'Well, are you going to kiss me?' I demanded, impatient.

He leaned forward and placed a featherlight kiss upon my left cheek.

'Enough?' he asked.

'No,' I replied. 'More.'

He bestowed another on my forehead, his lips lingering a moment longer.

'Enough?'

'No,' I answered honestly.

He kissed me now on the lips, pulling back after a few seconds.

'Still not enough,' I said. 'I'll show you, boy.'

He laughed at my teasing. I tugged him towards me, impatient, and kissed him properly. A kiss that demanded an answer, and his arms tightened their grip on my wrists. After a minute, a kiss was not enough to satisfy us. He picked me up and carried me to one of the sofas, and setting me down, began to undress me, pulling my tunic over my head. In our impatience, I got tangled, and giggled as he freed me.

'Do you laugh at Caesar?' he asked, smiling over me.

'I do,' I said.

I reached for his belt and unbuckled it. I wondered that we'd waited this long. I did not think about the slaves busy in the villa, nor of Brutus at his uncle's house. I only thought about this man, the feeling of his fingers on my bare skin, his lips kissing my throat and my breasts, his murmurs of love and lust. I felt drunk with the way he looked at me, eyes wide with delight. He did not see the marks on my body from bearing Brutus, the fading stretchmarks, the slight softness on my belly, or if he did, he accepted them as part of my story, just as I caressed the scars on his forearms. He pulled back for a moment, simply to look at me.

'How did we wait this long?' he asked, amazed, voicing my own question.

'I don't know,' I said.

Turning and shifting on the sofa, he pulled me onto his lap, covering me with caresses and muttering words of love.

'I choose you,' I said. 'Whatever else happens after, I choose you.'

This is who I want to be, I realised. This woman of desire who is desired and loved in return.

11

CLEOPATRA

They find Ptolemy just as Ra is finishing his nightly journey through the underworld, and rising again in the east, as a flaming beetle to heat the world. The guards drag Ptolemy back to the palace under arrest. I can hear him cursing and calling down the wrath of the gods upon me. My heart hurries in my chest. He needed to be caught, but now he's here, I wonder what Caesar intends to do with him. Soon he'll discuss the matter with his portentous advisors. They share the same cut of beard and the same sense of doom, and I can't tell them apart. And yet, he often wants to know what I think of their advice. He listens to me carefully, never interrupting, and I know that he is starting to value my counsel as much as that of any Roman.

Caesar rises from the bed, leaving the chamber, and my

slaves wash and prepare me in his absence. I stand with my arms above my head as they sluice me with warm water, watching in silence as the early morning light drifts in through the shutters. I don't like that Ptolemy is now lodging within the palace, the worm inside the apple. Something has shifted again. Before the fires were further off, now they burn right here. Charmian dresses me for Caesar's company, adorning me in gold and jewels so that every part of me glisters. My serpent amulet pinches into the flesh of my arm like a too-ardent lover. The door opens and Caesar returns as I finish my toilet. He eyes me as a dish of plump olives set before him. He reaches for my wrist, pulls me close and bites my lip. Charmian and the other slaves withdraw.

'Your brother can wait,' he says. 'He must sit quietly for a while and fester before we grant him audience.'

'Because now that you have him, you're not sure what to do with him,' I say.

Caesar laughs, and bends towards me, capturing my chin in his hands. I want to turn away, impatient to hear his intentions, but I don't for it would be impolitic. His kisses warm into something else, and soon, as he shoves at me, I exaggerate the pleasures I feel. I don't want him now, I only want to know what he plans to do. After we are finished and lie breathless side-by-side, I can hear the hurry of voices just outside our chamber.

'Don't shuffle and whine, come in,' calls Caesar.

The old men enter, feigning not to notice that we are naked and in bed, but carry on as if we're seated discreetly upon adjoining sofas. Charmian has slid back in with the advisors and I gesture to her to come and dress me so I can leave them to their discussions, but Caesar stops me, saying in Greek, 'Stay and listen.'

The old men flinch with dislike. They hate that Caesar beds me, and worse still that he heeds me; I'm a woman, a licentious Egyptian and a queen. I'm not sure which they dislike most, I'm a triumvirate of distaste. Charmian slips a shawl over my shoulders, and wrapping myself in it I sit up unabashed that I'm naked underneath, and answer Caesar in Latin, switching easily between languages. 'I will gladly stay and offer you my thoughts.' I smile and nod towards the advisors. 'But you know what they're all saying about you, don't you, mighty Caesar?'

'You want me to say no, so no, what are they saying about me?'

'You conjugated with Cleopatra when you should have declined.'

Caesar laughs uproariously at the old joke, carefully deployed. There is truth in it. None of the men around us are pleased that I am in his arms. They do not laugh at the joke.

'Well then, what shall we do with the prisoner?' he asks, frowning and rising from the bed to be dressed.

One of the greybeards scowls and coughs. 'You can't kill him, but so long as he lives, he is trouble.'

'Troublesome in life, and troublesome dead,' says Caesar. 'How long till our legions reach Alexandria?'

'Still weeks if not months. The winds have not been favourable.'

Caesar's might is in his reputation but also in his armies and, cut off from them, he's a body without fists. Since I can recognise his present vulnerability, so can all his enemies. If he was shielded by his usual number of legionaries, the eunuch crows would never dare to insult and threaten him as they do. They tug at his weakness like a loose thread, and I fear the vestiges of his power will unravel. I've never found myself praying so hard to the gods to hurry the arrival of Roman legions into Egypt.

Ptolemy's arrest has incensed the crowds in the street, and I can hear the noise outside the palace like the roar of the sea. Even in here, with the shutters closed, the air is thick with smoke. The city is burning and we are cut off from our troops. Our position here is precarious, we are nesting on the edge of a cliff.

'What do you think I should do?' he asks, turning to me.

His advisors recoil, horrified. It's bad enough that he beds me, an abomination that he listens to me. I hesitate. The advice I wish to offer does not need an audience. Caesar senses my hesitation and dismisses the old men with a wave, snapping at them to 'Go, apace.'

I take a moment to put my thoughts into words. I'm relieved he is including me and my interests in his decisions. I consider for a moment. I must flatter Caesar as well as offer my solution.

'You must address the crowd yourself. I've heard that you are the greatest orator of them all.'

'An exaggeration,' he says with a wave, but I can tell he's not displeased.

'Tell them that you are keeping Ptolemy here for his own safety. He's not under arrest but your protection. But it also falls to you and to Rome to stop the confusion and the warring factions. Declare once and for all that I am queen. That I rule alone, with Rome's backing.'

He looks amused by my audacity, but I know that he could not have expected anything else.

'And your brother? What do we do with Ptolemy?'

'Keep him here for now. Then you cannot be accused of murder. But, you must kill the eunuchs. No one keeps a viper for a pet. They will bite you at any moment. It's what they do, they cannot help it any more than rain can help falling from the sky.'

He looks up at me, propped on his elbow, expression quizzical.

'You enjoy me not merely because I am a woman but because I am a queen. So, do not listen to the woman, hear only the queen.'

'Men of Rome do not like kings or queens.'

'You are not in Rome.'

'I am not.'

'And you are not only a man, you are Caesar. I ask you to be Caesar now. Swear to me that you will do this thing. Mark them with blood. Or give me leave and I shall do it in Caesar's name.'

He stares at me, taken aback by my grisly determination.

'If no man is willing to touch the eunuchs, then a woman shall.'

My hands tremble, I hide them behind my back as though they are already streaked with blood. I do not want to murder. But, for the good of Egypt I will do it and end this war. Caesar surveys me, his expression unreadable.

'First of all you must declare me as the only Pharaoh to the Alexandrians. But that's not all you must do.'

'There's more?' asks Caesar, entertained by my presumption.

'Yes. For while your rhetoric is, I'm sure, peerless, you don't know Alexandrians. You must ply them with compliments like sweet wine but you must also give them something they want.'

Caesar studies me, his expression hardening, no longer amused. 'It is you who must give to Rome.'

I want to tell him that I've already given to Rome again and again and again, and what I've given should be enough, but I don't. I force myself to smile.

'Give, in order to receive. You want peace. Seem generous. Give us back Cyprus.'

'The isle your father lost in order to pay his debt to Rome?'

'Yes, and he lost it along with his people's love. Give it back, and if they do not love you for it, they will certainly hate you less.'

'That is a high price for a miserly affection.'

I don't answer. He is a Roman, used to setting high prices, not paying them. We have paid out to Rome again and again, in slaves and gold and grain and blood. He may or may not choose to give us Cyprus, and my trying to persuade him will only seem like weakness. I can sense his irritation, whether at me or at the disadvantage of his position, I cannot tell. He stands and quits the room without taking my leave. I know where he's going: to speak to my brother. He does not ask me to accompany him. My mouth is suddenly dry as though I've sucked on sand – he has not confided in me his thoughts or intentions.

I stand beside Caesar on the balcony of the great palace. It's a stone platform jutting out, so we can see the twisting streets beneath and can also be seen by the throng gathered in the street below. I'm arrayed in royal purple, my gown heavy in the heat, the diadem on my forehead stopping the sweat trickling into my eyes. I glance down at the mass of people gathered in the street below and their roar is so loud it's like the smashing of the waves upon the shore, and I want to put my hands over my ears and slide back into the palace. I can feel their hatred for me and Caesar, it lands on my skin like spittle. Charmian kneels at my feet, and I watch beads of perspiration trickle down her neck. I gaze at her and think of all my followers and know that it is for them I stand here, pretending to be unafraid.

Still, I'm relieved we're out of reach of the missiles of filth that they hurl at us, and that the globs of cow shit, other excrement and rotting fish land on the walls beneath and slide back onto the crowd. Caesar's expression reveals no revulsion, concern or a hint of his intentions, and he makes no move yet to speak. We stand and listen and wait as the noise crashes around us, echoing off the stone. The heat is bitter and cloying. Charmian is swaying on her knees, and I wonder if she's going to faint. I cannot help her. A queen cannot stoop to concern over her slave, even if she is her friend. Then, I realise that the soldiers and slaves and the members of the court gathered on the balcony are beginning to shuffle and bow, and I see to my astonishment Ptolemy waddling out to join us. He doesn't appear as a prisoner but a swollen prince, adorned in purple robes that perfectly mirror mine. His round face is flushed with satisfaction and shiny with heat, his small eyes are pebbles squashed into his face. He doesn't look at me, but grins at Caesar, who nods at him in acknowledgement. The note of the crowd changes, from rage to excitement, for these are his friends not mine, those souls left in the city belong to him. I think of my devotees stuck outside the city, death circling them with black wings, and I'm filled with cold rage.

At last Caesar steps forward, grasping my hand so I must join him or yank my arm away. That, I don't dare to do. And then, I see to my absolute dismay that his other arm is draped around my brother. He clears his throat and begins to speak.

'Rome brings you good tidings, great and worthy Alexandrians. Ptolemy is here under our protection. I return to you, out of the generosity and largesse of Rome, the isle of Cyprus.'

I stare at him, trying to catch his eye, gratified that he's taken my advice. He doesn't look at me, and annoyance tugs at me. I realise he wants the audience to believe the return of Cyprus is entirely his own idea, not in response to my suggestion.

'And as a friend of Egypt and Alexandrians, I'm here to help restore order,' he continues. 'You are blessed sons and daughters of Egypt, for you are blessed with two living gods and two Pharaohs, Cleopatra, father-loving daughter who rules alongside her brother-husband, Ptolemy.'

I'm no longer annoyed but dismayed. I glance at Caesar, pricked with fury, but he doesn't look at me. This is betrayal. There is nothing that I can do in this moment. I cannot remonstrate or contradict him, but his disloyalty lodges in my chest. He takes my hand. I long to snatch it away, but I don't. He gives my hand to Ptolemy, who hesitates only for a second and then takes it, holding my fingers as though they're steeped in poison and just a touch could kill him. I stare across at Caesar, aghast. Charmian swivels round to look at me, astounded and afraid. I'm dizzy with rage and hurt. I was a fool to think Caesar was my friend, he belongs only to Rome.

That evening, I lie upon a sofa in my chamber, feigning composure. I want to pace and rage and hurl pots against the walls. Instead, I lounge and feel the sea breeze upon my cheek. Charmian and Apollodorus watch me, brittle with worry.

'I cannot rule with Ptolemy. It will end in death,' I say slowly.

And, here in Alexandria without my army and friends, it will probably be mine. I try to push away my anger at Caesar's speech.

'Did he give you his word that you would rule alone?' asks Apollodorus.

'I thought he did. Half a dozen times. But he would not swear to it even though I asked him.'

Whether he promised me or not, this feels like betrayal. I've paid the price in flesh for him to choose me. Outrage scratches at me, and yet I try to cool my rising temper and consider why Caesar made his proclamation. I know he has no love for my brother. This was a decision made by Caesar out of weakness. We're surrounded by Ptolemy's supporters, his army is the noose around Alexandria. This palace is a sinking island in hostile seas. Caesar's speech was to still those waters, give us more time until his legions arrive. But I need to survive until they reach us. When they're here, they can clear the way for my own army to join them and I'll be protected. Until then, we're two gods stranded on mortal soil without our thunderbolts.

Caesar's words have only made me more vulnerable. Despite being my lover, he has been careful not to declare his absolute loyalty, an apparent ambivalence that Pothinus and Achillas will view as an invitation to try harder to murder me. If Caesar won't act and do what needs to be done, then I must.

'Tell me the whispers,' I say to Apollodorus.

'I'm listening. I've heard nothing useful yet.'

'Listen harder.'

Fear makes me snappish. They all watch me; Charmian's eyes are wide, startled by my displeasure. 'As I am Egypt's queen, be stirred. Let us remind Caesar of our brilliance and let him glimpse our witchery. This is an evening for marvels.'

Apollodorus and the others continue to stare at me, half afraid of me as well as for me. I make myself smile at them, hoping I exude confidence I don't yet feel. 'Listen to me now and the gods will still make this a happy day for Cleopatra.'

Isis is goddess of witchcraft and magic. She tames Death himself so that he is giddy with love. I am her creature in this world, and she will help me when I ask. I order offerings and present them at her shrine and command the priests to pray to her in my name. I need to borrow her power and magic and show them who I am and what I can do.

That evening Caesar hosts a banquet, not in the guest palace but in the royal quarters of the palace itself to celebrate the reunion of Ptolemy and me. He has taken over the main palace in a display of strength and bravado. This is my old domain; these are the golden halls I roamed as a girl. I chose the designs of the mosaics arrayed in gold, grey, blue, emeralds, rubies, rose and milk agate, and ordered the carvings in hippopotamus ivory. I selected the panther-skin rugs and the silver-dipped horns of the ibis and the vast wooden doors inlaid with jewels and carved with cavorting gods.

Candles sway suspended from the roof beams, their light refracting in the golden ceilings as well as on the surface of the indoor streams that run through the palace. The trickle of the water mingles with the shimmering chords of lyres and everywhere pools of light shimmer and play. The very air itself seems gilded and set with spinning jewels. The night is thick with the scent of jasmine and jacaranda blossom. In the gardens beyond, ten thousand torches shine out in the darkness, so bright that they snatch away the night and it seems the sun god Ra himself has been tricked into coming out early. If the gods ventured into my palace, they would not realise that they have left Mount Olympus or the celestial Field of Reeds.

My tricks with light are just a hint of what's to come, for tonight my power has a whiff of the divine. Ptolemy calls me serpent of the Nile and believes it is an insult, but it is not. The serpent god has many names, and I have learned them all. She is chaos and power and beauty. I know, for I speak the language of their gods and of my people. And in return, the gods speak to me. If Caesar does not understand who I truly am, then he must be made to learn.

For this one night, Pothinus permits fruit, meat and non-mouldy grain to enter the palace, showing that he can withhold and also provide. This is his earthly and petty demonstration of power. Mine shall dazzle. I wear a robe of purple silk, fat, bloody rubies in my ears and gold bangles of emerald-eyed vipers twisted round my arms, so heavy that I can hardly raise my wrists. Caesar sent the ruby earrings to my apartments with a note requesting me to wear them: at once a gift and an order. I oblige with quiet fury. The jewels aren't even his to give, for they are from my own treasury and are not in his gift. I itch for this war to finish, and to be free to remind the Roman that the wealth and prizes he raids like one of the pirates in his stories are not his but mine. For all his charm and kisses, he's a thief. I am waiting to be paid and my price is a kingdom.

All the other guests are assembled and waiting, the cronies of my brother's court. They wear his favours in the form of emeralds and shining gold upon fat fingers. They gossip in Greek, not wanting to dirty their tongues with native Egyptian words. As I arrive at the banquet with my train of slaves, they cannot help but stare with grudging admiration. I want to laugh at them. They've picked the wrong side in this struggle. Soon, they'll be begging me for mercy, stripping the gems from their fingers and placing them at my feet alongside their grovelling apologies. I might forgive them. For now, I shimmer as Isis and I wield my serpent wand. My retinue are all dressed as nymphs and demi-gods and Caesar greets me with a kiss.

'Fairer than a spring morning,' he says. 'Persephone herself would be slighted when she saw your beauty.'

I accept his flattery with a smile as though nothing has shifted, when in truth I feel as if he is stepping on my gown, and I want to tug it free. I feel Charmian flinch behind me at his remark, sometimes she is more my own self than I can be. I spy Ptolemy in the corner already at the banquet, stuffing olives and oysters into his mouth. There's a slick of grease on his chin.

'Come, my friend,' calls Caesar, beckoning to him. 'Stand with your sister-wife. Let us celebrate this peace and new prosperity.'

I stare at Caesar. Even as he declares me to be another man's wife, he strokes my cheek with the pad of his thumb, and places a kiss on the inside of my wrist as Ptolemy lumbers over, unsmiling and reluctant. For once my brother and I agree on something – this situation cannot continue. Even for us, this is peculiar: he is here as my husband and co-ruler in an occasion overseen by my lover. Caesar can't stop touching me, like a child unable to resist picking at a scab. He doesn't even play along with the pretence that I'm my brother's wife. Caesar is mistaken if he believes this absurd course will give him much respite from fighting or danger. I watch carefully which dishes my brother eats from and consume only those. Despite the glory of the palace and the sumptuousness of the feast, it's set out on earthenware plates.

'Why not gold?' I ask. 'Do you seek to insult our guest, eunuch?' I demand, turning to Pothinus.

The eunuch smirks and bows low in a feigned apology. 'Great queen and honoured consul and dictator, the golden tableware has had to be melted and sold to meet worthy Caesar's demands for money. Only earthenware is left.'

I'd laugh if it wasn't so absurd. The golden plates will likely be stacked in Pothinus's own suite. Caesar again pretends not to notice the insult, but the eunuchs are simpletons. Caesar sees everything. He only waits. I take his hand and lead him to a fountain that appears to have stuttered and stopped, and gesture to a slave to give him a cup.

'I'm not thirsty. And it's broken.'

'Is it? Let me fill it for you.'

I place my cup beneath the fountain and at once, through some enchantment, it spouts with a torrent of red wine. In moments the cup is overflowing. Caesar laughs, amazed, and takes another cup from the slave. He fills his own, watching the crimson fountain turn on and off, his expression bright, shedding years.

'It works for me too, so this witchcraft is not yours alone,' he declares.

'Ah, but I still command it,' I say with a smile. I can tell he's charmed and diverted. I'm relieved that Apollodorus and Charmian have carried out my directions with such care. Ptolemy, however, sulks in the corner, watching us. The guests circle Caesar and me, we are the fire that draws them. Any dish or drink that we touch, no ordinary guest is offered, it's kept for us alone. We anoint it with our favour.

There's a trill of birdsong and the air is full of coloured birds, flying above in jagged patterns. One of the mosaics is of exotic birds and as the real birds flutter before the glittering tiles, it appears as though they have flown out of the artwork, breathed into sudden, miraculous life. Caesar laughs and claps his hands, almost boyish in his delight. The other guests applaud, but Ptolemy hunches and scowls, stuffs another piece of sausage into his mouth.

The music from the lyres and flutes drifts around us, and

slaves sway in beaded dresses as the Roman soldiers stare, glossy with sweat and eyes glazed with desire. I know how the Romans consider us wicked and corrupt, and yet they travel to Egypt eager for dissolution and debauchery. They long to revel in their disapproval of me and tonight, I shall give them what they want – even if it's a performance shaped to mirror their own desires. Caesar's guards are shiny with drink and heat and they stare at the swaying slaves as the light creates rippling patterns upon the dancers' skin; the Romans are no longer soldiers but a legion of Echoes mesmerised by my dancing Narcissi. Their dreams pull Romans to Alexandria like moths to the moon – their desire for exotic enchantment is as potent as their greed for gold and grain. I shall send them scurrying back to Rome brimming with scurrilous tales. The dancers have painted themselves with gold and silver in exquisitely rendered designs, and as the sounds of the flutes knot and weave, they step out of their beaded dresses and undulate naked, save for the gold anointing their skin. The effect is mimetic, and the audience stares as if in a dream. The scent of myrrh, sweet rosemary and cedar is so strong, I can taste the bitter herbs on the back of my tongue.

And, then at once, with a loud crack, the massive carved doors to the hall slowly open, the wood grinding against the stone. It takes four slaves to operate these doors, they're ten men high and hewn from sycamore and studded with gold. Yet now no slave is touching them and the doors are swinging open by themselves. The guests rouse themselves from their trance, intrigued to see who or what has the strength to move them, but when the doors are fully open the entrance yawns empty. There is no one there at all. No monster stands in the gaping doorway, only the torches spit in the garden beyond. A hush descends like a snuffer upon a candle. Even the dancers are stilled.

'No one is there. They opened by some invisible force. Or perhaps it was the breeze made by the breath of a god,' I say softly.

'A god? Or a shade from beyond,' says Apollodorus. 'And what news or portent do they bring?'

'You mock my eyes with air,' says Caesar, turning to me.

And yet he stares intently.

'No, my lord. You have seen the signs. These are black night's pageants.'

The scent of incense and herbs is overpowered by that of smoke. It fills the air, so that the slaves start to run in search of the fire, fearing the palace is ablaze. After a minute or two, the smoke dissipates by itself, but then we see a figure now stands in the gloom, tangled in the last threads of smoke. Its eyes glow red. The slaves scream and run. The legionaries grab for their swords and rush forward, still half drunk on wine and fading lust, bellowing curses.

'Pompey,' says Caesar, stricken, recognising the figure.

The figure looms, holding something outstretched on a tray.

I step forward and Caesar moves to walk beside me – he cannot be seen to be reluctant or frightened, especially next to a woman and an Egyptian. The figure is a statue and yet it is so perfectly carved, the creases around the eyes and the soft sag of skin around the throat so real, he looks not so much a statue as a man frozen into stone by a gorgon. As I stare, I could almost be certain that he has the breath of life on his cheek. And yet, as I reach out and touch him with my fingers, he is cold, hard marble. There is also something terrible about the carving, his expression at once mournful and enraged. The eyes are bright with fire as if lit from within.

I can see now that this Pompey holds out a second head, his own, on a tray, proffering it to Caesar once again. This is Pompey resurrected and whole, yet he holds his own death before him, a reproach and an offering. I glance at Caesar and can see he is disturbed and unsettled, though trying not show it. The dancers cling to one another and the musicians forget to play.

'Who did this thing? Or is it the work of the gods?' he demands.

No one answers.

'It is wonderous terrible,' he mutters, half to himself.

Ptolemy stands in the corner of the room, his face pale and aghast. Before him is the man he murdered, the great general stabbed and gutted like a street thief on his orders. Achillas and Pothinus, his co-conspirators, seem less frightened than angry, as though before the statue was conjured out of the smoke, Caesar had forgotten their crime. They huddle and glower. I edge away from the statue. Caesar hesitates and then retreats. As we do, the doors begin to close again, still untouched by slave or man. The musicians have abandoned their playing, and the only noise is the creak of wood, and the bang as the massive doors shut. The noise rolls around the hall like thunder in the mountains and then is still. The silence is heavy as ash.

'Let us to bed. We must rest,' says Caesar at last.

He takes my hand, and my brother watches us leave, unable

to conceal his unease and displeasure. Caesar leaves me alone in my room so Charmian can ready me for his company. I'm weighted down with too many jewels, my dress too elaborate for him to take satisfaction in undressing me. She lingers over the task, dismissing Iras and the other slaves so that we can be alone as she strips me of the golden amulets and beaded necklaces.

'You did well,' I say, my voice low. 'The display was perfect. When the doors opened I almost believed it was magic myself.'

'It seemed like terrible magic. I don't understand how else the statue of Pompey came to life,' she replies. 'It was a malevolent marvel.'

I smile, amused. She peeped behind the curtain, knows how the trick was performed, she watched as the inventor set the underground pulleys, as he ordered slaves to heat pipes for steam, and Charmain paid in gold the sculptor who made Pompey's death mask. Yet she is still afraid. 'Man's genius is akin to magic, a divine gift from the gods,' I say, trying to reassure her.

'If it helps you, then I will do it. Magic or not,' she says.

Apollodorus opens the door, and Caesar enters. The slaves withdraw, leaving us alone.

12

CLEOPATRA

In the morning, Charmian shakes me, rousing me from sleep. I can see that as is his custom Caesar has already risen and gone – I wonder whether he slept at all. Charmian places a finger to her lips and beckons me to follow her. The other slaves eye her curiously. Apollodorus waits outside the chamber with a company of guards, who surround me on every side. I follow Apollodorus and Charmian in silence, my heart fluttering wildly in my chest like wings. We retrace the way to last night's festivities. Slaves and servants fall to their knees as I pass, surprised to find me strolling the halls. I pay them no more heed than I would blades of grass as I wander through the gardens. When we enter the great hall, Apollodorus leads me to the fountain that so enchanted Caesar the previous evening. Its crimson water no longer gushes in arterial sprays but has dried in muddy stains along the channel at the base of each layer, the colour of old blood. I observe that the tiers of the fountain are littered with small birds, their coloured wings drab and robbed of their iridescence in death. Some of the tiny corpses have collapsed into the residual wine, and lie on their backs, twig legs scratching the air, rigid, their feathers and beaks stained red.

I lean over and sniff the dregs of the wine. It has an unpleasant, bitter scent. Apollodorus beckons and a man edges over to us, bowing and trembling.

'This is the palace barber, Amun,' explains Apollodorus.

'The man who doesn't speak, but only listens,' I say. 'If only more were wise enough to realise they have nothing worth saying out loud.'

'But we are glad that some do speak when they should not,' says Apollodorus. 'Amun heard the eunuchs conspiring as he shaved them yesterday.'

The barber nods furiously. His skin is pale brown and flecked with hundreds of freckles. There's the sound of footsteps and Caesar himself enters with his Praetorian bodyguards and generals. Flavius strides over and takes in the fountain, picking up a bird between his forefinger and thumb, then drops it again with disgust.

'Have any of the guests taken ill?' asks Caesar.

Apollodorus shakes his head. 'No, my lord. This wonder was kept for you and the queen.'

Caesar is quiet for a moment, considering, then turns to me. 'The falcon you had as a girl?'

'I found him like this,' I say, gesturing to the fallen birds.

'Poison is a woman's trick, but eunuchs are not men. They are womanish in their wiles,' says Apollodorus.

Caesar says nothing for a minute, his face grave and sad, and when he finally speaks, his voice is full of emotion. 'Before Pompey was my enemy, he was my friend. The vision of him last night was a portent. He dragged himself back across the river Styx to warn me of this danger.'

The men of his guard mutter, half afraid, and make the sign of protection against the evil eye.

'Pothinus and Achillas thought to kill you both with the wine,' says Flavius, his voice low with anger. 'This fountain is the queen's toy, and they knew she would want to show it to Caesar. Once she had touched it, no one else could drink from it.'

The barber nods again, making extravagant gestures with his hands. Apollodorus watches him and then translates.

'Amun says he heard them discuss this as he shaved them. They think he is stupid, as well as dumb.'

Caesar and his generals retreat to the side of the hall where they hold a conference in low voices. Caesar murmurs something in the ear of his general, who listens intently and then quits the room. The eye of the sun is opening wide and peers in at the open window. The heat swells and I long to shed my sandals and step into the rills rushing cool spring water through the halls.

Pothinus enters the hall at a lick, sweaty and puffing. Ptolemy trails behind him, a huddle of slaves following in his wake. They are a ragtag company this morning, lacking their usual pomp. The eunuch stops abruptly as he sees the graveyard of birds. Pothinus stares at me. His skin looks waxy and drips like a sweating candle, and for the first time he looks afraid.

'We have uncovered your plot,' I say.

He shakes his head, blinks. 'This is not my doing.'

'So you are happy to find us in excellent health?' I ask, trying to keep the incredulity from my voice.

'Always, my queen.'

'Where is Achillas?' I demand.

Pothinus doesn't answer. Ptolemy shifts from foot to foot and stares at his advisor, as though he too would like to know where his other general has gone.

'Indeed, where is Achillas?' says Caesar, coming to join us. 'You are twin delights, a pair of shadows without the man who casts them.'

If Pothinus is insulted by the dig at his lack of manhood, he's for once wise enough not to show it. He licks his dry lips, his tongue a darting pink lizard. He studies me intently for a moment, and then says slowly, 'Caesar never drinks wine. It would be a poor method to employ, should I wish to harm him. And, we swear to you with our love that we do not.' He turns to me, his gaze cold and furious. 'And you, madam, did you sip from the fountain? Or did you know not to drink?'

'The court saw me take wine and drink,' I reply.

There is general murmuring, for it's true – they remember watching me. I showed Caesar, and then I drank.

'Praise fortune and Zeus. She was protected by the gods. They intervened and saved her from this vicious trick,' declares Caesar, taking my hand and kissing it with relief. 'My kinsman Pompey dragged himself from beyond the grave to deliver us warning of this plot.'

'Someone else did this foul thing. Look elsewhere,' beseeches Pothinus.

'As you open your mouth, you bring forth weeds and malice,' I say.

'I know nothing of this,' says Ptolemy, speaking for the first time. His voice is a pleading whine. 'If they did this horrible deed, it was not on my command.'

He is trying to distance himself from the crime, but his generals acting without his express authority makes him appear weak.

Caesar ignores him.

Flavius returns with members of Caesar's guard, red-faced and breathless. 'We've searched the palace, but Achillas is fled.'

'Guilty men run,' says Caesar, turning to stare again at Pothinus.

The eunuch looks around the room, snared by his own viciousness. I can see the whites of his eyes like a dog who knows he's about to be kicked. Now, my brother looks really frightened and glances between me and Pothinus, who falls to his knees before Caesar and begins to grovel.

'I swear, I did not do this. This is not my doing.'

Caesar studies him evenly then says, 'It's devious and malevolent. Like inviting a man to shore, offering him a hospitable welcome and then butchering him before his feet touch dry land?' Caesar's voice rises in uncharacteristic anger. 'Pompey's blood stains your hands and cannot be washed clean.'

Pothinus prostrates himself on the floor. 'That was badly done. And I have begged your forgiveness and that of the gods. But this I did not do.'

'Fie, you wrangle for your life, but if your ill deeds were fishes, your skin is the net stretched to bursting.'

Pothinus sits up on his heels and opens his mouth to plead again, but Caesar signals with his fingers, and at once his general Flavius steps forward, unsheathing his blade, and grabs Pothinus's head and yanks it back. He pulls the sword across the eunuch's throat in a fluid motion. Pothinus's eyes widen in surprise, and he claws at the gaping slit as he starts to drown wetly in blood. There's a sucking sound and bubbles of blood form on his lips, containing the last words he'll never say out loud. They pop and vanish. We watch him as we would a trout flailing on the shore; no one speaks or moves to his side. He's no longer a man, merely a grotesque spectacle we recoil from. His dying seems to go on and on, the blood rushing and rushing from his throat in a crimson waterfall, soaking his tunic and streaming onto the floor until we all have to step back so that it doesn't stain our shoes. There's no noise except for the gurgling and his hands tapping on the marble floor as if he is calling for Osiris the death god to come and fetch his soul. Then at last he stills and slumps face first into the spreading pool of his own blood.

I stare at the huddled figure. He has tormented me for so many years and now, when his end comes, it is swift and silent. He's been plucked out of this world and cast down into the dark and I shall not grieve for him. He yearned for my death as other men pine for a lover.

'Seal the palace. Find Achillas,' snaps Caesar.

Flavius hurries out of the hall with a company of soldiers. I stare at the corpse, transfixed, and have to force myself to look away. Several slaves rush in with buckets and rags to clear up the mess and viscera, but one of them misjudges the extent of the river of blood on the dark polished floor and slides over, landing hard on top of the corpse. The other slaves haul him to his feet. They sweep the mess into the rills with brooms instead, marbling the clear waters red then pink.

'Dearest queen, I am glad that you weren't plucked from me by this foul poison,' says Caesar.

He kisses me on the cheek and then, turning, leaves with his bodyguards.

The slaves haul out the body, leaving a slick of viscera upon the marble. The room smells of meat. I stare at the wet and bloody trail. Charmian and Apollodorus come to stand beside me. It's so quiet and still, the only noise the sound of water running across the stones in the open streams. Charmian reaches for my hand, I let her take it.

'Your falcon died of old age, his feathers grey,' she says quietly. 'We buried him under the lemon trees.'

I don't reply.

'Does Caesar know the truth?' asks Apollodorus. 'The barber played his part beautifully.'

I shrug. I don't know. The poison was added after the party, the birds tempted to drink by the sugar and honey stirred into the wine. 'It doesn't matter,' I say. 'Caesar needed a reason to kill them. I gave it to him as a sharpened blade. A bloody gift. More valuable by far than all the rubies he gifted to me.'

13

CLEOPATRA

Achillas has gone. The creature has fled into the city, summoning all mercenaries and thieves. There is a lull. We don't know where he's gone. The city is oddly quiet – everyone hides, waiting, like animals seeking shelter before a thunderstorm. Days pass. Then weeks. The air is a breath held. And then the storm sweeps in with twenty thousand men gathering outside the city like flies around a boil, Achillas the pustule at its head. Several thousand mercenaries march inside the city, intent on murder. Caesar watches in amazement as siege towers taller than a dozen men are shoved against the palace walls. He didn't realise that the Alexandrians had such ingenuity in them. We are resourceful and clever, although at this moment, I wish they were using their skills in my defence rather than in order to try and kill me.

Roman legions aided by my personal guard labour through the night to raise the walls, while archers rain arrows down upon the marauders. The towers are abandoned. We inside the palace are now under siege, cut off without food. But we are not fools: the deep streams flowing into the palace from underground wells bring us fresh water and are stocked with fish. We can outlast any blockade until Caesar's legions arrive. We are fat with complacency. Caesar writes his memoirs in the lull – calling for paper and ink. I know he's been writing an account of his life, his boyhood, the time he was kidnapped by pirates, his rivalry with Pompey, but while he's alluded to his past, he's never let me read it. Nor have I asked. Now I sit opposite him writing my own memoir; two versions of the same siege. Neither of us requests to read or hear the other's account despite our affection towards one another. We write like two jealous schoolboys, each shielding his work from the other. I wonder what he says about me. I have no desire for him to discover what I say about him.

And then we wake after a week to find the rills stinking and silted up with dead fish, the rest floating on the surface, bellies up. The eunuch's men have poisoned the waters, boring down and down into the ground water and flooding it with seawater until all the streams and springs that run into the palace are fouled with salt. Inside the royal quarters, the atmosphere crackles with panic like the air before a lightning strike. Slaves and freedmen weep, their lips parched with thirst.

Ptolemy sits in his apartments complaining that he's hungry and thirsty, fretting that we'll allow him to starve. I wonder what he thinks of his eunuch now, when he's condemned Ptolemy to suffer alongside the rest of us. I suppose

Achillas believes we will send out Ptolemy to haggle for our lives. He cannot think to leave him here to die, for Achillas's claim to power is only through my brother. This misspent war is in my brother's name. But we don't send Ptolemy out to bargain for peace, but keep him in his apartments under careful guard, where he shoves morsels of crispy polenta into his mouth and sends us messengers to whine that he's hungry and thirsty.

Caesar dismisses his own portentous advisors in preference of my counsel, and the two of us sit in the glittering halls together, quietly discussing what we should do. We are neither frightened nor dulled by panic – the only pair in the palace who are not. Some battles are won with might, others with careful thinking. We sit in Caesar's chamber, the shutters keep out the sun so it only spies upon us through the narrow slats. The dead fish have been pulled from the rills and are burning in pyres outside, and the air is thick with smoke and fish. We sip beer from the cellars since there is no fresh water.

I lead Caesar into the great library and call the librarian to bring me all the maps and scrolls pertaining to the watercourses. Inside the cool shade of its halls, the air is perfumed with the dry scent of its scrolls and manuscripts. The scholars work on, writing, reading, heads bowed as though just beyond the palace walls the city isn't writhing, eating itself like an ouroboros. Caesar turns a circle on the spot, marvelling at the elegance of the library, the vast scale of the knowledge it holds.

'One day we will hold a copy of the volume you scribble away upon,' I say with a small smile as we wait.

'No doubt. But where will it go?' he asks, as if wanting to

be shown the resting place for his unfinished tome, as a dying man seeks to inspect his waiting tomb.

'Oh, there's no room for it here. The shelves are overstuffed as it is. I'll put you down by the docks with the other scrolls we don't have space for,' I tease.

'You'll shove me in the old warehouses with the grubs and second-rank historians?' he asks, pretending offence.

I laugh. 'Oh, many of our most precious works are there. It simply takes so long to inspect them and sort them properly. Years slide into decades.'

The librarian returns and Caesar and I sit at one of the tables in the Egyptian section. The scholars continue studying as though they aren't in the midst of a war, and that they can ward it off through reading. And yet, their intuition may be correct, for the books and charts I have studied here may save us. I unfurl the pages and Caesar surveys me in silence as I trace my finger over the blue veins showing the watercourse as it threads through the island of Pharos and spurts along the Cape of Lochias. There's a complex series of reservoirs that filter and purify the waters of Lake Mereotis and freshwater canals carry water between the lake and the city. The ingenuity of the system interests me, and I explain its secrets to Caesar.

He kisses my neck as I talk, and I shrug him off.

'I'm busy. Listen.'

'You have the memory and temperament of a soldier. No, of a general.'

His voice is honeyed with admiration and desire.

'I am greater than a general, for I command Egypt. And sometimes Rome,' I add, allowing him to plant a single kiss on my ear lobe.

When I'm finished, I adjust the weights on the maps, so that they cover the entire surface of the table.

'We are close to the sea and the rocks below are veined with streams flowing into the bay. If we dig down, we'll find fresh water.'

Caesar examines the maps again and considers for a few minutes, then taps a spot with his finger.

'This. Here. This is where we must dig.'

On his command, the soldiers and slaves begin to tunnel through the muck and rock. They dig down and down. The sun rises and sets and rises again. We measure time in the emptying of the beer flasks instead of through the water clocks and through the telling of tales. If he's worried, he conceals it. We return to his apartments in the palace and each of us writes our thoughts and recollections for a few hours, and then, tiring of this task, we talk instead. He is good company and the hours slide past, he recounts stories to distract me of his campaigns, his kidnapping by pirates. I've heard rumours and echoes of these tales before but it's something new to hear them fall from Caesar's own lips, and he gives them their own shape. I listen, thirsty and eager. I shall gather these stories deep inside myself and recall them later, again and again. These are the moments where he sheds his outward self, puts to one side the general and dictator, and I see glimpses of the man; his half-smile like the sun dipping behind a cloud. He lies beside me, naked and unembarrassed, propped on his elbow. He runs his index finger along the ridges of my spine, his finger moving in the same way it does when he tracks the line of a manuscript as he reads. I wonder if I'm a text he's attempting to decode.

'When I was kidnapped, I was little more than a boy,' he says.

'Like my brother?' I ask with a wry smile.

'Nothing like your brother,' he replies. 'Older and wiser. I'd tarried a while with King Nicomedes in Bithynia and was starting for home.'

I have heard the rumours about Caesar and King Nicomedes. That the young Caesar stayed for months as he was besotted with the king. There are whispers that the two were lovers. Even now his enemies chant 'Caesar, Queen of Nicomedes'.

'Tarried a while?' I ask, arch. 'Doing what?'

'The king has excellent vineyards.'

'You don't drink.'

Caesar ignores my teasing. 'On my voyage back, I was captured near the island of Pharmacus by pirates.'

'Were you frightened?'

'Annoyed. It was an inconvenience. Then they insulted me. They demanded a mere twenty talents for my ransom.'

'Did they not know who you were?' I ask, amused.

'They did not. So I laughed at them, and told their leader that they needed to ask for at least fifty talents.'

'Only fifty?'

'Cleopatra, do you wish to tell this story?'

I mouth my apologies and settle back.

'Next, I sent my followers to procure the money so I was left alone with my captors. The pirates were profoundly irritating. Murderous, yes, but also loud. Although I did not entirely dislike them. For eight and thirty days, I shared in their sports and games. I also wrote poems and penned speeches I intended to give in the senate, which I read aloud to them, to observe the response. Senators and pirates are not so dissimilar.'

I smile even though I'm not entirely sure if he's joking.

'And then I'd threaten to hang them all and crucify them.'

'Which they also took as boyish mirth and good humour?'

'Exactly.'

He pauses and takes a long drink and then continues. 'After my ransom had been paid they set me free. They seemed almost sad to see me go.'

'Poor fools.'

'Nothing poor about them. They were stuffed to the gills with gold, much of it mine. The moment I reached shore, I raised ships and put them to sea to catch the robbers. We caught them still lying at anchor off the island.'

He still sounds outraged at the wound to his dignity, and there is a note of triumph as he recounts his retribution. It hasn't faded in the twenty-five years since.

'I had the men locked up at in the prison at Pergamum. I went myself to the governor and demanded that it was my right to punish the captives. All their money and treasure belonged to me as spoils. But the governor was greedy and cast longing eyes on the money.'

'But you did not let the matter pass.'

'I did not. I took the robbers out of prison, where they greeted me as an old friend, come to help them escape. Then, I crucified them all along the shore.'

I imagine the line of pirates crucified on the beach, like a gruesome variety of palm trees. I recall Pothinus, how he aimed his slick insults at Caesar, and I almost pity the dead man. He forgot what Caesar is. I know that the Nile will yet run with more blood.

'You are my captive now, what should I set your ransom at?' I ask, kissing him.

'All the gold and beauty in Egypt,' he says, smiling.

I pull away. He's naming the price of his friendship, his fee to win me this war, and it's a good Roman price: more than I can ever pay.

Neither of us speaks for a little while. He pulls me closer and trails his finger along my arm. I find myself wondering about the other women he has lain beside. Did he tell them the same stories, and did they wonder about the cost of his friendship? I have no other lover to compare him with.

'Do you miss your wife?' I ask.

He looks at me in surprise, then covers it.

'My wife? No.'

I noticed the pause before he answered.

'You miss someone else,' I say, now understanding.

Again, he does not speak at once and when he does it is carefully.

'Miss is too strong. I feel her absence. We have known each other a very long time. We were friends before you were born.'

I experience a pang of something, not jealousy, but awareness of how little he belongs to me. This time between us is but a verse in an epic poem, thousands of lines long.

'Can I know her name?' I ask.

He hesitates, and then says, 'Servilia.'

14

SERVILIA

My life with Caesar was always a caravan of partings – some tender and full of anguish. Others, hot with rage. We always came back together. Even though Pompey was dead, Caesar did not return to Rome or to me. While there were whispers that he'd found solace in the arms of the Egyptian queen, I had no reason to think that this liaison would be unlike his others – fleeting as the tide. I did not experience the sharp knife of jealousy; my discomfort was quieter and simpler. I missed him.

As was always the way when I missed him, memories of our times together turned over and over in my mind. I conjured the past out from longing. He'd never entirely belonged to me. He was married and for many years so was I. There was a brief, honeyed period – before I was obliged to take my second husband – when it was simply Julius, Brutus and me. Those were some of the happiest times of my life. We were not a family for Caesar had his own. And perhaps it is to my shame that I did not wonder how this might affect his wife, Cornelia; I was too happy to have him with us.

I loved those times together. We existed as a little company of three. Caesar would sometimes remain and eat with us rather than return home. He would tell Brutus stories of his campaigns in Gaul and Italy, and Brutus listened, wide-eyed and amazed, as though Odysseus himself was seated at the table, recounting his own battles in Troy, his bloody struggles with the gods. And when it was time for the slaves to put him to bed, Brutus would plead to stay up late and hear more, only reluctantly retreating when he'd extracted a promise from Caesar to return again tomorrow and continue the story. I was happy. And while I knew it could not last forever, I tried to exist only in that moment. If I thought too much about the fragility of it, then the glass would break, and it would be finished, the joy leaking away. And I knew I was playing make-believe, but that made it no less precious. It was an illusion of something I could never have with Julius, but the illusion was so beautiful, so longed for. That I wished for it so hard, and he did not, was a pain that I had to be careful not to allow to spoil the time we had. Julius was content to love me, have me, enjoy the company of myself and Brutus and not wish for more. He had other obligations and ambitions.

Caesar never suggested or allowed me to believe for a moment that he would leave Cornelia, even as he assured me of his love. And I was foolish to think that this could continue just because I might wish it. Inevitably, as I grew complacent hoping that things might simply drift on always as they were – Caesar having one family of blood, and the other of love – everything shifted again. One day, Brutus came home early from my brother's house. Caesar was there, we had already risen from bed and were simply talking together in the garden, and I was hoping he would stay and eat with us. But as Brutus found us beside the fountain in the viridarium, I saw to my dismay that he was not alone. He brought with him my brother Cato. Cato, his face pale and puffy, looked out of place in the garden surrounded by the scented shrubs and criss-crossing streams. He kept his arms stiffly at his sides. He was a man who belonged indoors amongst his papers. I registered his presence with dread. I did not wish for him to find me here with Caesar. I wondered, with unusual resentment, whether Brutus had described Julius's visits to his uncle. There were whispers of our affair in Rome. But those did not concern me. Rome was always full of rumours carried on the wind. Cato never usually listened to rumour, but I realised, with rising trepidation, he would try to find out for certain whether there was any truth to this one. And Caesar's casual presence in my garden, his hand trailing in the cool waters of the rill, loudly confirmed the fact of our relationship.

Cato stood as rigid as the statue of Neptune in the pool beside him, his face robed with its customary scowl, which intensified as Caesar greeted him with warmth, unperturbed. No, Caesar would no longer stay and eat with us, he said in reply to Cato's invitation, he must return and dine with his wife. I was irritated at my brother's assumption of the role of host, and then immediately saddened by Caesar's refusal.

His uncharacteristic reference to Cornelia. I felt a pang of loss as he took his leave. As I watched him walk away, I knew with a grinding of dread that these halcyon days had just been snatched away. I longed to call him back, dismiss my brother. Of course I could not.

Cato and I withdrew to the tablinum and sat as the slaves served us the dinner intended for Julius, plates of all his favourite dishes – simple fare but beautifully prepared. Cato and I barely ate; perhaps he sensed he was dining on another man's choices. Then, he was always abstentious, rarely drank wine; that he had in common with Julius. Brutus dined with us, the only one with any appetite and unperturbed by the uneasy silence, looking at his uncle with a reverence and loving awe.

After the tedious meal was finished Brutus retreated to bed and I longed to follow him, knowing what must come. Cato called for wine. He poured me a glass and walking slowly across the room pressed it into my hands, saying, 'Sister, drink.'

He did not take one himself. Then he sat back down with his head slumped, almost touching his chest, for so long that I thought perhaps he'd fallen asleep. Then, suddenly, he looked up at me and said, 'It's time. You've been a widow for nearly a year. You are a young woman, breedable, and it is your duty to marry again. And I see that you have recovered neatly from your grief.'

I ignored this arch jab at Caesar. I tried to formulate words that my brother would understand to express my love and need for Caesar. That he was necessary to my very existence, that I hadn't realised I'd been sleeping until Julius woke me. The words desiccated in my mouth. I said nothing. My brother did not understand such things.

'These appetites you have discovered, you will satisfy again in marriage,' he said as though sensing a part of my reluctance but failing entirely to understand. My desire was for Caesar, not for any other man.

This was all he thought Caesar was to me – all any relationship outside marriage could be – carnal and base. In that moment I hated Cato. I hated all of Rome for what they now demanded of me. And I could not argue against them. It would be like shouting at the moon not to wane and pleading with the tide not to turn. My only escape would be to marry Caesar. And he would not leave Cornelia. For a moment I almost hated him too.

I understood what was expected of me. I could not defy my brother, nor the rest of my family. I was still a member of the Servilii, one of the oldest and most respected clans in all Rome. As a woman I could not join the senate nor become a praetor nor win great victories against our enemies, but I could bear sons, join our family in marriage to the other noble houses of Rome. My duty was clear and irrefutable, to challenge it was to defy Rome and her gods. I listened, obedient and weary, as Cato suggested various matches. I felt dizzy, and Cato ordered me to drink some of the wine. It did not help. My heart was already claimed. And I couldn't help but note that these men were not the very best of Rome, they were the bruised apples. My choice was limited. Despite the prominence of my own family name, I was still the widow of a rebel.

Caesar visited me again about a week after my brother's first visit. We lay together, but now there was melancholy to our time together; the sun had retreated from us and we were already in shadow. He kissed me and I turned away; now my desire was sated, anger rose inside me like steam. I reeled off with distaste the list of men my brother had put forward. I hoped that discussing my prospective husband would rile my lover into action, that when I revealed the paucity of my choices to Caesar, he would at last decide to marry me himself, have mercy upon me. To my dismay, he betrayed no jealousy as I recited the list of other men, listening with acute interest, offering his opinion but never his hand. Hurt and humiliated, tears stung my eyes. He saw them and took my hand and kissed it.

'I cannot marry you, Servilia,' he said softly.

I snatched back my hand and refused to look at him. 'You can. You choose not to.'

'I already have a wife.'

'Men divorce their wives every day in Rome.'

'I don't.'

The pain was acute. He loved me and yet there were bounds to his love. Caesar wouldn't divorce Cornelia. He didn't divorce her on pain of death and confiscation of all his property, he wouldn't divorce her for me. Not for mere love. My choice of suitors was compromised because what I offered any potential husband politically was limited. My family and connections were good but I was tarnished. In marriage, Caesar only ever acted for political advantage and expediency, and I had nothing to offer him other than my own self. I was simply not enough. I was everything he wanted in his lover, but I was insufficient to be his wife. He accepted that his rejection meant I must marry another man, and this thought didn't seem to trouble him. I wanted him to defy pragmatism for love. But that was wishing for a river to turn course and flow upstream. He loved me, but his ambition was brutal and absolute.

I wouldn't speak to him again that afternoon, and after offering empty words of comfort, he finally left me alone to my unhappiness. For a while I tried to withdraw from him. When he called to see me, I instructed the slaves to tell him that I was out. He knew they lied, but left me alone, pretending to believe them. And yet, when I heard him leave, I wept, longing for his company, almost calling him back. Cato visited twice each week, bringing a possible suitor with him. I served them wine and listened politely with no interest. I only required that they would be a good and kind stepfather to my son.

They were all the same. I knew that I must choose one, but how to make a choice when I was indifferent to them all? And then Decius Junius Silanus visited me late one morning. He was an undistinguished politician a few years older than me. Apparently we'd met several times before, although I had no memory of him. He came alone, without my brother who was recovering from yet another cold. I served him wine and he sat on the sofa. We exchanged pleasantries and then lapsed into silence that I made no effort to fill. He set down his wine and looked at me, his expression thoughtful.

'You will not love me. I know that. I admire Caesar and I cannot compete with him. And I know how it is between you. If you agree to be my wife, I'd ask you not to stop but to pause. I need to know that my children are my own. After the children, I will ask no more from you. And, I will not divorce you unless you ask me to.'

I listened in surprise and then I looked at him and saw him for the first time, jolted out of my indifference by his kindness. His eyes were grey, soft. I understood that Silanus was a good man. He would not ask of me more than I could give. I agreed.

I sent for Caesar, and he came at once. I served him a meal beneath the vines. His favourite dishes like old times. We discussed poetry and the new threat of war and Brutus's education, but not what must come. When we finished eating, he unwrapped me with great tenderness, and after we had made love, we lay together naked in the open air. My skin was prickled with gooseflesh, as the sun now lacked any real heat. He stroked my back, running his finger along the ripples of my spine, and I told Caesar who I'd chosen.

'Silanus? A reasonable choice. A sensible man,' he said.

And then I told him that we must part, for a while at least. To my surprise he looked stricken. He kissed every part of me, my lips, my breasts, the soles of my feet as though bidding all of me farewell.

I ensured that I bled before my marriage to Silanus. After we were married, Brutus and I moved into his villa, renting out mine to a wealthy family arrived from Cyprus. I had inherited property both from my father and my first husband, learning to manage these estates so they ran smoothly with a profit. My new husband accepted that these were mine and not part of my dowry, and if he needed extra money to put on games or to invest in an upcoming election, he would come and ask me, explaining how it would benefit our family. I always gave it to him, but I asked careful questions as to how it would be spent.

I split my time between tending to my own financial affairs and serving my new husband. Realising that I had grown proficient in money matters, he soon asked me to oversee his estates in addition to my own, as well as his slaves and other property. He treated me with affection and kindness, taking an interest in Brutus's education. I hosted elaborate dinners to help further his career, where I served great toothy carp and oysters and stuffed pigs' udders and the sweetest wines to the senators, praetors and high priests of Rome. I sought out the finest musicians and hired only the most honeyed singers from Macedonia and Thrace. Our household soon developed a reputation for the most convivial hospitality and amusing company. All the time I missed Caesar. His absence was a hunger that I could not feed. I listened to the interesting and amusing chatter of my guests but I only pretended to be diverted, for like a too-often-laundered tunic, the colour had washed out of the world. I saw Julius amongst company but I did not speak to him. He avoided the gatherings at my house, accepting only when his absence would be noted. Seeing him merely split open the wound.

Now with more distance, I must accept that we were not parted for so long, although to me it felt that time had slowed, grown lumpen and sluggish. Within a year, I felt Silanus's child quicken within my belly. My joy was double. Firstly, that instinctive, reflexive joy which impending motherhood brings – the gods being benevolent – and secondly, while my belly was plugged with one child, I was in no danger of conceiving another. I could see Caesar again.

I informed Silanus of the happy news that he already suspected, and then only a little afterwards, I sent word to Caesar. He came to me at once, straight from the senate, my letter still tucked in his sleeve. He wished me all good felicities and then with only the slightest hesitation he folded me into his arms and kissed me. Our reunion was frenzied with joy. We knew now what it was to be without one another. As I led him into my bedroom, I worried briefly that he would not like my growing body, the soft swell of my stomach housing another man's child. My breasts, usually small, were strained and mapped with a tributary of veins. I needn't have worried. He saw only me. My pregnancy meant that he could be with me, so for him it was a source of pleasure and reprieve. He found me beautiful, whatever the waxing or waning of my belly and treated me with absolute tenderness. Silanus must have known about Caesar's visits – I did not bribe the slaves for secrecy, such subterfuge felt beneath me – but he asked no questions and made no demands upon my body himself and instead spent long days away.

As my desire increased later in my pregnancy, so did the frequency of Julius's visits. Silanus never objected. As I grew fat as the full moon, he rubbed my swollen feet and held me tightly while I wept in terror at the upcoming birth. I did not pretend to be brave with Julius. We both knew I might die when the child came. I did not want to leave either him or Brutus. And I was frightened of dying. I was frightened it would hurt. Julius, who had faced death many times in battle, never judged me for my fears. We'd both heard the inhuman screams of women who'd died in the birthing bed after hours or days of agony, their poor bloody and mutilated bodies as mangled as any legionnaire gutted on the battlefield. I saw my own terror reflected in his face. Sometimes exhausted, I fell asleep in his arms, and when I woke he was watching me, his face painted not with love but fear. He was more worried for me than he was for himself before any campaign. He did not want me to suffer nor to be without me.

When the birthing pains began, I sent word to Silanus. I spared Julius the worry and the terror. The birth was not as difficult as it had been with Brutus. Then, I had been only fourteen and I truly thought I would die. This time I expected the blood and rush of water and the endless twisting pain as my body turned itself inside out, breaking itself open to push out new life. The men were sent from the house, and the midwives arrived with the family women. The world shrank to this room. This bed. This pain. The noise. The noise was me, my screams coming from some other part of me. I screamed with my feet and my mouth and my eyes and I split apart and did not die. And then she was in my arms, slippery and still draped jauntily in her caul. Her whimpering screams took the place of mine. She was pink and bruised and angry. I held her. I was so full and so empty. I bled and bled, soaking the sheets and the mattress so thoroughly it had to be burned.

We stared at each other in wonder, my daughter and I. We were together and alone. I had survived. I had a daughter. I slept. I woke and looked for her. Panic rising, until I saw her asleep in a cradle beside me. The room was warm and full of women. They fed us both. This room was all the world. Neither my daughter nor I fully belonged to the mortal sphere, not yet. There were still hours, days when we might slide away. Time passed. How long, I do not know. We grew stronger. They opened the shutters and we blinked in the light. We chose to stay in the world, to live.

As I healed, I sat with my daughter propped on my knees and stared at her, the perfect bow of her lips. The black eyes. The pink gummy mouth, clamping to suck on my finger like a fish. I watched her suckle the wetnurse's breast, my own breasts swollen and leaking milk until my dress was wringing. Caesar sent me his love and good wishes. My belly contracted with a final echo as I read his note. He and I must part again. I could not see him until my belly quickened once more.

Our lives would be a series of partings. I grew better at them. I came to understand that they were pauses, not endings. We'd always come back together. And yet, with Caesar in Alexandria, I wondered when the reunion would come. I wrote him letters and put them in my drawer, unsent.

15

CLEOPATRA

On the third day, Caesar and I hear the shouts of triumph when our men reach fresh water. We shall not die of thirst. We toast our small victory with crystal goblets of cool, clear water. Cunning has saved us from Achillas. The streams and rills refill with fresh water spurting from the new wells but it's too late to save the fish. We must survive on the palace stores, already depleted. I have the slaves bring Arsinoe and Tol to me in the mornings. I spend time discussing various topics with them. Arsinoe listens rapt, her falcon eyeing her from the silver-tipped horn of an ibis across the room. Tol struggles to concentrate. He's soon bored and restless, staring at the gardens outside the windows with a lover's longing. I take pity and release him. Soon, his shouts reverberate through the afternoon. A slave brings Arsinoe and me chilled rosewater sweetened with honey. Arsinoe eyes me carefully.

'Will you kill our brother Ptolemy?' she asks, her tone sharp and accusatory.

'No,' I reply, taken aback. 'Why do you ask such a thing?'

She frowns, neat furrows on her brow, and picks at a tiny scab on her knee. 'He's scared. He thinks you're going to murder him. He's drunk most of the day now. It dulls his fear. He knows you contrived to have Caesar kill his eunuch.'

'Murder is his habit not mine, Arsinoe.'

The colour rises in her cheeks. She's never spoken like this to me before, and I look at her in surprise. Only now recognising she's no longer the child she was. Perhaps she hasn't been for a while, but distracted by war, I haven't noticed.

'And when do you see him? Who takes you to him, little one?' I ask.

'Am I a prisoner? Can I not see who I like? He's my brother too,' she retorts.

'He lies as he breathes, my darling. I worry.'

'He isn't lying. He only told me that he's afraid. His fear is not a lie.'

I say nothing for a moment. I expect that Ptolemy is afraid. And he will be sharing his terror with anyone who will listen. It's partly his character – he has no self-restraint nor shame – but it's also sensible. If he tells everyone that he's afraid I will kill him, then if anything happens to him, all eyes will turn to me. His supporters already loathe me and rage a war on his behalf; it will set them further against me, make it difficult to rule them even when I win. Arsinoe and I talk for a while longer, but her answers are by rote. Eventually, I dismiss her, promising that we'll talk again tomorrow. She's leaving childhood behind, and I need to be ready for her. I don't like the distance between us, the antagonism of her questions. I suppose it's to be expected for a teenage princess, but I feel deflated and weary.

Charmian and I walk in the gardens in the late afternoon, the sky steeped in blue ink. The sun dangles low, a polished gold coin on a thread, it lacks only my image or Caesar's stamped upon its face. Charmian plucks a lemon leaf, inhales its sharp scent, tucks it behind my ear. Then, she thrusts out her arm and stops me from stepping forward. Silently, she points to a viper in the dust just in front of my feet. It oozes along the ground, its skin molten metal. A fat lizard pauses at the base of a tree, stupefied with sunshine, and the snake leaks closer and closer in fluid curves, never directly. When it's within striking distance, the viper fires itself like an arrow. There is now no lizard, only snake.

I look into the face of my oldest friend. Her brown eyes, the black braided hair. She doesn't smile, her lips are a tight line. She wants me to survive. I know what she wants me to do. She wants me to be the viper and swallow my brother whole. Despite everything he's done, everything I've already done, I balk at this mortal taboo. My family is not like any other on this earth and while Ptolemy lives, the dagger hovers over my breast, nicking at my skin. Even though as a god I shall reign in the next life, I want to rule for a little longer in this one.

I don't sleep. I only think about the problem of Ptolemy. The thought is gristle stuck between my teeth and no amount of teasing can poke it free. My mind is already stained with red, my thoughts slippery with blood. There's a thudding on my bedroom door at dawn. Charmian pads over to answer it and Apollodorus follows her inside, his expression panicked, and his sword belt is askew.

'She's gone,' he says.

'She?' I ask.

'Your sister. Arsinoe fled the palace and has joined the enemy troops outside the city.'

'No,' I say. I shake my head. If I deny it enough, it can't be true.

'She has gone. She's gone to Achillas and your enemies. She declares herself queen, and that when she has killed you, she'll marry Ptolemy and they will rule together. Brother and sister Pharaoh.'

Bile rises in my throat. I feel sick. The blood leaves my cheeks. I think of the teenage girl. Her thin arms. The falcon on the wrist that seems almost too slim to hold it. And before that, the baby who slept in my arms, suckled my finger for comfort.

'Not my sister,' I repeat dumbly. 'She would not leave me.'

But I left her first, a voice nags in my head. I left her alone in the palace with my brother and his cut-throats while I journeyed down the Nile. While I was gone the eunuchs must have dripped their sweet poison in her ear, turning her against me. They could not tolerate her loyalty towards me. They did not kill her but they killed her love for me. I cannot blame them for it is my own fault for abandoning her. I deserve this betrayal. How did I not see that her love for me had guttered out?

*

The sky is never dark. Fires burn beyond the walls all through the night. Arsinoe's presence has rallied my enemies with renewed enthusiasm, and their ships prevent ours from reaching us with fresh supplies. The palace stores dwindle faster than we expect. The freedmen blame the slaves for stealing it and beat them, until Apollodorus orders them to stop – the slaves don't have enough energy to heal their wounds without food, and we need them to work. Beyond the palace walls Arsinoe and Achillas's army swells into a sea of men. Mine are stranded outside the city, cut off from Caesar's men. They will be mown down if they try to join them and divided in two, our strength is weakened. I pray to the gods for favourable winds to carry Caesar's fresh legions to break the siege, but I grow restless. I want to do more than pray.

I hold private counsel with Charmian and Apollodorus.

'We cannot fight them until we have more legions. Then, your army can join with Caesar's and we can push back properly,' says Apollodorus again.

'There are other ways to fight. We must wait for more soldiers, but until then, we must be clever.'

Charmian looks at me, her expression hopeful for the first time in weeks.

'Take us to Caesar,' I say. 'I need an audience with the consul.'

Caesar is busy with his commanders, but he dismisses them as I enter.

'You must release Ptolemy. Send him to Achillas and Arsinoe,' I say.

'To be rid of the noise of his weeping?' asks Caesar, attempting a joke. 'I could just call for musicians to drown him out.'

I try to laugh, but I don't have it in me. 'If you allow Ptolemy to go over to the enemy camp, he and Arsinoe will fight. Achillas will be caught between them, snared in their ambition unable to properly command the troops.'

Caesar leans back, sweating, and closes his eyes as he considers. I sigh and press my argument. 'My siblings cannot be together for an hour without trying to kill each other. Their hatred will split the enemy, cause squabbling and division. One of them will die without our having to wield the knife.'

I know what I'm saying is true, but plotting against my sister causes an ache in my chest, even as she schemes to hurt me. I feel as if I am putting a beloved pet dog into a fight-pit alongside another, even if this pet dog has just bitten my ankle.

'I shall tell him that I'm sending him to sue for peace. And, I'll send two Roman envoys with him to help him argue our cause,' says Caesar.

I'm silent – he does not want to hear my warning – but I am confident that there will soon be two more widows in Rome. I only say, 'You mustn't tell Ptolemy that it is my suggestion that he should go, or he will refuse. Instead, tell him I am against it and then he will be tempted to leave. But you must accept that he'll betray you the moment he can.'

He smiles at me, indulgent. 'Caesar inspires devotion. There's a chance that his love for me is enough to plead our cause for peace.'

I look at him, meet his eye. 'There is none.'

*

Of course he betrays us. It's reassuring in a way, like the ebb and flow of the tides, the constancy of my brother's nature. He has the two envoys sent with him by Caesar killed as soon as he arrives at the enemy camp. His guards stab the Romans so many times they bleed like perforated wineskins. The first man dies at once, they allow the other to crawl back to the palace, where he dies of his wounds, leaking blood all over the floors in a sloppy trail, staining the grout between the tiles. The message of my brother's betrayal is inscribed in the stab wounds on the Romans' bodies. If Caesar is surprised by my brother's actions, he does not say so. I am sorry for the men's deaths, but I gave Caesar warning. He listened to me as Menelaus did Cassandra, disbelieving the truth.

I try to imagine the reunion between my siblings, my sister's feigned delight at Ptolemy's sudden arrival. Only the eunuch will be genuinely pleased to see him. With Apollodorus's help, I dispatch my spies into my siblings' camp. They come back with stories of bickering but not outright division. I'm frustrated as I have never known them keep peace with one another for more than a few hours. Their hatred of me has unified them. Apollodorus counsels patience until I lose mine.

Over the next weeks my brother's ships strike at ours, causing inconvenience and irritation but not disaster, with neither side winning a real victory. Pompey's ships sit in the harbour. They belong to no one. His men hate my brother for murdering their general but they hate Caesar too, the deep-rooted enemy. The ships do nothing but bob on the tide. They neither return to Rome nor join the fight. I watch them from the high window of the palace tower as they sway in the wind, swinging on their moorings as the sailors carouse and declare for no one. The immobility of the ships in the harbour symbolises our own stasis. I worry we're becalmed by fate, doomed to wait endlessly, nothing changing.

The war is stuck even as the seasons turn. The winter brings hot sandstorms rolling across the city. Unlike us walled up in the palace, the sand is free, slicing across the enemy army and Caesar's legions. We close all the doors and shutters in the palace but still the sand seeps inside, forming fine piles beneath each sill as though the desert is only waiting to reclaim the city, the final victor who shall outlast us all. The palace and the moon gate are ours, but the enemy still controls the other parts of the city. The great harbour belongs to no one and whoever controls it wins this war. We watch their ships sail up to our lines in the waters, close but not within arrow's reach.

Then, at last, something shifts. News arrives; good and ill. Apollodorus races to find me in the upper tower, where I have taken to sitting for hours on end, watching the harbour. Charmian is sprawled on a cushion beside me. Apollodorus is flushed not only from running but with excitement.

'You want Pompey's sailors to take your side in this conflict. Your brother and sister want them on theirs.'

'Yes, we all want those ships. And I have tried to get them. But no matter of argument or bribery persuades them. Pompey's men do not care for me one way or the other, but their loathing of Caesar is bone deep.'

'And your sister wants to win Pompey's ships and men to her side every bit as much as you do,' he says.

'Of course she does. Those fifty ships if on their side could cut off our access to the sea. When the legions arrive to relieve us, they wouldn't be able to land,' I reply, impatient. He is telling me nothing new.

'But she has a problem. Much like yours. While Pompey's men are not so full of hatred towards your sister, they despise your brother. And especially his eunuch, Achillas.'

'Yes. This is why we are stuck. Stranded in this endless impasse.'

'Ah, but your sister, spider that she is, has found a way through. Arsinoe has killed the eunuch. Poisoned him.'

I stare at Apollodorus. 'And my brother is outraged and spitting with betrayal?'

'Yes. The camp is full of bitter divisions. It writhes with hate.'

My triumph is momentary. I look at Apollodorus in understanding. 'But, Arsinoe murdered the eunuch to appease Pompey's men.'

'Or so she claims. There was no love lost between her and the eunuch. But she has certainly told Pompey's crew that she has carried out vengeance for them, in Pompey's name.'

'Then, those fifty ships are now my enemies,' I say, rising. 'Come. We must warn Caesar.'

I find Caesar sitting at his desk in one of the chambers in the royal suite. The walls and ceilings are frescoed with scenes from the Book of the Dead, the eyes of the gods picked out in onyx, so they all seem to glint at me as I enter. Caesar listens in silence without interruption while Apollodorus tells him the news. He asks a few questions, and then considers for a moment.

'They will try to take the harbour,' he says.

'Tonight,' I say. 'They will not wait. They'll strike at once.'

My heart hammers in my chest, even though I knew this moment must come. We cannot lose the harbour or Caesar's relief ships when they arrive will not be able to land, and then there will be no end to this siege other than death.

'We must burn Pompey's ships,' I say. 'Set the harbour ablaze, before they try to take it.'

Caesar studies me for a moment. He turns to a slave. 'Bring the commanders to me,' he says.

We wait for them to arrive, neither of us speaking, but I can hear the hum and tick as his mind whirs.

'Once I've burned the ships in the harbour, I'll take Pharos Island,' he says slowly. 'We must hold the point where reinforcements can land.'

I nod once. His plan needs twice the number of soldiers and ships than we have, but I don't condescend to him by saying this aloud. He knows the danger and that we have no choice.

'I shall come with you and command my ships myself in this fight. I have only a few ships here in Alexandria but those I do have, I command,' I say.

Caesar laughs, and then seeing my expression, stops. 'No, good queen. A woman has no place amid a battle. I fight in your name and for Egypt.'

'Then I join you. You are not my proxy.'

He pauses for a moment, choosing his words carefully.

'When the way is cleared for your army to join with mine, then command them with my thanks and prayers. Do not risk your life in battle to command a handful of ships. I do not value your life so cheaply. And, as Pharaoh, Queen of the Red Lands and Black, neither should you.'

I frown and try to think of another reason that I should fight alongside him, but as I'm pondering, he turns and walks away, already intent on what is ahead. I stand in the quiet chamber, my fists clenched at my sides.

Charmian steps forward, her expression tense.

'Do not go,' she says. 'Please.'

'I do not like that they fight for me, and I am not there. I'm no coward.'

'Of course not, my queen. What if Caesar wins this fight for you, but you die in the onslaught? Then it will all have been for nothing,' says Apollodorus. 'You have so few ships here. When the enemy discovers that you are here, they will target you with all their power and you will be exposed.'

I'm furious but I know they speak the truth. If Caesar achieves his aim and burns Pompey's ships, takes Pharos Island, but I am dead, then what will be the purpose? Caesar would have no choice but to invite my brother to take my throne. Frustration at my helplessness buzzes in my ears.

A hush has fallen over the palace, all usual business is stilled. There are soldiers left here to guard the palace, but a fraction of the usual number. The rest march with Caesar down to the harbour. If the battle there is lost, there are not enough left to protect the palace from my brother's mob. I feel the energy across the city like a pulse. Everyone waits. Charmian paces, chewing her nail until I take her hand, pulling her close to me. I tuck her hair behind her small, shell-like ear and tell her, 'Go to the apothecary at once, and bring me poison. If Caesar dies, and they take the harbour, then death will find me tonight.

But I shall not die at their hands – murdered and hacked to pieces. I shall rob them of the pleasure of my death and die at the moment and in the manner of my choosing.'

Charmian blinks and pales but does not try to argue with me. She knows what I say is true.

'I will bring it to you, my queen, enough to still two hearts. Wherever you go, I follow.'

I hug her tightly, inhale the jasmine plaited into her hair. 'If we die tonight, then it shall be side-by-side amongst the lemon trees; we'll quietly step down into the underworld.'

After she has gone, there is little left for me to do but pray and talk to the gods, demand their favour. I order all the priests to hold a procession in their honour through the palace gardens. The priests arrive at dusk in their white linen robes, holding the emblems adorned with her golden stars, while the acolytes carry tiny golden palm trees and serpent wands. The high priest leads them, clasping a bright lamp in one hand and in the other a golden vessel shaped like a woman's breast where from the nipple streams milk that falls to the earth. Following the priests come the deities, Anubis with his jackal head and gleaming teeth, ready to take messages to the dead. He will be kept busy tonight.

With the prayers continuing below, I ascend the lookout tower, the highest point of the palace looking out across the harbour and east towards the isle of Pharos. My feet clatter on the stone, and as I emerge at the top I can see the sky is already bright with flames, the harbour filled with blazing ships, even the water seems to burn. From here, I cannot hear the noise of war so I watch it in a dumb show like a masque performed by players at court to amuse us, toy ships toppling upon a pond, the men only toy soldiers. Soon, the smoke blows towards us and the procession of priests in the gardens below is wreathed with smoke, and I can only hear the march of their feet and their drums. Charmian hurries up the steps, and stands beside me breathless, sliding her hand into mine. I glance at her and see that slung around her neck are two tiny vials containing the death we may soon seek.

We watch together as the sea blazes. My mouth is sour with fear as I watch. Far below sailors drown and bleed. I can do nothing but mutter prayers for the safe passage of their souls. Apollodorus hurries up the stairs to the tower, a messenger panting behind him. The messenger stands before me, breathless and sweating.

'Speak quickly,' I snap. 'Already your news cools as you stand.'

He swallows, wipes his face, smearing grime.

'Speak,' I say, impatient.

'Caesar has burned Pompey's ships, but he has been forced to set fire to much of his own fleet to stop them falling into enemy hands.'

All is not lost. We have not managed to take Pharos, but we have still struck a blow to the enemy. I absorb the news. 'So he returns to us now?'

'No. He says to tell you that he takes the ships he still has, and tries for Pharos.'

I shake my head. I don't know whether Caesar is brave or mad. He does not take his little victory but gambles on a larger one, despite the odds.

'It's possible he might take it,' I say, turning to Apollodorus and Charmian, wanting it to be true.

'Of course it is possible, for it is Caesar who attempts it,' says Apollodorus.

I taste fear in my mouth.

'Pay the slave in gold for his news,' I say to Charmian, turning back to watch the harbour.

The messenger hurtles down the stairs to return to the battle and gather the next scrap of information. Apollodorus remains with Charmian and me, and the three of us wait and watch together in silence, trying to decipher meaning in the swirl of smoke and ships below. We float like the curls of ash on the breeze, unknowing, adrift in the currents of fate.

I hate that I'm not part of this fight, that I'm here, waiting to live or die. I vow to myself that if I survive this, I will join the next battle. I'm not just a woman but a queen. I won't let Caesar dictate to me again.

My eyes weep from the smoke. Even up here, the air is thick. The island of Pharos is hidden by the fumes, the beam of the lighthouse is eclipsed. And yet, there is a strange light cast upon the city from all the fires, red glowing pools that blink through the fog of smoke. My city burns. I gather my shawl around my shoulders as the wind lifts my hair. A hot desert wind, warm as breath and dry as the dunes.

'The fire spreads,' I say quietly.

The fire will surely race through the wooden buildings lining the harbour. I can only hope it won't climb to the palace, consume the rest of the city. Most of the buildings in Alexandria are masonry to avoid this very disaster but those older warehouses around the docks are still wood, tinder-dry and hollowed out by dry rot and beetles. They are packed with goods and grain and silks. Biting my lip, I think of the half dozen buildings crammed with scrolls that cannot be housed in the overstuffed library of the mouseion. I mutter a prayer, let those be the ones spared – grain can be seeded and grown again, silks rewoven. But the writers of these texts have long since vanished into dust themselves, their thoughts desiccated, surviving only in the marks scratched upon these scrolls. The texts hold hundreds of years of knowledge and secrets and if they burn, the ideas will sputter out too.

I try to remember precisely which works are housed there. I don't know, and that frightens me. We won't even know what riches we have lost. Not the works of Plato or Aristotle or Homer, but scattered treasures by unknown hands. And yet no less valuable for being less renowned. Perhaps a new Plato lurked there, still waiting to be discovered, who shall now vanish unread. I glance down towards the vast building of the mouseion and the library, both still just visible through the smoke. Will the great library burn one day too? I always believed that its ideas would live on forever, the scrolls transcribed again and again from one generation of scholars to the next, the worm and time defeated. But that thought now feels as fragile as thistledown.

What survives our mortal death is our ideas. Transcribed in art and words and stone, they are the piece of us that remains. But if that can disappear in a single night, consumed by flame? What then for immortality? The sky is red and the smoke extinguishes the stars. Prometheus stalks amongst us; he gave us the great gift with one hand, but he also steals back with the other.

I turn to Apollodorus. 'Send half of the soldiers guarding the palace down to the dock. They're not to join the fight, but to put out the flames. Save the library warehouses. I want the scrolls salvaged. Soak any buildings not yet aflame with seawater.'

Apollodorus stares at me in dismay. 'My queen, there are not enough soldiers here as it is.'

'No. There are far too few. If my brother's men fight their way up from the harbour and reach the palace, we're dead anyway.'

'But my queen and Pharaoh—'

'Do it,' I snap. 'This is an order, not a discussion.'

He bows, and hurries away.

The next messenger arrives but I can't tell at what hour, for there is no water clock up here in the tower and the stars are sheathed. He stands before me, his face blackened with soot and smeared with sweat. Blood from a wound trickles down his cheek. He bows his head and does not speak for a moment and he clutches a bundle of rags in his arms.

'Speak,' I say, exasperated.

He kneels. 'My queen, our soldiers saw great Caesar jump into the water near Pharos Island. His own galley was sunk and he had to swim past the enemy. It's not possible that he lives.'

'Not possible? This is Caesar,' I say. I try to sound resolute but my voice cracks.

The messenger holds out to me a soaking rag. I recoil, disgusted, and don't take it, but he shoves it into my hands, and as I look down at the sodden mass, I realise that it is Caesar's purple cloak stained with water and blood.

'They pelted him with rocks and arrows, for his purple cloak made him a good target. And then some while later his cloak was pulled from the waters.'

I turn to Charmian, the wet cloak still grasped in my hands. 'So it's true then, he's dead.'

I have no time to grieve for him, although there is a tightness in my chest. If Caesar is dead, they will be coming for us. My death will not be far behind Caesar's. I look at Charmian. 'Pay the man for his words. Give him gold for he brought us news of Caesar and Caesar's name must be paid for in gold.'

After the messenger is gone, back to the battle – though to what good I do not know – I make my way down from the tower and walk slowly towards the lemon grove. I hear Charmian behind me, running to catch up with me, and I turn to her.

'You do not have to stay with me. Not in this moment,' I say. 'You can try to escape with Apollodorus. He will come for you.'

She shakes her head. 'There is no choice, not for us.'

I sigh, for what she says is true. They know she is mine, and when they find her, they will kill her too. It's better that she comes with me and chooses an easeful death. As we pad through the dust and smoke, Charmian sobs silently, shoulders shaking, her face slick with tears, two clean channels through her soot-lined face. We do not speak for there is nothing left to say.

I choose the patch where the trees grow tightly together, the spot where we used to sit as children and race our scorpions or play knucklebone. I am frightened and not ready for death. Will it hurt? There is so much more I want to do, to be. I'm impatient for life and outraged that I must now unwillingly surrender to the death gods to whom I offered so many sacrifices. They released their claim upon me only to summon me back again. I am cheated.

Snow begins to fall, fat flakes. I have never seen snow before. But as I catch a flake, I realise it's not snow but ash. Some curls are large, I hold one on my palm. It's a tiny scrap of papyrus. The words are coiled and as I watch it disintegrates into dust in my hand, the letters dissolve into nothing before I can decipher a single word. So, is this what is to come? The fragility of words and the stories they form frightens me. Even if I am to die tonight, I want my story – however short – and Egypt's to endure. The library must survive, always. Without it, the last specks of me and my history will vanish into spirals of dust, lost in the sand.

My heart beats in time with the priests drumming in the far side of the garden. Charmian takes the vials from her neck and places one in my hand. It's perfectly clear, pure as water, nothing about it suggests the poison within. I hope the death it promises is as flawless as the liquid. I open the lid and raise it to my lips but Charmian stills my hand.

'Not yet, please,' she says. 'They do not come for us yet. There is time.'

'Time for what?' I ask.

'A kiss. A song.'

We kiss, and she tries a song but her voice cracks with fear and grief, so I sing instead; the lullaby that our nursemaid slave used to sing to us when we were infants. Charmian and I were born within the same hour, it's only right that we should die within the same in our place beneath the lemon trees. I sing the lullaby twice through. I cannot sing forever, this thing must done. As I finish the song for the second time, we raise the vials towards our lips, ready to hurry death on his black wings, but then before we can drink, I hear an explosion of shouts. My heart thunders. Are they here already to kill us? Charmian shudders in fear, clings to me.

'Hurry now, swallow,' I urge her.

And then I realise the voice belongs to Apollodorus. We hesitate, the unstoppered vials ready.

'Hold! My queen, Charmian, do not drink!'

There are more cries, the sound of more people entering the grove.

'This is the place they always go,' says Apollodorus.

There is the snap of branches brushed aside, footsteps through the fallen leaves. Why is he leading them to us?

'Let me pass.'

I know that voice. Caesar. He reaches our spot beneath the lemon trees and comes to sit on the ground beside us. He's wet and bruised and bleeding. I stare at him in wonder.

'You fell into the water. You're dead,' I say.

'I am as you see,' he says. His face is cut, his eye swollen shut, but he smiles. 'Caesar is hard to kill.'

A noise hums in my ears, the hurry of my own heart.

I hug him, gripping him tightly, and he holds me fast, surprised and pleased by the warmth of my response. I don't want to release him, lest he should disappear like the ash that blizzards all around us.

He smiles at my expression of relief, I'm still too shocked to yet be happy. He strokes his thumb across my cheek. I hold his hand there, kiss it, and he looks at me, both of us taken aback by the force of my affection, a mild breeze that had built into a steady squall without my noticing.

'I threw off my cloak and managed to swim some distance to where a skiff lay. I heaved myself aboard,' he says, as though slightly bewildered by the audacity of his own escape.

'Pharos Island?' I ask.

'It's ours. Yours. We've won. For now.'

I kiss him.

'And the library warehouses?'

Apollodorus steps forward. 'Most of them burned. We were too late. But we saved one.'

He proffers a bundle to me. I look down and see that he's passed me a packet of slightly soggy papers, stamped with the great library seal.

'Caesar's men helped us save that which we did,' he says.

Caesar wipes a hand across his forehead, smudging it with black.

'When I saw Apollodorus trying to save the library warehouses, I ordered my men to stop their looting and to help. I'm only sorry we couldn't save more.'

Caesar is a brutish soldier, but he's also a man who understands the value of words, and their value to me. It's a gift of knowledge, both in and of itself, but it also reveals his understanding of me. He knows what matters to me. I kiss him. He smiles, taken aback at my affection.

*

The enemy is wounded, but not yet defeated. They withdraw, hissing, to the edges of the city and the desert beyond. We need to finish them, but we lack the strength for the final blow. Days drift past like scudding clouds. I'm sitting in the tower, staring out across the waters, smooth and blue-tipped with white. The waves are high, but there's only a light breeze. I stand and go to the edge of the parapet, leaning over the edge as far as I dare, shading my eyes against the sun. The white tips aren't foam or waves, they're sails.

'The Roman fleet arrives!' I yell.

My cries are carried down, the news passed from person to person until the entire palace vibrates with it. Within the hour every street in Alexandria teems with legionaries, and the air is busy with Latin instead of Greek, noisier than the dawn chorus. After months of being outnumbered, now we have many more men than the enemy, and ours are better armed and trained. That evening, I watch the beam from the lighthouse race out across the harbour illuminating the sails of hundreds of galleys like gulls on white wings.

At last, I issue the command I've been waiting months to give: I order my army to join with Caesar's. They've been stranded outside the city for so long, and yet they remained loyal to me, waiting, certain that the order to fight would come. I watch as they flow into the city, the narrow streets piped full of men. Outnumbered, my brother's men scuttle away, withdrawing from the city and vanishing into the desert, regrouping there under his and Arsinoe's command.

I have supplies carried from the port into the palace. All the goods that have been unable to reach us for months:

grain, fruit, linen, vivid silks, wine, olives, oils, perfume, beer, salted fish, rare woods and pigments. I order a feast, but while the court gorges and drinks and vomits with joy and excess, Caesar and I talk together, eating only bread and fruit and drinking cups of sweetened wine.

'My brother and sister flee with their ships and armies. But we must chase them down. End this,' I say.

'I've readied all the ships. Tomorrow, we sail.'

'Good,' I say. 'This time I'm coming with you.'

He opens his mouth as though to object, but then, wisely, says nothing.

My brother and sister make camp near Pelusium. There are fortified villages nearby and the soldiers take control of them, while the surviving ships from their fleet are moored on the Nile, a few miles away. We sail to meet them. The river is calm and wide, herons fish and the wind stirs the reeds. Above, kites surf on warm currents of air. The peace is almost deceiving me as to what lies ahead, beyond the curve of the river. Caesar and I lie on silken cushions, surveying the banks. It could almost be a pleasure cruise except we discuss the battle and our tactics. We decide to meet them on land, for they expect a water battle.

For the rest of the day, we prepare for the attack. All through the night, we assemble the men. We have thousands of soldiers, all eager for war. At the far end of the barge, I can see Charmian pacing, jittery and anxious. I'm glad of her restlessness and fear, for it's as if she holds mine for me, so I can be calm as Caesar and I debate how best to attack.

We talk for hours, arguing over tactics, until finally we're agreed. We'll take the enemy camp just before dawn.

Caesar looks at me. 'I will lead the men into the battle. You wait here with the fleet.'

'We agreed. This is my fight,' I tell him.

'And you are here. We need you to command the fleet. If we are chased back to the water, you must be waiting here with at least a thousand men and our ships, ready. If it comes to it, you must finish the battle on the river. You know these waters.'

I do. I know them better than Caesar. I agree.

Dawn is still a couple of hours away and I'm sweaty and dizzy. Charmian plies me with cool rosewater and gives me a herbal poultice. I thank her, drink the water and then vomit. Caesar appears at the door of our tent.

'You are frightened,' he says. His voice is kind, but I hear the note of disappointment. He had hoped for more from me, only to discover that I am womanish after all.

'I am not frightened,' I say, my voice sharp. This is only half a lie. I am frightened for I am not a fool, but it is not fear that has made me sick.

He looks at me again, more closely, beginning to understand.

'It's not fear in my belly,' I say softly. 'It's something else.'

Then, Caesar smiles, a broad, boyish grin. 'The soothsayer foretold it. This child lives. So we shall surely win.'

I smile back, more confident than I feel. The soothsayer said the child would outlive Caesar. His death might yet be tomorrow.

*

A narrow tributary flows between where our ships are moored and the road which Caesar intends to march up to reach the enemy camp. I send Apollodorus with Caesar and the armies, with instructions to return to me with news.

'I forbid you to die. You do not have my permission,' I tell him.

'No, my queen. I would not dare.'

Charmian and I wait. The sun rises, a polished golden plate spinning against blue. Birds circle, every now and then swooping to snag a fish. A jackal rustles the reeds. We hear nothing. Just the wind and the mosquitos. The sun starts to fall again. The cicadas tick. The light starts to fade. Charmian scrambles to her feet.

'There!'

Narrowing my eyes, I see the figure of Apollodorus on the bank. The minutes it takes for him to row his skiff to us last forever.

'Tell us,' I say, the moment he scrambles onto the deck.

He's brown with mud and smeared with sweat, his breath is short.

'Caesar charged at dawn, the cavalry rushed through the water but the banks are steep, much steeper than we'd reckoned with, and the horses were slow to climb, some even slipped and fell. And then there was a storm of arrows upon them. The river turned red with blood. The living rode over the dead. But then we noticed a clump of trees and the legionaries cut them down, and used them to bridge the banks. We were able to cross quicker and all at once. As soon as the enemy saw us come in such numbers they retreated towards the village.'

I'm silent for a second, picturing it. The smoke and cries and the water churning with blood. For weeks to come, the banks will be stacked with the dead, open-mouthed, bloated and gutted, stranded on the mud like fishes.

'What then?' I demand.

'Caesar launched a full assault on the villages, taking their forts. They were outnumbered. Your brother and sister's men hurled themselves over the ramparts.'

'And my brother and sister?'

'Your sister escaped. I don't know where. Your brother rushed down to his ships. There's a company with him. I'm ahead, but I don't know how far.'

'We are ready for them,' I say, resolute.

My ships are prepared for battle. I don't know how many boats will come with my brother. They'll sail along the tributary that feeds into the Nile, trying to reach their fleet down river. The tributary is shallow, and only small skiffs can navigate it. Only a few small boats will be able to sail with him, he'll be ill protected and he surely guesses that we wait for him to appear, our ships larger and in greater numbers, our archers poised. His cause is desperate, hopeless, and he must know it. I almost feel sorry for him.

Our ship stays in the deeper water in the centre of the Nile, but we watch the mouth of the tributary, waiting like a cat with its paw poised outside the mousehole. I will finish this before Caesar returns. My heart races in anticipation. It's nearly dark. Ptolemy will be trying to hide under its blanket. I order all the torches lit and the priests to offer sacrifices that the clouds will peel back from the moon. The air is filled with the sound of their voices raised to the gods, and the smell of burning flesh. The smoke curls upwards towards the clouds which slowly draw apart like curtains to reveal the bright eye of the moon. It blinks on the surface of the Nile.

And then, I see a small boat, rushing down the small stream. It's overloaded with people. Then, in the light of the moon, I see a gleam of golden armour. Ptolemy.

I realise how to end this.

My archers raise their bows.

'No,' I say. 'Do not fire. Sail closer.'

'Yes, my queen.'

We chase them. It's the work of a few minutes. I stare at my brother. His armour flashes like golden lightning in the torch light. We're almost alongside.

'Order twenty men to swim to the skiff, and climb aboard.'

I watch from the deck as twenty slaves swim with easy strokes to my brother's skiff. He and his men realise what's happening too late. As the swimmers clamber onto the low-slung boat, it sinks lower into the water, then begins to flood with water, toppling. Men are thrown into the river. They shout and swim. My brother clings to the side of the boat, crawling to the last part afloat. If he screams, I can't hear it. In his golden armour, he's brighter than the stars. I see him flail, cling to the side, but the boat disappears under the tide and then, so does he. He sinks at once. He does not come up again. I know he cannot, his armour is too heavy. He will be like an arrow sailing to the bottom where he will strike the mud and lodge. His men swim down and down, trying to save him, but come up empty-handed, spitting out water. He will be too heavy to drag to the surface. His armour anchors him to the river bed. I picture him under the water, the gold river king. Already he sails across another river, blacker, colder, to Osiris and Anubis.

When Caesar arrives back at dawn, bloody and triumphant, I'm having the river dredged.

'Why?' he asks. 'A thousand men saw him drown. Let the fishes eat his corpse.'

'We can't let the people start to think of him as an Osiris. The god's body was cast into the river and then rose again, his soul nurtured by the mud of the Nile. We need Ptolemy's corpse, bloated and broken.'

They've been dredging for hours. Then, at last, they drag him up. His golden armour is streaked with brown, a gold coin dropped in shit.

His corpse lies on the bank, starting to stiffen. Something pokes at my happy triumph, not as sharp as sadness, perhaps regret. His death means peace. Like the sun and moon, there was never room for us both in the sky. He's now passed into night. And yet, I no longer feel any pleasure at his death, and the way he scrabbled for life tugs at me. I see him drowning at the bottom of the river in his gleaming armour, deep beneath the waters. His eunuchs are dead with him. Everyone who loved my brother is gone. He has slid out of the world, regretted by no one.

I lie under a canopy on the royal barge, listening to the burping of the frogs, and the smack of the oars. Birds score patterns on the unbroken blue of the sky. I'm sticky and swollen with heat and an unfamiliar feeling pricks at me. I think this is happiness. I clutch at it, for it won't last long, so I hold it in my hands like ice, delighting in the sensation before it melts away. I'm dressed in a glistening white dress, trimmed with crocus-yellow silk and embroidered with flowers and fruit. I'm drowsy and yet not quite ready for sleep, though I'm lulled further and further in by the steady slap of the water against the hull. Caesar runs his fingers through my hair, tugs at my braids, and then leans low to kiss me. I want to stay here, drift in this moment. He tucks my black silk mantle around my shoulders. It's fringed and stitched with the moon and stars in gold and silver thread.

'You mustn't get cold,' he says, fussing like a nursemaid.

I laugh. 'Cold? I'm drunk with heat.'

He lies beside me, and we remain still, shaded by the silken canopy stitched with coiled serpents, our hands almost touching. Neither of us speaks, and I realise that it is comfortable to lie in silence beside a man for whom, if I do not feel love, I harbour the tenderest of affection. I no longer need to try and charm him or perform, for he is caught. He is mine, for today at least, and tomorrow too. He has gifted me back my kingdom. His finger runs up the down on my arm. I shiver and smile. His expression darkens for a moment.

'Your sister was captured. We'll take her back to Rome. Parade her there before she is—'

'Hush,' I silence him, place my fingers on his lips.

I can't hear about Arsinoe. Her betrayal aches in my chest. It's acid rising in my throat. I have a letter in the bag around my neck from her, begging for forgiveness, pleading to come back to my court, my affections. It's a letter full of love and lies. I have not replied.

Caesar places his hands on my belly. I know it is only an echo of love that I have for him for it does not touch how I feel about this tiny secret, this secret as small as a leaf inside me. I must survive now, no longer for me or even for Egypt, but for my son. I glance to the side of the barge where Charmian stands, Apollodorus behind her, his chin resting on the top of her head. She smiles at me. When Caesar returns to Rome in a week or two, she and Apollodorus will remain. We are a family of sorts – not like my blood family, where we scheme against one another for power and death – but one created out of friendship and love. They will do anything to protect me and my son.

16

SERVILIA

Caesar had been away from Rome for more than two years. The silence was so long, so absolute, that it felt like a little death. And I knew he had not returned to me at the first possible moment. Once the war in Egypt had been won, he lingered in the east with Cleopatra, drifting down the Nile on her golden barge to see crocodiles and the pyramids of the old kings, if the rumours are to be believed. The distance between us spun and stretched like wool on a spindle. Perhaps he stayed with Cleopatra for political reasons, to cement an allegiance. But for once I agreed with the gossips – it was not politics which made him remain by her side but Cleopatra herself. I decided that I would not ask him directly if this was true, or why he didn't hurry back to me. I feared that the truth might not make me happy.

He always had the capacity to hold more than one woman in his heart at once.

Then at last Caesar returned to Rome, and he came alone, leaving the Egyptian queen behind. The afternoon of his return, the sunshine clarified like butter. I now lived in an estate on the banks of the Tiber surrounded by vineyards. I was nervous at the prospect of seeing him, excitement heating the blood in my veins. I strolled down to the lower gardens, feigning calm. I saw him before he noticed me, and I watched him sitting on a low bench set before a swirling pool. He looked older, thinner. His hair was entirely white, like dandelion fluff. Then, he saw me, and rose at once and started towards me, his arms open. I hesitated and stood back, at a little distance.

'I missed you,' he said.

I searched his face for dissemblance but found none. He just looked tired. He was far from the youth I'd first loved. I said nothing. He'd been away a long time, and in a queen's bed. We needed to find our way back to each other. Sensing my reserve, he stepped towards me and looked at me steadily.

'You are the love that I choose, Servilia. No. That's not true. I have no choice in loving you.'

I stared at him and felt something clenched within my chest unfurl. I still did not speak.

'Please, sit with me.'

Sighing, I sat down next to him. Before us the green waters foamed and roared. A kingfisher dabbled by the banks, the light gilded and iridescent on its wing. Caesar clasped a box on his lap so tightly that his fingertips were white. He opened it, and inside I saw the largest, smoothest pearl I'd ever glimpsed, like he'd snared the full moon and secreted it inside this box, pale and glowing. It was a jewel belonging to the heavens, not the earth.

He cleared his throat and began to speak. He'd rehearsed his speech, but to my surprise the great, unrufflable senator sounded nervous.

'Servilia, tides wash in and roll away, but you remain, as everlasting as the sands and as infinite. I've never wearied of you or of loving you. This pearl isn't enough. Not for you. You deserve the best of what belongs to the gods, but this is the choicest offering a mortal can give.'

I let him place the pearl in the palm of my hand, it rested there as large and round as a bantam egg. Its surface was smooth and luminous white.

'It was always you, Servilia,' he said, his voice soft.

I would never wear such a jewel, it was not my style. I was always simple in my taste and dress, rarely wearing jewellery or decorations of any kind. Yet, the gifting of it would tell all Rome what I was to Caesar. Even his wife must know. And Cleopatra. The pearl itself would sit hidden in my room, unseen. To the rest of the world it was a symbol of my power and my sway over Caesar. But I understood what it really meant: the pearl showed Caesar's love and also his fear. He could not bear to be without me. He loved me, not beyond everything, but almost. I accepted his love along with his pearl. I chose to believe him and to accept what he could give me of himself. What choice did I have? I loved him.

*

I had him to myself for more than a year. Although even before Cleopatra's arrival, her presence still infringed upon us. I tried hard not to resent it. I heard that she'd given birth to a child, a boy, called Caesarion – son of Caesar. I asked Caesar if the boy was his, and he simply replied, 'The boy is Cleopatra's. He's not a Roman. But I do not dislike his name.' This, I understood, was his acknowledgement that the baby was indeed his. By this time Caesar had been married three times and only ever had one child, a daughter, Julia, now dead. His third wife, Calpurnia, never conceived and was unlikely to do so. I'd come to accept Calpurnia. Often, to my surprise, I felt sorry for her. I did not marry again when my second husband, Silanus, died and it had stung when Caesar didn't choose me and instead married Calpurnia but I was in my forty-second year when Silanus passed after a long illness, and it was no longer certain that I would bear a new husband any children.

When she'd married Caesar, Calpurnia was a young teenager, small and birdlike with the black eyes of a thrush, a fine down lining her skinny arms. She was pious and grave and whenever I visited the temple, she always seemed to be there, deep in prayer. I don't think I ever saw her laugh. Even though Caesar chose to marry her in the hope of sons, they had no children. Perhaps that's what inspired all her visits to the temple: to beseech the gods to ripen her womb. Despite her piety and offerings, the gods didn't listen. I must admit that there were some in Rome who muttered that he might as well have married me for love, instead of Calpurnia for youth. I listened to them, not entirely without satisfaction, but I no longer wanted to be his nor anyone's wife.

I wondered how he felt with his only son not only a

bastard, but a foreigner. I found myself thinking of that boy often. I used to wish that Caesar and I could have had a child together. But, over the course of a long life, it's a small sorrow – the niggle of a pebble caught inside a shoe, and I was kept busy with my children and grandchildren.

For the time being, Cleopatra stayed in Egypt, tending to both her baby and her court. New mothers are vulnerable, when they are also queens that danger multiplies like locusts on a wheat crop, and I was not surprised by her staying in Alexandria. While I was curious about her and the boy, I preferred to be curious from afar. I liked a sea between us. I told myself that there was no reason for the Egyptian queen to journey all the way to Rome. A little later, I heard that she'd married her youngest brother, a child of about ten, in the peculiar and unsavoury traditions of the Egyptians and the Ptolemies. I almost pitied her in this. I could not imagine any woman, queen or not, wanting to marry her brother. I had not sought to change my widowed status. I'd observed my friend Clodia and her freedom in her widowhood. I liked that my money was my own. And, for myself, I didn't need or want a husband, I had children – two daughters and a son – and I had Caesar. Other than my children, I had no one to please but myself. My brother Cato had died, and while I grieved his loss, it was not without relief. From my safe distance in Rome, I allowed myself to feel pity for Cleopatra.

Then, the whispers began: Cleopatra was coming to see Caesar. And soon, all anyone could speak of was her arrival in Rome. For all that Rome was a republic, they were transfixed by the arrival of the Egyptian queen. They thrilled with disapproval. I felt them all study me for signs of jealousy. For more than two decades Caesar and I had endured despite five marriages between us, numberless foreign paramours as well as the steady trickle of Roman matrons and senators' wives. I learned, if not to take interest in these other women, to accept them, for their relationship with Caesar had no bearing on his with me. He never lied or tried to conceal their existence. Between us there was the ease of familiarity and affection, and yet also an edge of unknowable otherness. Caesar desired many women, bedding plenty for he could not see a dish without sampling. In the beginning, I would watch him, wondering if he was the same with them as with me. But as the years went by, and women continued to pass through his bed, never staying longer than a year or two, I understood that I was the only constant. Rome was no longer titillated by our relationship.

But the arrival of the Egyptian queen set the tongues wagging again with great excitement. They all wondered how I would manage with this sudden rival. This exotic and exquisite queen, the same age as my own daughter. I bore it outwardly with fortitude, complaining only to my friend Clodia of my annoyance. At fifty, I hoped to be beyond the reach of the scurrilous tongues. But unfortunately, it was my age and widowhood that seemed to provoke and delight the gossips. It was me who Rome seemed to think would be mad with jealousy rather than Calpurnia. No one seemed to trouble themselves as to what she would feel. Perhaps wives are safer when a new lover appears than the old mistress. Especially when she herself is, if not old, then not in the first bloom of youth.

That brief year after Caesar's return my life had been a

sheltered mooring, away from the squalls that continually swept through Rome. I should have known that nothing ever lasts. Calm and delight are never permanent – only ever a lull. Some periods of tranquillity are longer than others, but the wheel will always turn. And it was Cleopatra's arrival that spun the wheel round and round, dizzying us all.

I hosted a dinner party shortly after her arrival in the city. It was for the matrons of Rome, my closest friends; I invited only the wives, telling them to leave their husbands at home. My parties were renowned. I often hosted them for Caesar – my entertaining was more ribald and joyous than Calpurnia's and senators knew that by gaining my ear, they'd gain Caesar's. But, that night, I wanted to be free of politics and manoeuvrings and wanted simply to be amongst my friends. I served more wine than was respectable at a dinner for matrons and hired musicians from Persia to entertain us. My daughters came, my eldest, Junia, and the younger, Tertia. I invited my daughter-in-law Portia, hoping she would not accept. To my relief, she sent regrets. Brutus had always sought my opinion, but to my dismay, I discovered recently that I had a rival for his ear in Portia and her advice was mostly defective. Portia was my brother Cato's daughter, and she had all her father's certainty and self-regard but none of his wisdom. We did not argue but treated one another with absolute politeness. I invited her scrupulously to my house and she sent scrupulous regrets.

My daughter Junia was lucky in her husband, Lepidus. He was a politician of a different ilk to Caesar. Where Caesar charmed and persuaded, Lepidus wore them down with dullness. I sometimes wonder if senators agreed to his proposals merely to stop him talking. He was also unlike Caesar in his chastity and was utterly devoted to my daughter. Junia was happy, basking in the sunshine of his adoration. Happiness for those outside its bubble is wearisome in its monotony. She had that rare ability: to be content. I do not know how I produced such a tranquil, easy child.

Tertia was prettier than her sister and rebellious. From the moment she could walk, she hid from the slaves at bedtime. We'd discover her in the kennels hours later, sleeping fast amongst the dogs, a small figure amongst the heap of snoring hounds. She and her husband, Cassius, each had an impetuous streak, both of them choking on their own ambition but lacking Caesar's patience and foresight.

At the party, we all reclined on couches in the triclinium, listening to the mellifluous song of the hired flute players mingling with the music of the fountains. Junia and Tertia shared a couch, squabbling amiably as they had when they were children. Junia was the drab copy of her sister, the faded, quickly rendered fresco completed by the apprentice and not the master. Yet, seeing them together filled me with a warm delight, richer than sipping any fortified wine. I liked to listen to their chatter. They became the children that they'd once been and I almost forgot that they were now mothers themselves. Together, they were simply the girls, my girls.

Everyone else was wondering loudly and all at once about Cleopatra. She'd arrived in Rome with a great retinue of slaves, and now lodged in one of Caesar's villas. But no one had yet seen the queen herself. She remained cloistered within the villa and with no visitors apart from Caesar. The estate where he had established her was on the other side of the Tiber from us. I could just see it from the high bank at the top of my garden, the lights burning in the windows at dusk, although I was too far away to catch sight of the queen herself, even if she ventured out to take some air. For the first time in many years, I wondered how Caesar split his time between the two of us. I pushed the thought away. Yet there was something that irked me. Caesar was expedient in his choices of lovers, and his relationship with Cleopatra was not sensible. To bed her in Egypt was one thing, understandable since he was far from home and it served to remind her of her place beneath Rome, but to bring her here, host her not only as a foreign dignitary but as his lover, was impolitic. Romans might be fascinated by royalty but even now as the women chattered, their disapproval was loud and resolute. I'd never seen Caesar act outside of his own interest before.

Everyone looked to me for confirmation of the rumours, expecting that Caesar would have told me, firing a quiver full of questions at me.

'Is she really married to her brother? He's a child. Not even ten. He is here, is he not? Surely they don't share a bed? And has she brought her son? The boy. Is the child truly Caesar's? And her hair. Is it true that she wears it loose in braids, plaited with golden thread? Her teeth are painted black, and a third eye is painted upon her forehead. She's a witch with magical powers in her tits. I heard she shits pearls.'

I held up my hands and their questions guttered out. 'I don't know the answers to any of these questions, although surely common sense must resolve some of them for you.'

I had never pressed Caesar for details regarding his other

lovers, and I was not going to start now. 'We must wait to satisfy our curiosity.'

There was a pause, and the conversation turned to discuss Caesar's upcoming triumph, celebrating his conquest in Egypt. There was a hum of excitement as it had been some time since Rome had seen such a pageant.

'Ten thousand slaves will walk through the streets.'

'Who cares about slaves? I've heard there will be dragons and zebras.'

'Zebras aren't real! Don't be stupid, Fulvia.'

'And the conquered Egyptian queen.'

'Cleopatra?'

'No, silly. Her sister.'

At this point, one of the women clapped her hands, asking with a smile, 'Who here has been conquered by Caesar?'

More than half of the room raised their hands. I did not. Everyone already knew about me. And, besides, I conquered him. They all laughed to see the forest of raised hands. I forced a smile but felt a nudge of humiliation. To be bedded by Caesar was a rite of passage, it seemed. Then, to my dismay, I noticed some of the women eyeing Tertia with interest, looks of disbelief on their faces when she did not raise her hand. There were rumours in Rome that I'd encouraged her to become Caesar's lover. I knew that some soft-headed fools listened to such nonsense, but I'd hoped for better from my friends. I took a sip of wine, disappointed. To my surprise it was Fulvia who voiced an objection on my behalf.

'What imbeciles are you, to listen to the base fantasies of men? Tertia might be an echo of her mother in youth, that does not mean she echoes her mother's desires.'

There was embarrassed silence. Fulvia laughed loudly. 'So it's acceptable for you to harbour such filthy imaginings, but when I voice them aloud, you're all suddenly shy. Oh, you are so easily offended, good women of Rome.'

I smiled, grateful to Fulvia, and exchanged amused glances with Clodia. Fulvia was not my friend, but I'd invited her as she was a woman with whom it was dangerous to quarrel. She was easily the most forceful woman in Rome, fearless, resolute and always outspoken. She governed her household and her husbands like Caesar his empire. I enjoyed the company of forthright women. I looked at her, rosy-cheeked, as pretty and plump as a well-tended dove, and yet I knew that her wholesome appearance belied her ruthlessness. She surveyed the company with eyes watchful and astute. She was also one of the wealthiest landlords in Rome and collected her rents with absolute precision and alacrity. The fact that Marc Antony had married her despite her fearsome reputation endeared him to me. Until their marriage, I'd considered the man a drunk and a liability, and had often urged Caesar to find a superior lieutenant, not to trust this licentious spendthrift as his proxy. And yet Antony's marriage to Fulvia made me reconsider him. A man who is unafraid of a woman and confident enough to let her rule him has a strength beyond that in his arms or fists.

I tried to imagine Cleopatra reclining here with the rest of us, discussing who had bedded Caesar. Would the Egyptian queen have raised her hand? Smiled with the rest of us? The thought was so absurd, I laughed aloud.

'Will you host the party after the triumph, *mater*?' asked Junia.

I shook my head. That honour must surely belong to Calpurnia.

I did not see Caesar for several days. He was occupied with business, but I did not mind. Time had taught me patience. That afternoon when I came to see him in the garden of his villa, he was quieter than usual, and I sensed a caution in him, although perhaps it was my own.

'Is Calpurnia hosting the celebration for you after the triumph?' I asked.

He hesitated; the silence twanged.

'No. Cleopatra asked to have that honour.'

I stopped walking and turned to face him, appalled. I looked at him in horror. I was glad that there was no one to see me, for they would take my dismay for jealousy. It was not. It was shock at his foolishness. Every senator in Rome wanted to be the one to have the honour of celebrating Caesar if the revels were not to be hosted by his wife. But instead, he was granting the honour to Cleopatra. It made it appear as though he was sharing with her a morsel of his victory in the East. It was reckless and unconsidered. Every senator would be insulted. Caesar was making a political miscalculation giving her this honour. I'd never known him guided by anything other than his usually perfect political acumen. Then, Cleopatra wasn't only his mistress, nor simply a queen. She was the mother of his only son. As I looked at Caesar, he would not meet my eye. A small space opened up in my chest, a hole that had not been there before.

17
CLEOPATRA

I like Rome no better on the second visit. The city has gained neither wisdom, beauty nor better drains since we were last here. Even though I'd prefer to remain in my palace by the sea, it is time for me to visit Caesar. I want his assurances that Rome will lend me support without interference. I am no puppet queen. My throne is my own. And yet, beyond the necessity of the visit, there is something else. I want him to meet his son, but even this is not the only reason I want to see him. After some wine, I confess to Charmian that I miss him, just a little. His smile. The way he listens when I talk. How his hands feel on my skin.

'How much do you miss him?' she teases. 'I yearn for Apollodorus like I do for spring at winter's close. Or as I long for the soft arms of sleep at the end of each day. Do you miss Caesar like that?'

I hesitate, for I do not long for Caesar with such ardent need.

'No, as I crave a taste of honey after a salty feast.'

'A taste only?' she asks, laughing.

I do not answer. My affection for Caesar would not be enough for me to leave my court in Egypt and travel to Rome, if it were not also politically expedient. And yet the thought of seeing him again gives me considerable pleasure. It's an image I turn over again and again in my mind, as though his face is a favourite fresco.

Last time I came here with my father, now I arrive in state as queen, with my brother as my husband, in name at least. Tol does not wish to be in Rome, he wanted to stay behind in Alexandria, training his falcon and roaming the palace gardens. He's been lost since Arsinoe's betrayal. He's sullen and quiet, and I don't know what happened to the sweet-natured, open-faced boy. Our family destroys people, the snake eating its own tail. I couldn't risk letting Tol stay in Egypt without me. I don't believe that he will seek to snatch my throne – he is still a boy, and he used to be fond of me – but so was my sister once. His advisors are not as rancid as Pothinus or Achillas, but I forbid them from accompanying us to Rome. I watch from the window as the now tall and skinny boy trails around the gardens that slope down the Tiber, one of his hunting birds on his arm, a wagging pack of dogs following behind. I will protect him as best I can. He doesn't need to like me. Fondness won't keep him safe.

This journey to Rome is different for I am not only Pharaoh and Queen of the Red Lands and the Black, Isis on earth, Mother of Egypt, but the mother of a boy. My son Caesarion is eighteen months. When he was born, I felt first my body split open, then my heart. It now lives with him, apart from myself. I did not know I could feel such love, bright and fierce. Now I have seen the sun, I do not want to go back into the dark, and I know that I could. My love is latticed with fear that the gods will take him from me if I do not please them. Nothing else matters. Only him. All I do now, each course I take, is for Egypt and for him.

The house Caesar has lent me is pleasant if small. To my relief it stands a little outside Rome, away from the stink of the city. I too would have preferred to remain in Alexandria, in my own palace surrounded by date palms, tumbling fountains and scented by sea air. In Alexandria, Caesar belonged only to me. Here, I must share him, not only with other women but with Rome.

He comes to visit me the day before his triumph. I try again to persuade him not to parade my sister in the pageant. He smiles and takes my hand, kissing it.

'Cleopatra's womanly scruples and kindness do her much credit.'

I pull my hand away, indignant.

'You think it's kindness? Pity? Have you forgotten who Cleopatra is?' I demand. 'I ask you not to parade my sister in front of this crowd because it is impolitic. They will not want to see her whipped or to watch her die.'

Caesar is not riled by my hiss of temper, he only smiles, unperturbed. He likes my fire. 'Ah, you do not know the appetite of Romans for blood.'

I imagine it's much like the hunger for savagery elsewhere, but I do not press him. There has been time and distance between us, and I am not yet sure of him. He wants to please me, but I can't tell whether it is to placate the Pharaoh of Egypt whose treasuries he wishes to raid again, or if he simply desires to make me happy. He has granted me the honour of hosting a celebration for him after the triumph. I must be satisfied with that for now.

He takes my hand and leads me towards the villa. As we approach he kisses me, and I warm to him. He holds my face in his hands, and I see that he is tired and yet he smiles at me, small papery creases appearing around his eyes.

'I am yet Caesar and you are Cleopatra,' he says, kissing me again.

There is a pleasant familiarity to his touch, and I kiss him back, wrapping my arms around him. Then, from the villa I hear crying. Caesarion has woken and is angry, wants me. Unthinking, I turn away from Caesar and start to move to the house. He catches my arm and pulls me back to him.

'The slaves will take care of him,' he says.

I try to ignore the sound of my son's screams, but I hear them from inside my skull. I can think of nothing else. Only his cries. His distress. Caesar isn't concerned by them at all. His only interest is me. Turning over my wrist and laying a soft kiss on the tender skin, his lips linger. It's both a suggestion and a command. I have no choice but to obey.

Later that evening, I sit on a bench in the nursery by the light of a single candle, keeping watch as Caesarion sleeps. Smouldering incense fills the room with the scent of oil and musk roses. Miniature carved figures of Horus, Bes and Bastet cast shadows as their godheads seep out of the figurines to guard my baby boy from death and terrors. Trails of tears are drying on his cheeks like snail tracks, and his dimpled fists are tightly curled. His mouth is open, soft and pink with the pearlescent gleam of his first teeth. This is love, I think, as I watch him. It's so sharp, it pricks like fear.

I hear a noise behind me, and turning, I see Charmian beside me. She looks as tired as I feel, and I lay my head on her shoulder. We stand before the cradle, watching my baby as he sleeps. The goddess and queen have been stripped from me and put to bed for the night, and now there is only the woman left: thin and tired with shadows beneath my eyes, scrubbed clean of all makeup, my hairpiece unstitched. Beneath my tunic, I run my fingers across the pale stretch marks scoring my belly and hips from carrying Caesarion. My exposed skin is chafed raw from the weight of the golden jewellery.

Charmian rubs my back with strong fingers, teasing the knots, and I lean into her. I wonder if she can smell Caesar on me. I am sticky with sweat and his pleasure. I gaze down at Caesarion, the brush of thick lashes. He's on his tummy, his knees tucked up beneath him, his bottom in the air, his small toes coiled. He's just a baby and yet Rome is a writhing viper pit seething with those who want him dead. A son of Caesar, foreign-born with a queen for a mother.

I nibble my fingernail and stare at him. I'm so full of love and worry that I can hardly breathe. All mothers fear for their children: death and accident lurk always. Yet I fear for him as much from men as I do from the ghouls of pestilence and disease. I stare at him, greedy with love, and experiencing the thoughts of every mother from peasant to queen that this child, mine, mine, is perfect. He is so perfect that he wounds the heart that loves him. Unable to bear it any longer, I reach out and brush his plump and perfect cheek with my fingertips so that his eyes flutter for a moment and opening them, he stares at me with wide black eyes, and then ebbs from me back into sleep.

I sigh and stroke his small hand, the dimpled knuckles. Charmian tries to slip away and leave us, not wanting to intrude. I catch her hand, tugging her back.

'Stay.'

I want Charmian with me so she can share with me not only my worry but my joy. For joy must be spoken aloud and witnessed. With her beside me I've loved this boy, delighting in each new word as he tastes it, rolling it between his lips as he begins to discern the shape of the world. Leaning over, I check beneath his pillow for the small bottle of Nile water that is always hidden there for his protection. In his sleep, one small fist grasps the gleaming bulia amulet around his neck. I want the gods to spin a cloak around him to shield him from the eyes and evils of the world, from sickness and age and from jealous men.

My thighs are damped and chafed. There is a bite mark upon my shoulder. I hope I gave a good performance of desire. Power must be satisfied. I took Caesar's gifts and the victory he bought for me but there is always a cost. And only I can pay it. My brother Ptolemy died. My sister is sentenced to death, and thousands of Egyptians are now dust in the desert. This is the price of the dead, that I must lie there and pay Caesar with my flesh. I use my body to buy respite for Egypt from Roman greed. I am the mother not only of this boy, but of a country. And this is what a queen does. A king does not have to lie on his back and pretend his pleasure.

I look at Charmian and for a moment I envy her. She loves a man and he loves her back. She can choose to give him her body or not. Their affection is simple and uncomplicated and only involves one another. There is no transaction, only love. I will never be able to give myself to a man where there is not something to be gained for Egypt. It would be reckless. A pregnant queen risks death in childbed just like ordinary women. When Caesarion was in my womb, I watched all the courtiers whisper and plot, wondering if I would survive. Sex with a man is a calculation that I must assess as carefully as the taxes due to my treasuries. I will never be able to love and desire a man just for himself. That freedom is not for me.

I wake in the morning to find Charmian is gone. A surge of worry pulses through me. She is always here. Is she ill? Has something happened to Caesarion? I call out for her and in a moment she's beside me.

'What is it? Why weren't you here?' I demand.

'I beg your forgiveness, great queen.'

I look at her and can see that there is something troubling her.

'Tell me?' I ask.

She hesitates. 'Apollodorus's sister has come from Sicily.'

'A social visit? How pleasant.'

Her face is tight with anxiety. Impatience pricks at me.

'Speak, what is wrong?'

Charmian takes a breath, then says, 'She brings gold. She wants to buy his freedom.'

I laugh. That a farmer could give me enough gold to buy what I do not choose to sell.

'She will not leave. She insists on seeing you, great and worthy queen.'

Charmian's face is pale and tight with worry. I'm irritated that a farmer's daughter has disturbed the peace of my morning.

'And what does Apollodorus say?'

'He's furious. And tells her to leave.'

I relent on hearing his loyalty towards me. 'We will hear her petition, for Apollodorus's sake.'

When I am dressed, I go out into the garden and sit in the shade of a pomegranate tree. The sky is watery blue with scribbles of birds like inky hieroglyphs. After a few minutes, Charmian and Apollodorus appear with a young woman. She is pinched and thin, with the same dark hair and brown eyes as her brother. Her feet are dusty, and she fiddles with a leather bag tied around her waist.

'I beg your mercy, great queen,' says Apollodorus. 'I ordered her to leave.' He looks at his sister, his voice pleading. 'Return to Sicily, Tulia.'

'I can't, not without you,' says Tulia with a flash of temper. 'Queen Cleopatra—'

Apollodorus flinches with barely concealed rage and interrupts her. 'Do not speak. You do not have permission to address the Pharaoh.'

Tulia opens her mouth to speak again and then closes it again. Her eyes are full of fire but she looks exhausted and worn down.

'You may speak, girl. I would not grant this privilege but I am grown fond of your brother. Why have you come to us?' I say.

She kneels at my feet – not the usual Roman way, but she is Sicilian, I suppose.

'My father is now dead. I have no other brothers. My mother is old and sick. There is no one to run the family farm. Apollodorus was taken as a slave in war ten years ago. I beg you now to return him to us. I will pay for his freedom.'

She brandishes a bag of coins at her waist.

'I pity you for your hardship. But you cannot buy what is not for sale. He belongs to me. Now leave us. Do not return.'

She looks at me with hatred and blinks back tears, opening her mouth to speak.

'Do not speak again. I have gifted you with profound kindness by allowing you into our presence. If you were not his sister, then I'd have had you whipped and sent away.'

Apollodorus puts his hand upon her arm and half drags, half carries her away. From the other end of the garden, I can hear her shouting and him hissing at her to be quiet. A pomegranate drops to the ground at my feet, bursting when it falls, spilling its guts onto the earth, bloody and oozing.

'If I see her again, I will have her killed, not whipped,' I say. 'Make sure her brother knows this.'

Charmian bows, nods.

All around me the slaves are preparing the villa for the party. It must be splendid beyond Rome's imaginings, for then they will no longer wonder why Caesar has given me this honour.

Caesar has lent me the villa, but I've already altered it according to my own designs. I did not ask either his permission or opinion on the changes, and I paid for all the improvements myself, using workman brought from Alexandria. I do not trust the skill of Roman craftsmen; I've seen their shoddy statues and ugly houses.

The villa is situated on what is considered the wrong side of the Tiber, but I am sure that within three months, all of Rome will be mimicking my designs and searching for houses nearby. I glance around the room to where the finest artists in the Hellenic world are finishing stencils of budding nymphs. On the opposite wall, Hatshepsut hunts wild fowl amongst the lush marshes of the Nile. They are so exquisitely rendered that now, in the trance-like flicker of the candles, the nymphs appear to dance and the Nile marsh reeds quiver as a lurking heron eyes the speckle-bellied fish that flick through blue waters. Just beyond the windows lie the vast gardens where soft lawns are edged with torches, the wobbling flames reflected in a series of recently completed rills and pools, stretching on and on down to the river. I can just make out the spreading arms of a grove of cedars, black in the dark, from where the song of a nightjar echoes. I've created a world with no borders or edges, the boundaries between inside and outside, day and dusk have been removed. This is a realm of the unreal: Rome and not Rome, a piece of Alexandria transplanted like a dream where anything might happen.

The mosaic laid into the floor displays the Egyptian and Roman gods feasting together, a divine union. Isis wears an emerald necklace, but the beads are not tile or fired glass but real jewels. Every time anyone treads upon it, I observe with wry amusement as Apollodorus winces, for it was he who settled the bill. I hear the low murmur of the slaves as they prepare the feast, the metal clang as gold and silver plates are set upon tables, the ceramic knock of wine flagons. I take a deep breath. I've always liked best the moment right before the party, when I can imagine the rooms filled with guests like future ghosts. Soon the villa will be brimming with the great men of Rome talking and drinking, but beneath the surface laughter and smiles, the murmur of plotting and intrigue will run under the conversation like a hidden stream beneath rock.

I'm supposed to wait here for them, knowing that a short distance away my sister is waiting to die. I might hate her for her betrayal, and yet I do not want her to suffer. I still remember the girl she was before. My blood fizzes in my veins. I feel only dread. I know she must die, but in my mind I don't see the woman who betrayed me, but the little girl I loved. The baby who wrapped her tiny fingers in my hair. Her milk-soft smell. I do not want to see her humiliated and degraded for the entertainment of a Roman mob.

'Charmian,' I say, summoning her to my side. 'Bring me items of yours. We're going into the city.'

'No, my queen. You can't. It's too dangerous for you.'

'Not if you dress me carefully as a fellow slave.' Her face is still painted with horror. 'We'll take Apollodorus,' I add, relenting.

My two friends are furious with me. I hear their simmering anger but neither dares to voice it, which suits me fine. Once I am ready, we venture out into the city streets. Rome after sundown is the kingdom of whores and thieves. The air is filled with the thudding of drums and the slap of soldiers' feet across the cobbles is so loud that I feel it in my chest as a second heartbeat. For once, the road is cleared of all the usual night-time traffic of wagons and oxen while the regular slanging match between carters as they get stuck in jams and the housewives yelling at them from windows to be quiet is replaced by the caterwauling of an immense crowd. It seethes all the way along Palatine Hill and into the distance, ten men deep. They've been standing since dusk, clutching banners, waving flags, swigging from flagons of wine and boasting of Roman victories, tales that grow more improbable with each rendition. A song rises up amongst the crowd, tossed from side to side like a ball. *Men of Rome, keep close your women, for here's a bald adulterer. Lo! Now rides Caesar in triumph as he rode Queen Cleopatra.* It was accompanied by jeers and thrusting. I snort in contempt – was this the best the supposedly great empire could muster? All the same, I feel Apollodorus tense beside me; I know his hand has gone to his knife. A man, barely able to stuff his gut into his toga, nudges me and leaning close, hisses in my ear, 'What do you think of our poetry, pretty one?'

'I prefer the Greeks,' I reply.

He roars with laughter.

'Only because you've never been fucked by a Roman,' he shouts, grabbing his crotch. I turn away in disgust and push my way further into the crowd to escape, hearing him call after me with a series of increasingly elaborate obscene suggestions. I doubt that a man of his immense proportions could achieve any of the contortions he is suggesting we try. A moment later, I hear a groan and I know that Apollodorus has knocked him to the ground.

This triumph is not only over Caesar's enemies but over night itself. Rome is lit with a hundred thousand torches, blazing along the route with such brightness it is as though the power of the empire encompassed the heavens too and it can order the stars to fall to earth in neat rows. Despite the press of bodies, the evening is cool for autumn and I tug my cloak close around my shoulders and low over my face.

'We can leave, go back to the villa,' whispers Charmian.

'No,' I reply.

I try not to succumb to the heavy feeling lodged deep in my stomach. *Let it be quick. Don't let her suffer.* My eyes water from the smoke of the vast bonfires lit on the top of every hill, where they blaze with tongues of scarlet, spitting volleys of sparks upwards like red shooting stars. Trumpeters call out long bright notes into the night air. Other noises are tossed out into the darkness, feral and unruly. I watch a massive lion leading a company of leopards. They patrol the street eyeing the crowd, a slave strolling behind ready with his whip. A few of the drunken men at the front poke at them with their laurel boughs, yelling and then cringing back with frightened laughter when the lion roars, ready to pounce, only distracted by the snap of the slave's whip across its haunches. Next come legionaries carrying standards decorated with the scenes of battle and bloodied enemies writhing in agony and defeat. They march for what seems like hours in an endless procession of men, the forest of thin wooden spears like the skinny trunks of a winter forest.

The wagons are decorated with dozens of flags dyed in crimson and purple, visible by the blazing lanterns. On top of each wagon is constructed a platform where a marvellous scene is laid out. There's a cart bearing a model of the Pharos lighthouse, its light shining out across silver painted waters, where toy ships bob in the harbour amongst cresting waves of white plumes of feathers. A slave works a set of bellows to make the silken sails flutter in the wind. At the foot of the lighthouse is a golden island formed of treasure: spoils from the war, gleaming statues and silver plates and jewelled goblets that glint in the lights of the torches like tiny suns. The crowd gasps and screams with delight to see such plunder. I wince for I know that this gold was bought with blood.

Then, out of the gloom emerges a seemingly endless train of prisoners, bony and ragged with their arms bound, legs of each knotted to the prisoner before and behind so that they stumble along, half-tripping. When one man falls sprawling upon the hard ground he cannot rise, for the column marches on and the unfortunate soul is dragged across the cobbles screaming, leaving his skin behind in a wet slick.

And then I see her. She is on the last wagon, draped in a fine linen sheath so sheer that I can see the frail rigging of her ribs. Her skin has been oiled and glistens in the torch light. Around her neck she displays a gleaming chest plate, brighter than the stars above and studded with lapis and rubies. The thin bones of her wrists and ankles are manacled with gold chains but she does not tremble, only raises her chin upwards and dares the crowd to heckle her in her moment of wretched humiliation. I want to shout at the crowd: voyeurs and villains all. The night swells with music, the banging of drums and the smack of sandals on stone.

Charmian takes my hand, and together we wait for the chants and jeers, obscene songs blown forth like foul breath.

And yet, after a minute I realise that the crowd has fallen silent. No one heckles or cheers or hurls handfuls of filth at her. It is like the stillness before dawn. The drums fade and there is only the sound of marching feet and then, I hear mutters of unease. They like to watch their enemies murdered, to see them writhe as the bones in their throats are crushed, and the whites of their eyes turn speckled and bloody. But they do not want this for her. As I stare at her, I can see that she senses it. Their lack of bloodlust.

The wagon stops beside us. She surveys the crowd, and for a moment her gaze rests on me. I look at her and she stares back at me. Neither of us smiles. I am here for her, my sister, despite all she has done. There's a jolt, and the wagon moves on and she's gone.

The procession continues on up the Capitoline Hill and to the temple of Jupiter. I see the wagon pause for a moment before the pillars of the temple, and then it continues on its way. Relief pours through me, warm as heated oil. They cannot kill her tonight. Not here, not like this. Satisfied, I turn to Charmian and Apollodorus. 'Let us return to the villa. We must be ready.'

Within an hour the villa is crammed with guests like flies around a rotting carcass. I watch concealed on the upper gallery as the men try not to marvel at frescoes so finely rendered they appear as a window into the boundless world of the gods. The scent of roses drifting inside from the garden does not mask their stench of stale sweat and envy.

These great men of Rome do not fool me. They finger the

linens estimating their cost and I see more than one senator slide his napkin into his pocket once he's dabbed his mouth. At other parties in Rome, guests are obliged to bring their own. Not at Cleopatra's. If only I could win them over, one napkin at a time. I've insisted that the best wine is served to all guests and not the cheaper variety to the lesser men. They may gossip about me and suspect me of all manner of wanton misdeeds, but they will not accuse me of parsimony. I know that many of them have only come to gawp at me and then scurry home, eager to spread lascivious gossip like a spray of cow shit upon a ploughed field.

I'm fidgeting with unease. Caesar isn't here yet. He called at home for a little while, and then he'll come as guest of honour. I must assemble myself before he arrives; be easy and charming, hide my discomfort. I look down upon the long dining room below. The walls are painted with trees so that the room inside seems to dissolve into the garden beyond. I watch the politicians in their togas lying side-by-side on the sofas, like landed trout lined up on the river bank, shoving morsels of food into gaping mouths.

It's time to let Rome see me. Charmian signals to the musicians; they change the song and play a different melody, not one of Rome but Egypt. At once, the chatter changes key too; everyone waits expectant, looking for me. I slip down the stairs at the end of the landing and out into the far side of the gardens, unseen by the guests. There, a hundred slaves dressed as nymphs are waiting for me, each bearing a torch. On Apollodorus's signal, they process before me, lighting the way. I pass between an avenue of statues, Roman and Egyptian gods. The final two, leading into the vast hall where the guests wait for me, are of Venus and Isis, they flank me on either side. The marble is bleached bone in the semi-darkness; the smell of honeysuckle, mint and thyme mingles with the scent of burning pine logs and sweat. The music rises, and the guests cease their conversations. I step forward, lit by a thousand torches, and linger for a moment between the stone goddesses, allowing the men and women of Rome to see me at last.

As I walk slowly forward, I notice a woman staring at me. Everyone stares, but there is something about her expression, at once intelligent and grave. She has large grey eyes, and she doesn't smile. Her face isn't beautiful, and even in this light I can see the lacework of fine lines around her eyes – she's a woman who's laughed a great deal. Strung around her neck is a pale ball that shimmers and snares the light, the moon on a string. Then I see that it's a pearl and at once, I know who she is.

Servilia.

18

SERVILIA

Clodia insisted that I came with her to Cleopatra's party. I didn't want to. Perhaps I was the only woman in Rome not curious to see Cleopatra. But Clodia was adamant that people would only talk more if I didn't attend, and reluctantly I decided she was probably right. For the first time, I decided to wear the pearl Caesar had given me. I would remind Rome of what I meant to him, in case they'd forgotten.

Cleopatra had sent dozens of boats to row us across the Tiber to the party on the opposite bank. The boats had been conveyed here all the way from Alexandria – or else the craftsmen had, for they were in the style of those on the Nile, low and narrow with sharp bows, with Egyptian oarsman to row us across. Clodia took one look and shook her head.

'Absolutely not. We're taking mine.'

To my amusement, her own vessel and boatman were already waiting. I was nervous about the party, unusually so, and as we were rowed across I watched the swaying lights of the lanterns and torches with trepidation. As we disembarked and walked through the gardens I sensed all eyes upon me. I felt sticky with their curiosity. To my surprise I felt an odd sympathy for Cleopatra. Their curiosity to see her was greater than it was about my reaction to her.

Brutus arrived with Portia, who to my relief melted away into the crowd, suddenly spotting a friend at the far side of the garden. Brutus moved quickly to my side.

'How much did you hate the triumph, Mother?'

'She loathed every moment,' replied Clodia before I could speak.

'But you were magnificent, my darling,' I said.

'Nonsense. You left before you even saw me. I know you, Mother.' Brutus laughed and kissed my cheek. As he leaned in, his face grew suddenly serious and he whispered, 'Cleopatra won't stay long in Rome. And she has nothing on you.'

I laughed at the sweetness of the lie. Surrounded by my children, and in the company of my son, the evening was becoming tolerable. With a glass of wine and amongst friends, I allowed myself to share in the curiosity about the Egyptian queen.

Initially, I found the pageantry of her entrance absurd. Anyone would have thought that the party was to celebrate Cleopatra and not Caesar. As the music changed from Roman melody into a lascivious foreign ditty, I noticed to my amusement that everyone else was transfixed. They were all butterflies in her net. This was a display to rival Caesar's own entrance. Not wise perhaps, but then she'd timed it just before his arrival.

I lingered at the edge of the loggia, beside Clodia and Brutus, and watched as the Egyptian queen stood in the doorway at the entrance to the villa, between the marble statues of two gods, waiting there so that the assembled company could marvel at her. She was a goddess amongst other gods, or so her gesture insinuated. The statues were painted marble renditions of Venus and Isis, most skilfully done. Isis bent to kiss the baby Horus in her arms, a kiss offered in perpetuity, never given, love infinitely bestowed. Beside her the Venus was exquisite, with the perfect tilt of her upturned throat. Yet these women's marbled beauty was cool in its perfection while in contrast Cleopatra had a vividness that even I could sense. She smiled, and looked about her, and appeared to buzz with life and thought. She was short in stature, and her face was pleasing enough but her forehead was too high, her eyes too wide-set. Even though her beauty might be less perfect than that of Venus, she seemed to exude warmth. Candlelight played on her skin. I'd always known she was clever, so of course she knew how to display herself to her best advantage. I was not surprised for Caesar always valued that more than beauty. The intelligent young princess I'd met years ago had grown into a skilful politician.

'The problem is,' I whispered to Clodia and Brutus, 'can a man bed a queen, without sooner or later yearning to be a king himself?'

Clodia laughed, although it was not a joke. Brutus said nothing, only sipped his wine.

'She's looking at you,' whispered Clodia.

To my surprise I realised that she was right, and that the Egyptian queen watched me steadily, her expression pensive. I'd wondered about her; it never occurred to me that she might be curious about me. Did she remember me?

After a moment, Cleopatra disappeared into the villa to await Caesar. We lingered in the gardens, grateful for fresh air. I didn't attend to the conversation, my mind crowded with thoughts of the Egyptian queen. After some minutes there was an eruption of shouts to the east. Men yelled and there was the frenzied whinny of a horse, the iron clatter of hooves upon stone, and I assumed at first that it was Caesar arrived at last. Brutus, however, gave a small sigh and thrust his cup at a slave, saying, 'Take this and get me a bucket, will you?'

He hurried away, easing between the other guests, and I heard the bellowing get louder. It was followed by the sound of breaking pottery and a waterfall of laughter. I followed behind, curious. I discovered Brutus standing in the vestibule with Marc Antony draped over his shoulders like a cloak. Marc Antony was tall and broad with thick glossy curls and the rosy cheeks of an infant. Yet, this softness was at odds with the solid bulk of his arm muscles, their tendons like coiled rope. There were livid scars criss-crossing over his arms and neck and I guessed that they continued beneath his tunic, hatching his chest and back. Here was a warrior who displayed his battle scars as Cleopatra did her jewels and diadems. The man himself was so sodden with drink he could barely stand, but grinned through wine-stained teeth and began to sing crude songs about the women Caesar had bedded. To my relief, he omitted my name. Then, if he'd uttered it, I would have slapped him. Fulvia hurried to him, her lips a narrow line of distaste.

'Antony, come sit and eat something to soak up the wine in your belly. I can hear it sloshing about like a ship on rough waves,' said Brutus, interrupting Antony's lascivious ballad.

He ignored my son and began to sing again.

'Antony, do shut up,' snapped Fulvia.

Antony made to reply and then leaned over and retched. The slave was ready for it, holding out the bucket underneath Antony's chin. Fulvia stepped forward and now supported him with surprising strength, as a narrow stake holds up a leaning tree. Antony vomited loudly into the bucket, chatting amiably between heaving bouts.

'Well, fair ladies? What did you think of the show?' he asked, glancing at me and Fulvia.

He could not hear our reply over the sound of his own spasms. I was thoroughly revolted by the spectacle and wondered why Fulvia would choose to marry such a specimen. If he had hidden depths, they were truly submerged.

On finishing, Antony handed the bucket back to the slave with good cheer, totally unembarrassed. He grabbed another cup of wine from a passing slave, swilled the liquid round his mouth and then spat out the contents into the bucket.

'I liked the lions best. I think we should have lions to draw our chariot, Fulvia,' declared Antony.

'No, thank you. We shall not,' she replied sharply.

Antony laughed with apparent delight. 'I love it when you fight with me. But you know I always win.'

'I know no such thing,' replied Fulvia.

While they bickered, I noticed a change blowing across the other guests. Voices softened, becalmed. It was as if the air itself had suddenly stirred and thickened. I glanced about for Cleopatra and saw that she alone did not react. Through the archway, she moved smiling amongst her guests and did not look towards the door.

'Come, Antony, Caesar approaches,' said Brutus.

Antony, like Cleopatra, was unperturbed. He grinned, pleased as Caesar entered flanked by his Praetorian guards on either side. Everyone watched, and one by one, senators scurried forward to shower him with compliments. For all their grovelling, none of them bowed as this was Rome and there are no kings here. Cleopatra observed from a little distance away in the tablinum, making no move towards him. Yet, I noted that she was careful to stand beneath the most gilded spot on the ceiling, surrounded by a constellation of candles, so that she was heavenly lit. Whatever the chatter of my fellow citizens, I understood that she was no concubine of Egypt, she did not need to rush over and join the band of sycophants. She waited for him to come to her. I remained still, watching them all.

Antony, unabashed and apparently indifferent to protocol or ceremony, strode forward and pushing the others aside embraced his friend, kissing his cheek. I noticed Caesar wince and recoil on observing how drunk he was, his kisses sour with drying vomit. His gaze rested on me for a moment, our eyes met, and he gave a tiny smile, acknowledging me, and I could tell that he was pleased I had come. Seeing his pleasure, I was almost glad I had.

Senators continued to crowd him, lobbing congratulations and obsequious praise at him. In their white togas they made me think of woolly ewes crushed around a bale of hay. I watched in amusement as Caesar extricated himself; he wanted none of them now, he looked only for Cleopatra. Noticing her through the arches, he strode towards her, guests parting before him.

Turning, she smiled at him and opened her arms. In the candlelight, dressed in robes shot through with gold thread, her skin seemed to glow. Her black hair was woven in tight knots upon her head, so dark it blended with the shadows, and the massive jewels hanging around her chest made her throat appear naked and impossibly slender.

I felt a pang, not of jealousy, but sadness and concern. It was clear to me now that if he did not love her, then he was infatuated. I worried that his judgement was off, spoiled like old meat. Her slave had traced kohl around her eyes, and now they shone with an appearance of mischief and delight. For a moment, I saw her as Caesar did: an earthbound star, shimmering amongst sweating mortals. I was conscious of my plain dress, the grey streaking my hair. Even the pearl around my throat seemed absurd gilding, I never should have worn it. I felt ridiculous. And then I chided myself for my foolishness. Caesar did not love me for my face, but for my mind, and that had only sharpened even if my jawline had softened just a little.

Clodia tried to tug me away, clearly concerned, but I shook her off. I had to watch them. I admired the queen's skill. There was witchery in it. She conjured a whiff of the divine from the air like a naiad is summoned from its tree or pool. I might not approve, but I could understand his fascination with her. He took her in his arms then leaned forward and whispered in her ear and she gave a small, private smile. Everyone else was watching them too, silent.

I didn't like seeing her beside Caesar. Not out of envy, but because her youth and energy showed Caesar's age in sharp relief. Beside her, Caesar appeared mighty but worn, a marvellous statue with its nose chipped by years of winter frosts, edges sloughed away. The bare spot on the top of his head was mottled and sunburned, starting to flake. For the first time, I could see it as the fading of the light at summer's end. I had not noticed it before. And, if I sensed the decline of Caesar, so soon would the rest of Rome. He kissed her slowly and deliberately on each cheek. There was a dangerous stillness all about them. I wanted to stride over there and shake him, hiss at him to be careful, beware.

The guests shuffled aside as a small procession came into the room accompanied by the sweet music of a dozen flutes. Several slaves acting as nurses were dedicated to the care of young Ptolemy, Cleopatra's younger brother, who trailed behind. He looked about twelve, gawky and scowling, a child on the edge of adolescence. The guests looked on, fascinated. Little Ptolemy was not only Cleopatra's brother, but her husband. As I glanced around their faces – all petrified with delighted horror – I knew they were all trying to decide whether they had fucked. Caesar told me they had not. I would not tell though, let the rest of Rome be mesmerised by their prurient imaginings.

Cleopatra gestured to a young female slave carrying a stout and wriggling toddler to come to her. The slave passed the writhing baby to its mother. The child had golden skin like Cleopatra and the curling hair of Caesar before it started to thin. The babe began to buck and howl, tired and unhappy in the crowded room full of strange and hostile eyes. Caesar's son. Now I felt a fierce pang. In this sobbing, wriggling boy with his tear-streaked cheeks and runny nose, Egypt and Rome were united, but so too were Cleopatra and Caesar, joined in parenthood. She shared something with him that I could not.

'What's he going to do?' whispered Clodia. 'He ought to ignore the brat if he knows what's good for him.'

'How do we even know it's Caesar's issue?' wondered Brutus. 'They say she's bedded half her court.'

I waved at them both to shush. 'I taught you better than to listen to rumour. Look at the child, let your own eyes answer your question. Of course he is Caesar's.'

For once, I realised that I did not know how Caesar would react – erupt in fury that she'd allowed the child downstairs amongst company? Dismiss him in contempt? Either would surely spell catastrophe for Cleopatra. Was this what I wanted? I didn't know.

Then, Caesar stepped closer still and bestowed another kiss upon Cleopatra's upturned face and a moment later, before the array of senators and citizens of Rome, he placed a kiss upon his young son's forehead, publicly acknowledging him. The boy continued to howl, turning rigid in his fear and rage, oblivious that he'd just been recognised as the son of the most powerful man in the world. Everyone else understood the significance. The last of the air seemed to be sucked out so quickly that I wondered that all the candles did not extinguish. I felt the hiss of disapproval and contempt as poisonous vapour. Neither Cleopatra nor Caesar appeared to care. I clenched my fists at my sides, furious at their obliviousness.

19

CLEOPATRA

I recline on a sofa in the first tablinum, lit by a hundred wavering candles, a scroll dangling between my fingers, unread. The air is heady with the scent of beeswax and night herbs drifting in from the garden just beyond the open windows. Charmian is slotted beside me. There's no one else here, we're as we were when girls, lying nose to nose, fingertips touching.

'Why do we stay here? You've persuaded Caesar to acknowledge his son.' She stifles a sigh and asks, 'Can we go home, my queen?'

I look at her and smile. Her forehead is creased with longing, she pines for Alexandria. The sea and the clear blue air.

'Soon, dearest one. When I leave, he forgets me. I must

give him something more, so he remembers me. Only then will we be safe.'

This is true but what I don't confide is that I'm also not ready to leave him yet. I want our son to know his father, not merely through his deeds and renown but as a man. I loved my father, for all his flaws. I don't want Caesarion to share only a name with his.

Within a few minutes, I realise from the steady huff of Charmian's breath that she's snoozing in the drowsy heat of the fire. I must have drifted off myself, as when I awake, it's to find that Caesar himself is come, and is watching us, smiling, his expression tender. I nudge Charmian, and her eyes blink open and on seeing Caesar she immediately stands up and leaves the room. Caesar comes and settles in the spot still warm from Charmian's body. He lies beside me, his fingers stroke my hair, trace my lips, my chin. I allow myself to relax, soften into him for a breath. I'm always on guard, watchful, but here in Caesar's arms, I am safe for a moment.

'You will declare me a friend of Rome?' I ask softly.

'You are this Roman's friend,' he says and kisses me.

I stiffen; this is not what I mean, and he knows it. My father gave away Cyprus in order to be declared a friend of Rome. I have given Caesar something no less valuable and now I need the title in return. To call me 'friend' is to declare that Rome shall not seek to absorb Egypt into its empire for as long as I rule. I will find a way to persuade him to name me so. I know that Caesar is fond of me. He desires and admires me, recognising his own ambition reflected back like Narcissus at the mirror pool. Yet, his affection is neither strong enough nor blind enough for him to give me what I want unless it's also expedient for him and for Rome. These limits do not hurt me or wound my pride for I understand the edges of his affection, and mine is no different. My own desires come second to what is good for Egypt.

Caesar is subdued and does not speak for several minutes. His thoughts are opaque to me – but I can tell that something is nagging at him, a pebble in his shoe.

'Rome despises all kings,' he says at last.

At first, I think he's telling me that he can't give me the title of friend, but then I realise it isn't me he's talking about at all.

'They killed their last king,' he adds, half to himself.

'Yes, but long ago,' I reply.

And then with a slow realisation, I understand what he wants. He longs for the power I have. As I examine his face, I know what I must do: voice his own desires. He will not confess this desire to Servilia or another Roman. Only a queen can understand the longing of a man to be king. He is half-afraid to speak aloud his own greatest desire, so I shall say it for him. This will be my gift to him; to show him that Rome is ready for a king, so long as that king is called Caesar. He has been to Egypt, he has seen how we rule. Kingship is the only feat he has not yet achieved. I can see how it nags at him. If I help him become king, then he'll owe me a debt of gratitude sufficient to give me what I want.

I hesitate for a moment, then prop myself up on my elbows and meet his eye.

'What's the difference between you and a king? You have the power of a king. What is "king" that Caesar is not? It is but another word, and a smaller one at that?'

As I speak, I see the longing in his face. He's conquered half the world, killed a million men, and is draped in accolades and adulation, and yet still he hankers for more. I understand his yearning, more than anyone in the world. I killed my brother and defeated my sister to win my throne. He watches me intently, lit by his desire. I lick dry lips and continue.

'Rome despised kings long ago. But those kings were tyrants. Caesar is no tyrant. He is bountiful and just. All of Rome loves Caesar.'

Caesar looks at me narrowly and gives a short laugh. 'All of Rome does not love Caesar. Most of Rome loves Caesar, the rest is merely afraid of him.'

He is silent, thinking. I can hear the click and whirr of his thoughts like a death-watch beetle in old oak beams. I clear my throat and say carefully, 'No one can be loved universally. Such a thing is not possible. But do enough men in Rome love you? I would hazard so, but you are quite right, we cannot trust to guesses. A man does not step out onto a new-laid bridge across a stream without trying the plank first to see if it's steady and can bear his weight. Why not test the people, see if they're ready to accept a king?'

He stares at me, now intrigued. 'It is not possible. Not here in Rome.'

Yet his voice lacks conviction, and I hear the note of hope, eager beneath the surface.

'Have you not been declared dictator for life? That would be impossible for another man,' I say.

I understand the stark difference between a dictator and a king: a dictator dies and turns to dust; a king's son rules after his father's death. Upstairs, our son sleeps. He will one day rule Egypt. Is it possible that he could also become king of Rome? I am dizzy at the thought. I had not dared to imagine such power for him, and yet it is not only power but danger – a foreign-born bastard king to rule over Rome. A voice whispers to me that they will never allow it. They will kill him first. Already there are those in Rome who hanker for my son's death. Might this not make them more determined to murder him? My dizziness deepens to a sick feeling deep in the well of my stomach. Caesar has acknowledged our son, but he has not – as far as I know – made him his heir. The law here forbids it. Yet, laws can be made new for Caesar. There is heaviness deep in my belly, a tossing fear, reminding me how much our fate is bound to that of Caesar, for good or ill.

Yet the possibility of such power for my boy is too much to turn away from. I have never acted out of fear and I won't start now. I will advise Caesar so as to advance the future of my son. Caesar watches me steadily. He's greedy for more words, for me to tell him that what he wants is possible. I've finally said aloud that which he's longed for in secret, thinking only alone in the dark. With my words, I've made it real, possible.

His ambition and his decisions are entirely his own. As I meet his gaze, I understand with a tug of sorrow that he has no fear for anyone other than himself. He does not worry about us for our own sakes or how his actions might ripple outward from himself. But this is the way of a king. It was mine too, before I had a son. Caesarion is ours, but truly, he belongs only to me. Caesar is fond of the boy, and amused by his likeness to himself, but his affection is selfish. He will not choose what is best for his son at the cost of his own good fortune. His love is brittle and shallow. He will not hold him when he sickens, for fear of sickening himself. This path that Caesar seeks poses not only possibility but also danger for our son; a danger that Caesar does not consider nor would make him hesitate for a moment, even if he sensed it. I feel some of my affection for Caesar dry out like damp sand in the desert sun. Yet, I must play my part: lover, confidante, advisor. It is what is best for Caesarion. I take a breath. Try not to picture my boy's small form in the nursery, snoozing under his blankets, the pink upturned lip, the feathered lashes.

'And how would Cleopatra suggest I discover if Rome is ready?' asks Caesar, eager.

I shove my worries further down and think for a minute.

'Is Lupercal soon? That's a festival here in Rome, ribald and joyous?'

'It is.'

'Then, have someone offer you a crown before the crowd. A senator, white-haired and honest. Someone you trust absolutely.'

'Marc Antony.'

I hesitate. Antony is loyal beyond reproach, but he is certainly not white-haired with wisdom, and I am yet to see him sober. Still, I defer to Caesar.

'Antony then. He will offer you the crown, and the crowd will urge him to place it upon your head. But if you sense any reluctance or hesitation amongst them, you must demur and refuse it. They will love you for your modesty.'

'I shall decline it,' he declares, resolute. 'And only accept it if they urge me with full-throated ardour.'

I smile, allowing him to take the idea on, have it become

his own. He is picturing the scene, the crowd in the forum, their frenzied urging.

'And it shall not be a crown of gold but instead a wreath of laurels,' he says.

His eye is feverish in its brightness. He has never wanted me – nor, I suspect any man nor woman – as he wants this.

He takes my hand and kisses it. 'You are to me as Venus is to Mars,' he says.

He flatters me, but I pocket his compliments all the same. I enjoy his personal endearments, but I treasure his public declarations of regard. I am already transformed from Isis into the Roman Venus in her temple. My likeness sits on her dais, benevolent and beautiful, ready for all citizens of Rome to pay tribute.

I understand Caesar's desire to be a king. And, for better or worse, it is my task to help him: that's what he wants from me. I must pray to the gods to watch over my boy. That the ambitions of the father don't wound the son. I remember the words of the soothsayer in Alexandria – that the fruit will outlive the tree – and am comforted. There is not only the possibility of danger for Caesarion, but also power and an empire.

And yet, after Caesar leaves me to return home, I find I cannot sleep. I am hot and restless, and when I rise early in the morning, my eyes are red-rimmed as the dawn sun.

It's damp and the smell of rain is in the air. I do not like this cold season in Rome and it's not only Charmian who pines for the steady warmth of home. I want to inhale the breeze scented with figs and date palms, not open drains.

Charmian and Apollodorus have the slaves light fires in every room and toss herbs upon the flames. Now at least the smell of mint and thyme mingles with the scent of burning pine logs in the grate disguising the stench of the city. There are shouts and cries and then Iras enters, prostrating herself upon the floor as she says, 'I beg forgiveness, great queen, but I couldn't stop her.'

I see a tiny woman, bent in two like a windblown tree, her skin cracked as bark and her white hair in tight curls. She glares at me with black eyes: Apollodorus's eyes.

'I'm here for my son.'

She tosses a bag on the ground and gold coins spill out, rolling across the floor, tiny spinning suns.

Apollodorus strides forward, his face contorted in fear and anger. 'Mother, you should not have come. The queen told my sister that coming here again would mean death.'

'If you don't come home, then I will die anyway. If she kills me, then it will be quicker,' she snaps.

Apollodorus tries to take her outside, clasping her around her tiny waist. He's several times her size, but he doesn't want to hurt her and she wriggles free from his grasp and she turns to me, hissing.

'They say that Apollodorus is one of your favourites. If that's true, great queen, then let him go. Not for gold but friendship. There are no men left in our family. The farm goes to ruin, it falls away into the hillside and our neighbours steal our animals. His sister and her children will starve. We will have to sell them as slaves.'

'Such things are unfortunate, but they happen every day. I am sorry for you,' I say.

'But not sorry enough to give him back to us,' says the old woman, resigned. 'I see that it isn't true. They lie. For you do not love him. He is just a chattel slave like any other.'

Her voice is gnarled with disdain and flecks of spittle lodge in the corners of her mouth. She screws up her face and then glances away, as if she can't bear to look upon me anymore.

Anger rises in me, and I turn to Apollodorus, my voice soft with fury. 'Take her away from here. It is out of affection for you that I do not have her whipped and crucified.'

'I thank you for your mercy, great queen,' he answers.

Then, as the old woman shouts and mutters, he hustles her away, braving the blows that rain down on his face and arms. I sit beside the fire, but the chill doesn't leave me and the scent of burning incense is bitter and catches in my throat. I'm irritable, and even when the slaves bring Caesarion to me, I can't recover my good humour. Apollodorus wisely keeps away from me. Charmian tries to read to me, but I tell her to leave me alone. I look into the fire, but in the flames, I just see the old woman's face, her eyes black with hate.

Fulvia has responded quickly to my summons and I'm grateful. It does not matter that it's more likely out of curiosity than obedience. She enters the chamber looking about her with shrewd dark eyes. The customary refreshments are set upon the table. Fulvia doesn't even glance at them, she just watches me steadily, interested as to the reason that I have specifically asked her to come.

'Are we to be friends, great queen?' she asks. 'For if a queen orders friendship, then it must be granted.'

There is no warmth in her voice.

'I hope we are to be friends. Allies, certainly.'

Now, she is intrigued. I gesture for her to sit on the sofa opposite me and I take a seat myself. I look at her, the polished curls, the bridal flush on her cheeks and the girlish pout. I'm not fooled. I know what this woman is: clever and ruthless. She is a knife secreted in a pretty sheath.

I tell Fulvia of Caesar's intention on Lupercal. 'I urge you to persuade Antony to agree to his suggestion.'

She studies me with those clever black eyes.

'You would be married to the proxy of the king,' I say softly.

Fulvia's cheeks are pinker still, flushed with the glow of anticipated power. She does not answer just yet, but I am confident that she will do as I ask. Not out of any love or loyalty towards me, but because of her own desires. Sometimes as women our power is indirect, we must persuade men to move in the direction we choose; they are the ships but we are the breeze that fills their sails and pushes them across the oceans. Fulvia meets my eye and I know that she understands this too.

I signal to Charmian, who brings me a box. I unfasten it, and removing the jewel within, I present it to Fulvia, laying it on her lap.

'A hairpin set with jewels from Egypt. As exquisite as it is sharp,' I say.

She inclines her neck forward and I slide it into the twist of her hair. The rubies gleam amongst her dark hair, bright as drops of blood. We are allies now indeed.

★

That afternoon, I walk through the gardens alone, ordering the slaves to leave me. My head aches, and the feeling of prickly irritability has stayed with me, like a fever in my soul. As I walk to the fountain, I hear the sound of weeping. The sound mingles with the trickle of the water. I'm about to turn back – I have no interest in the crying of slaves – when I see that it is Charmian. She's huddled on a bench beside the water, her face puffy and blotched. Hearing me, she looks up in surprise and hurriedly wipes her eyes and nose on her tunic, leaving a trail of snot. Her eyes are red and swollen.

'I'm sorry, great queen. I did not mean for you to find me.'

I look at her for a moment. Her sudden sorrow separates her from me and for the first time I do not know what to say to her. Am I her queen or her friend? Then, I sit, and put a tentative arm on her shoulder. At once, she wriggles closer and sobs on my lap, her shoulders shaking as I stroke her hair.

'What is it, my love?' I ask. 'What grieves you?'

'Apollodorus.'

'Why, have you fought?' I ask. I have no experience with lovers' quarrels.

'No. He is despondent. Filled with grief and despair, and rages against fate and his helplessness. He was taken as a slave in war. Then gifted to you. He does not own his own life and he accepts this. There's nothing he can do. He can't leave you. He loves you and does not ask to be freed. But, he can't look after his mother or widowed sisters. His mother will die, she's too old to be bought. His sister and her children will be sold as slaves.'

Her words fall away into sobs. I stroke her hair, it's soggy with tears and sweat.

'You can't want me to free him. Then he'll leave you.'

She looks up at me, her face shiny with tears. 'But I do want you to free him. I love him. And love is freedom. He will leave me and I will be happy for him and my heart will break.'

I stare at her, unsettled by the force of her love for this man. I do not care for Caesar like this. My affection is a pleasant warmth.

'If you really want me to free him, I will consider your request,' I say. 'You've never asked me for anything before.'

'I do,' she says. 'I love him. Free him. Let him go.'

I'm preoccupied with Charmian's appeal and relieved that my day is strewn with visitors to distract me, some more agreeable than others. I understand that they are all come to peer at the Egyptian queen with dread and delight as they would a tiger or elephant dragged back to Rome. And yet, I need their favour, so I endure their insolent curiosity. I hear the bustle of arrival, and then Iras enters, announcing the newest visitors. I signal for them to be brought into my presence and the two women enter. The day is cool and a fine mist of drizzle falls, and both wear soft woollen shawls draped over their stola. Clodia is baubled with jewels, Servilia wears none at all. I am pleased to see Clodia, for she is entertaining and full of mischief, but I had not invited Servilia to my villa, and Clodia pushes the bounds of civility by bringing her along like a flagon of olives or a present of silks. I admire her, and yet, I know that Caesar loves her in a way that he does not me and her presence irritates me like stiff leather on new sandals. She is the woman who he has adored since before I was born.

His affection towards her seemingly never faltered in all those years. I examine her face, trying to understand the attraction, the allure that has captivated him beyond all others, but apart from the soft intelligence of her eyes, I cannot see anything remarkable about her face. Then, I do not expect to. Beauty fades, and Caesar did not love Servilia for hers.

She says, 'Caesar is building a library. He says it will rival that at Alexandria.'

I laugh. 'It's not possible, but I always admire Caesar's ambition.'

Servilia gives a sigh full of longing. 'I heard the originals of Plato and Aristotle are in Alexandria. Will you lend them to Rome?'

'It is not a loan when an item is not returned. Once those volumes entered Rome, my love should not let them leave again. Caesar may keep my heart but not my books.'

Servilia studies me for a moment in silence, shuffling her thoughts like a sheaf of papers, before asking softly, 'Does he truly keep your heart, great queen?'

I do not reply. The affairs of my heart are my own. And the awkwardness of my silence is cut short as Charmian enters, bringing with her Caesarion, who is clutching his toy crocodile and sobbing.

'He wanted only you, madam,' she says, apologetic. 'You said to bring him to you if we couldn't settle him.'

I hold open my arms, grateful for the interruption. He climbs onto my lap, and I play with the silk of his hair.

'What's the matter, little one?' I ask, as his cheeks are flushed crimson.

He doesn't answer, only chews his fists, saliva trickling

down his chin. I pick him up but he twists away, crying. His distress is a bruise, and as if sensing my unhappiness, Servillia looks at me, saying, 'May I try to help, great queen?'

I study her, searching for some agenda, but see none other than a mother offering her support. I nod and she comes over to us and kneels on the floor beside us. She puts her face down close to his, and smiles, covering her hands and peeking at him. Then a moment later she produces a feather from her sleeve and tickles him with it.

'Is your knee tickly?' she asks. 'Or your nose?' As she plays, she smiles and her face is suddenly bright with warmth and mischief.

Caesarion stops grizzling and giggles.

'You're a mother,' I say.

'Yes, and a grandmother,' replies Servilia. 'See? His cheeks are swollen, and he dribbles. Poor babe is teething. Have the slave bring cloves, honey and a pestle.'

I nod to Charmian, who hurries out.

Servilia continues to play with Caesarion, tickling first him and then his toy crocodile, which she pretends is snapping at her fingers. Clodia moves to sit with us and joins in the game. Charmian returns with the cloves and Servilia begins to grind up the mixture. When she has finished, she places a little on her finger, pretending to smear it on the crocodile's mouth, saying, 'He has such sore gums, we'll make him feel better. But he's a little afraid. Can you be a big, brave boy and show Croc that he has nothing to be scared of?'

With only a little reluctance, Caesarion nods and obediently opens his mouth and lets Servilia gently spread the concoction over his swollen gums. She smiles at him and as she does, she looks younger, a woman full of life and fun. I feel the last of my instinctive hostility towards her begin to trickle away. I wonder what it would be like to have such women as Servilia and Clodia as friends. I push the thought away. I do not have friends other than Charmian, and I am not foolish enough to forget that she is also my slave.

Caesarion takes the pestle and starts to smear the mix all over his toy, muttering words of tender comfort, and the three of us glance at one another. We are connected for a second. It's a moment of easiness where I could almost believe us friends, or that it might be possible if we were different women, these different times.

It's apparent that the medicine has eased Caesarion's discomfort, and he suddenly looks tired, smudged with sleep. I gesture to a nursery slave, who takes him from me to settle him for a nap. I watch him go, feeling a tug of love. A moment later, Clodia rises and excuses herself, taking her leave in what is clearly a careful pretext. Servilia and I stare at each other with open curiosity. I remember her from when I was a girl. She was kind and clever and already Caesar's lover. And he loves you still, I whisper in my mind. His affection is split between us, do you resent me for reducing your portion? But then perhaps love does not divide and dwindle but swells and multiplies. I think of Charmian and her selfless affection for Apollodorus. I wonder how such love would feel.

I dismiss the slaves, for we need no audience. I pour her a glass of wine with my own hands and give it to her. She drinks it all in one long swallow, and I realise to my surprise that she's nervous. I wonder what's troubling her. She bites her lip, hesitates. The easiness of a few minutes earlier has entirely gone. Then at last she says in a low, clear voice, 'We are tethered to one another by our love of Julius.'

Any other woman who dared to suggest that we shared a bond, I'd dismiss in contempt and anger, outraged at the insult, and yet there is something about Servilia's sweet gravity that gives me pause. I cannot dislike her.

'I have loved him, wanted only what is best and good for him, for thirty years. That has never altered,' she continues.

She pauses, as though waiting for me to speak, to reassure her of my love for Caesar. I do not. My regard for him is my own, not to be pored over even by her.

'We are not enemies but allied through our affections. What is good and right for him is also in our interests.'

'Your voice suggests a question, but you ask none,' I say.

'Be careful,' she pleads. 'This is Rome. You sharpen his ambition, where it needs no whetting. We both want what is best for him.'

'Yes, but perhaps we don't agree on what that is.' I pause and examine her closely. 'Do you ask me to return to Egypt?'

'I would never presume upon such a request.'

Though I'm certain she will not weep when I depart.

'I only ask you not to stoke his desires and ambition. I ask this not out of jealousy but love,' she says, a note of pleading still in her voice.

In that moment, I pity her. She is soggy with love. Where I admire Caesar, she needs him. My affection for him is sincere yet it is also tempered by caution. I know what he is, and that Caesar's greatest passion is neither me nor Servilia but himself and his own restless need for power. I suspect that she knows this too yet is devoted to him anyway. Her love for him is absolute, and it has softened her reason. I turn and walk from the room without another word, leaving her alone.

I return to my chamber and lie on the bed amongst the silks and cushions, but I don't sleep. A bee thuds gently against the ceiling, and I watch it for several minutes, its futile determination. I go to the table and fetch a wooden box, simply inlaid with ivory and ebony. Then, I summon Charmian and Apollodorus to my chamber. They stand before me side-by-side, not touching, and yet I can feel the connection between them, the tautness of an invisible thread. Charmian's face is still pale and swollen. Apollodorus looks pinched and drawn. Neither of them speaks. I look at them both and then open the small wooden box at my side and take out a scroll and pass it to him, saying slowly, 'Apollodorus, I grant you your freedom. This is a gift. You are at liberty to return to your family and home. Go with our love and our blessing.'

He stares at me, as though not quite believing what he's heard. Then, he looks at the scroll and, reading it, sees that it is true. My lawyer has drawn up the deed, declaring he's a freedman, and giving him back his family name. Apollodorus passes it to Charmian, who reads it in silence. She glances up, her face a contradiction of pain and joy, and then she begins to sob, shaking as hard as if she had mosquito fever. Apollodorus holds her close, and she smiles up at him through her tears.

'You will go and be happy and think of me sometimes,' she says softly. 'But only if the thought makes you happy, for I cannot bear you to be sad.'

I don't hear his reply, for he hugs her close, whispers in her ear, and she buries her face against his chest. I feel hot, my palms sticky, and yet my mouth is dry. I both want this next moment over, and for it to never come at all. I force myself to speak, to keep my voice from shaking.

'Charmian, we have been together since our births, an hour apart. You are the sister of my heart. I grant you your freedom and gift you a new name.'

I take a second deed out of the box and pass it to her, saying, 'Your name as a freedwoman is Charmian Cleopatra Beloved. You are free to go with Apollodorus. To marry him and have his children with our love and our blessing.'

In her shock, she stops crying and stares at me in confusion. I can see that she is too surprised to speak. Apollodorus, realising it too, goes down on his knees before me, in gratitude, tugging her down beside him.

'We thank you, great queen. For your love and generosity.'

I wave away his words for I do not want to be thanked. The pain that I feared now starts to build in my chest. I fear it will overwhelm me, a vast wave over a stone, and Cleopatra does not cry.

'Go,' I say. 'I only ask that you leave at once.'

Charmian rises and flings her arms around me. She kisses my cheeks, but I can't look at her for I can't bear to see my own pain reflected in her eyes or worse, that I don't see it.

'I'll miss you,' she whispers. 'Every single day.'

'Go now,' I say.

Apollodorus takes her hand and tugs her away from me, as though half afraid I will change my mind. When they have gone, I sit, slumped on the bed. The room is empty. I am alone. I have never loved Caesar or any man how I love Charmian. And for her, I have committed a selfless act, perhaps the only one in my life. There is no power to be gained for me by granting her freedom, there is only pain. And yet I would do it a hundred times over. I sit and listen to the chattering of the starlings outside the window, but other than the noise of the birds, it's absolutely quiet. I can almost hear the cracking of my own heart.

That night I cannot sleep and I wander through the gardens in the dark. Slaves trail after me, sticky with sleep, and I dismiss them, wanting only to be alone. I try to take comfort in the knowledge that Charmian will be happy. She will have an ordinary life – a husband who is kind and who loves her and, in time, children. I picture the farm in Sicily, the vineyards and silver olive groves where their unborn children will play. Perhaps they will have daughters who'll race scorpions beneath the lemon trees. It must be enough for me to know that she will be content and delight in simple joys. And yet, there is an ache in my chest that will not ease. It hurts like a physical pain and I want to walk and run to outpace it but I know that I cannot. The loss will follow me, and I cannot shake myself free however fast I run.

The night is restless, and I am not the only one awake; birds swirl, flitting from tree to tree in dark clouds when they should be roosting. The river rushes in the distance and the air is cool on my skin. I shiver, drawing my shawl tight around my shoulders. The wind lifts the leaves and catches the fountains so that I'm spattered with the spray. My forehead is damp despite the chill and I can smell my own sweat, sharp and animal. There's a restlessness in the air, a hum, and glancing up, I see the moon is smothered by clouds. I realise I'm holding my breath, and then, suddenly, there's a snap of lightning, and the garden is illuminated for a moment, the statues of the gods bright and white across the gardens for a heartbeat. And then a storm snarls up out of nowhere, the snaps of lightning are the clash of armies, and the sky is teeming with cries, souls of the restless dead. The slaves rush to me, their faces full of fear, hurrying me towards the house. I try to offer words of comfort to them, but I can't be heard above the clatter of celestial armies in the heavens above. The rain starts, a sudden sluicing, and in moments, I'm wet to the skin. I walk back to the villa, glancing upwards, my face dripping. There was no warning of this storm, it has blown across the city in a whorl of wind and rain and white light.

I stand on the veranda and look out at the flashes across Rome, the rents in the sky. The slaves strip off my sodden clothes and redress me. From above, I hear Caesarion wake and begin to cry. His whimpering is a tug I feel in my chest and, shaking off the slaves, I hurry up the stairs to him, stumbling in my haste. He sits in his crib, his face slick with tears and snot. Iras reaches for him, but I shoo her away and pluck him from his bed myself and clutch him to my chest. I can feel the rapid stutter of his heart against my own. He is warm and damp with tears and sleep, and I blanket his soft head with kisses. He burrows into my neck, and I inhale his soft, milky scent. His small body trembles with fear and rage at being woken by the storm. Iras comes to find us, her face grey.

'This storm isn't natural. It's the raging of the gods,' she whispers.

'These paltry Roman gods can't hurt us,' I soothe. 'Let them spill out their rage, like milk onto wool.'

Iras' face stays tight with anxiety, and Caesarion sobs on my shoulder. I sway, and rub Caesarion's back, feeling the downy skin of his back beneath my fingertips. At last, his sobs slow and falter into nothing and he becomes heavy in my arms. I don't lay him down straightaway but let him sleep against me, even though he's stout enough now that my arms ache. I am empty when I'm not holding him. All must be well, it must, for I have a secret that no one else knows.

As I think about it, I feel once more a flickering in my belly like the coil of a leaf turning over and over in the wind. I clasp one son in my arms, as my unborn son quickens in my womb. All shall be well, for I will make it so for these two boys, the one in my arms and the one yet to be born. My joy is muffled, I experience it through a veil of fear and loss. As the rain continues to fall, I feel a seeping grey dread slide across my mind like a sea fog on a damp day that will not lift.

20

SERVILIA

I walked out in the garden, placing tributes to Mars and Diana on their altar. I'd not forgotten how they'd delivered my retribution upon Pompey, and I gave them regular offerings in gratitude. I had not seen Cleopatra since I'd called upon her and played with her little son. I hoped her boy would never suffer the same fear and loss as mine. As I laid nuts, wine and a small bouquet of spring flowers – narcissi, primroses and columbine – before their statues, I found myself murmuring a prayer for the safe-keeping of both our boys. They too were connected, not through blood but love; Caesar loved them both as his sons. As I took deep, cooling breaths laced with the scent of new spring flowers, I experienced something like peace and hope, the tickle of early sunshine on my face.

There was discussion of Caesar taking his legions and defeating the Parthians. Usually, I'd learn of his departure for a campaign with a mixture of resignation and dread, yet now I heard of his plans with something more like relief. I thought it best that he journey far from Rome and from Cleopatra. I worried about the influence she had over him; she put kindling onto the furnace of his ambition. Until her arrival, I'd never sensed in him a desire to be king. Perhaps he could exorcise some of his more reckless ambitions on the battlefield.

I heard a familiar voice calling my name and turning, I saw Brutus walking towards me. I smiled to see him. The sight of him was always as the sun sliding out from behind a cloud. Today, however, he did not smile back and I could tell from the way he strode towards me that he was out of spirits. He'd barely greeted me before he said, voice rising in anger, 'I do not like to speak of Caesar with disrespect for I know what he means to you, but I fear his mind is overturned. By age or excess of power, I cannot tell.'

'Careful, Brutus,' I said, a note of warning in my voice. However annoyed I was with Caesar, I did not like anyone else to speak ill of him.

'Believe me when I say that I am trying. This is the most civility I can muster.'

His face was pale, and there were little round suns of anger on each cheek – the same tell as when he was a boy – but it was with tremendous calm that Brutus recounted to me how Antony had offered Julius a crown of laurels in front of the Lupercal crowd. I could hear no more and interrupted.

'This is not real. You come here to tease and provoke me. For what reason I cannot tell.'

Brutus started, affronted. 'Mother, when have I ever behaved in such a way? Least of all towards you. This is a faithful account of what happened. Marc Antony offered Julius Caesar a crown of laurels, three times. And three times, Caesar refused. But, there was hope in his hesitation. It was clear that if the crowd had urged him enough, he would have accepted. And he was disappointed that they did not. Consul, senator, dictator for life, none of these are enough for your friend, Mother. He hankers now for a crown. And not one of plaited laurels but gold.'

'Peace. He's not only my friend, but yours too, Brutus,' I said, my tone sharp.

'And that is why I'm here. I love Caesar. And I love Rome. Until now, I believed those two loves not only compatible, but commensurate. That by loving Caesar, I did also love Rome.'

I stared at Brutus. The flowers on the altar already looked drab and several had blown away in the breeze. 'It is still true. To love Caesar is to love Rome,' I insisted.

He said nothing, only looked at me. I never wanted my son to lie to me, but now I wished his account was an absurd fabrication, a false fireside tale. Yet, as I studied my son, serious, set now in earnest middle age, his brow furrowed and lips pursed with worry, I knew he told the truth, or what he believed it to be. Brutus could never lie to me, even as a boy; caught in some misdeed and fibbing to the slaves to escape punishment, he'd confess to me, the moment he was summoned into my presence. I taught him that the lie was worse than the misdeed. There was no crime he could commit that I would not forgive, but he must never lie to me. With dismay I knew he told the truth now.

I felt a snag in my chest as I tried to picture the scene as Brutus described it: the boisterous crowds, thick with wine and good cheer and brimful of affection for Caesar, singing raucous songs of his victories. Then, Antony strutting alongside, busy with his own self-importance, and conjuring a bouquet of laurels like a cheap magician. Caesar waving at them to stop, but full of expectation that they would not. Expecting that this would be his first, unofficial coronation, a display of false modesty and sham spontaneity. The thought of it made me wince for I'd always held Caesar and his judgement in the highest regard. I considered him capable of cruelty and self-regard, but never did I think he could display such hubris or stupidity. Had he forgotten that this was Rome? I did not blame Cleopatra, for all that she infuriated me. Queens always have their own schemes, and it was up to Caesar to recognise that. She did not know either Rome or Romans and if he paid heed to her then that was more of his own foolishness.

'I'll talk to him,' I promised Brutus.

Brutus shrugged. 'He listens to no one anymore. Not even you.'

Years later, people would tell one another of the strange signs that supposedly appeared across Rome at this time, and every citizen, even those not yet born, are now certain that they saw graves spew out rotting corpses, lions whelp in the forum or are eager to recount how they witnessed a bloody comet smear the sky with scarlet entrails. I do remember the comet, but not that it was red. Clodia told me breathlessly about a pig that delivered a litter of piglets without eyes. I sent out a slave to make enquiries, for if this was true, it was indeed an ill omen. The slave could find neither the pig nor a person who'd witnessed this strange happening. The monstrous litter was always at one remove, but that everyone believed these tales while eagerly searching for more signs unsettled me.

I'd been too angry to see Caesar since Lupercal and had avoided meeting either him or Cleopatra. Yet, time dulled the keen edge of my temper as fury cooled to fear. I was invited to dinner at my daughter and Lepidus's villa and despite knowing Caesar was likely to be there too, I accepted. Simply, I missed him.

The evening was bright and cool. The villa was lit with so many candles and torches that it shone out into the darkness like a second moon. Brutus was invited too, but of course he declined, having no wish to be in the company of Caesar, nor his sister Junia or brother-in-law Lepidus. It saddened me, for I wanted my son and daughters together, and I resented how this quarrel between Caesar and Brutus was spreading through my family, souring the relationship between brother and sister. Brutus avoided Junia, for he knew that she sided with her husband, and was devoted to Caesar by proxy. For the rest of Rome, this quarrel was political, but for me it was in the heart of my family and cut into my own heart.

The party that night comprised of a small gathering of intimate and old friends, but Lepidus always liked to lavish displays of friendship upon Caesar, so the villa was crammed with borrowed slaves and the tables of the triclinium were crowded with more food than ten-fold the number of guests could possibly consume. Junia frowned, overanxious about the comfort of everyone, so worried we would not take pleasure that she could take none herself. I kissed her, whispering, 'It is beautifully done, my love. All is well.'

From each room wafted the scent of roasted boar and game, caramelised nuts, every kind of poached fish and mulled wine. I strolled through the villa, eager to search out Caesar amongst the gathered guests. And at last, there he was, lounging on a sofa with an air of absolute assurance that drew all eyes to him. His gaze met mine and for a moment, as he smiled, I was a girl again wanting to be kissed, filled with hope and longing.

I settled on a sofa close to him. I would not share his sofa amongst company, but I was close enough to hear him charm everyone with his stories of bloody conquest and glory. As he described it, Rome was the only civilised city in the world, the one place worthy of the gods and their benevolence. The talk turned to war, for in only a few days Caesar was departing for his new campaign. Yet, as he discussed supplies and routes, I sensed a weariness in him; he sounded like a priest grown bored of his prayers, the words now rote, detached from their meaning and power. He was almost the same age as me, and I wondered if any part of him simply longed to stay at home. But lying still and growing fat on past success, adventuring only through his stories of old well-trampled glory, was not his way. Still, there was a shadow on him, the breath of Hades. What remained of his thinning hair was the colour of ash, and as he reached for a plate of figs, I noticed the protruding veins in his hand, the blotched skin.

As the evening progressed, the barrels of wine were emptied, and the chatter grew wilder, rumbunctious, and then, as is the way amongst old friends with many years between them, maudlin. Lepidus leaned forward, his teeth stained bloody with wine, and asked, 'Do you not fear death in this new campaign, Julius?'

'Fear it? No. But I shall be careful to avoid it. Like stepping round a large puddle,' replied Caesar.

Lepidus did not seem to hear him, as he continued to speak, wine sloshing from his goblet onto the floor. 'Battle is a good way for a man to die. Fast and glorious.'

Caesar snorted. 'There's rarely anything either glorious or fast about death in battle. Infection and agony perhaps. Glory only comes later, in the account.'

He turned to me and smiled, his voice softening. 'And you, Servilia? How would you like to die? Surrounded by your grandchildren?'

'No. I should not wish for company. Death is a lonely business. I should like to slide from sleep into death. Unwittingly.'

At this Caesar sat up. 'I do not want it to steal upon me in my dreams. That is a slippery, underhand death.'

'Then what is the best sort of death for a man?' I asked.

'One that is sudden and unexpected.'

I don't remember what anyone else said or wished after that. I wish we'd enjoyed some time alone together, Caesar and I, but we didn't. I don't believe that I even spoke to him particularly again, only addressed some general remarks to the company. I was spendthrift with our time for I thought we had plenty of it, and I could waste hours, minutes. I expected that I would see him tomorrow or if not, then the next day. There were so many tomorrows ahead, too many to be miserly with. I was worried about him leaving to fight in his new war, but not unduly. He'd been away before and he always returned. He was Caesar.

So, I left early. He smiled at me as I departed, but we did not speak or kiss. There were no words for me to hoard later. And perhaps it is not even this last smile that I truly remember, but another assembled from a lifetime of partings.

When I arrived home, to my surprise I found my other children there. Brutus was holding court with Portia and Tertia, her husband Cassius, and a few other of their friends. I was relieved that at least two of my children were friends. They greeted me with affectionate warmth. 'How was your evening, Mother?' asked Tertia, taking my hand.

'Come, sit with us a while,' added Brutus.

I did, not wanting to offend even though they seemed a little drunk and too bright, the slaves attending them looking overly fatigued, and I paid them scant attention – I'd left one party wearied only to discover another in my own house, when I wanted only peace. If only I'd listened to their chatter properly. They discussed nothing of their plans before me, but if I had paid closer attention, maybe I would have suspected enough to draw it out of them.

I wonder, as I have a thousand times since, if I'd stayed and discovered their plot whether then I could have convinced my son of the disaster he would unleash, reminded him again of his love for the man who'd been as a father to him. Brutus always listened to me, heeded my advice. Then all the world and its future would have been different, the earth moulded from a different clay. But it was not, because I was tired and exhausted by their high spirits, and I bade them good night when I ought to have asked questions, and insisted on knowing why they drank so much and were in such a state of excitement. If my bed had not called to me. If my head had not ached. If I had not wished to remove myself from Portia's braying laugh. Such small and fickle things decide the fate of an empire and a man.

They say that Calpurnia could not sleep that night. That she had premonitions, of Caesar's body streaming with rivers of blood from every vein. Perhaps that is true, or perhaps she conjured the memory of her premonitions later. Afterwards, Cleopatra told me that she too was restless, filled with nameless dread. I only know that I had no shadow-filled dreams. I slept deeply and well, and for the last time.

21
CLEOPATRA

The loneliness is a weight I carry with me everywhere, like the golden amulets shackled to my wrists. I think of Charmian and hope that her happiness is enough to balance out my pain. I don't think of Apollodorus. He took her from me. She chose him instead of me. Time has not yet scabbed the wound.

I distract myself with Caesarion, chasing him through the long grass. He screams with delight and hurtles from me, intent on joyous escape. I let him run further from me, feel the space between us lengthen until he's too far and the tug of him is like the pull of an invisible thread and I sprint to catch him, sweeping him up in my arms, and cover him with kisses, tickling his neck and belly as he shrieks and giggles.

'Again! Again!' he shouts, wriggling free and setting off once more, tottering and unsteady as he weaves along.

It's spring and the air is threaded with birdsong, and yellow sunshine spills along the path. There's a scent of turned earth and damp green things and dandelion seed pods feather the breeze. My feet are bare and smeared with mud, and a tiny beetle with a glossy carapace squats on my big toe. I flick it away, and prepare to run again, anticipating catching my boy once more, the feeling of his squirming warmth, his hot breath on my cheek.

Then I stop abruptly, for at the far side of the garden I see three slaves running towards me. They are shouting. There is something about their frenzy that unnerves me. I can't hear their words, tossed away by the wind. Caesarion continues to play, shrieking happily, but I no longer chase him. Shading my eyes, I glance at the slaves who still race towards me. A coldness trickles into my chest. I glance back at my boy, and for a moment can no longer see him amongst the tall grass, and I feel a sudden panic as though he is really lost to me. I can hear him still, his echoes of delight, and my heart rushes in my ears. I want only to follow him. A voice whispers that if I don't, I will lose him, and I know that is foolish for he is only playing in the grass, quite safe, and there are slaves and guards all around. I know my fear is not sensible yet cool dread rises within me like a spring tide. I want to chase him and play this game while we have time, and I am frightened as to what will happen when we stop. Time dilates, and then contracts again. The slaves draw closer, their shouts louder. I catch a single word caught on the wind and carried to me.

Death.

22

SERVILIA

I woke early and refreshed. The villa was still, the only noise that of the slaves busy about their morning chores and the pealing notes of spring. From a tree near my open window, a lark called. I smiled to hear it, gladdened, and decided that I would walk amongst my roses. I grew a profusion of them in every hue of white and pink and red and had mounds of manure carted in from my country estates for the gardeners to shovel into the beds. I am not vain of my own person, but I am vain of my roses – they are more exquisite than any in Rome. I meandered over to the window and glanced down at the beds beneath. Soon, the first buds would burst, and the air would be sweetened. I closed my eyes, happy in anticipation of a small pleasure. I'd heard Cleopatra had planted some that were new to me in the garden of her borrowed villa. If we shared a lover, we could share rose clippings.

Even as I was pondering this, I heard voices raised in the house below, but my thoughts were still scented with future roses, and I barely noticed. The shouts grew louder, and I felt a tickle of annoyance. I did not want visitors. Not yet. It was too early and they were unkind in their intrusion upon me on this bright spring morning. I would remain here in my own bedroom, secreted with my thoughts, and they would leave their message and depart, and the house would regain its stillness. Then to my dismay I heard the scuffle of footsteps on the stair. I sighed. I did not want them here. Let me stay in my room, alone and content and in peace considering my roses.

The door opened.

Brutus stood in the doorway, dipped in blood. His cheeks and hands were caked in crimson, sticky and wet, so thickly spread that it had not yet begun to dry. His white toga was torn and sprayed with gore. I stared at him for a moment, unable to understand the horror of the apparition before me, the living ghost of my brutalised son.

'Who has mauled you? Who has done this? What crime?' I cried, rushing to him.

Yet, he held me off, edged away from me. Something about his expression made me pause. I did not touch him. He smelled of meat.

'It is not my blood, Mother,' he said.

'Then whose?' I asked. The stillness around me swelled, it stretched and grew until I felt I must drown in it. I didn't want him to speak the next word. Do not say it.

'Caesar's.'

23

CLEOPATRA

I cannot think. My thoughts are thick and heavy and lined with blood and tumble over one another. There is no grief. Only shock and dread. I hear their voices, raised in fear and horror, but they sound as if they are coming from underwater now. Caesarion has stopped running, realising that I'm no longer in pursuit, and he stands swaying in the grass and frowns, his small face painted with disappointment. I rush to him and scoop him up, and he wriggles and cries, no longer pleased with the game, and I hold him too tight, frightened, and will not let him go.

Everywhere there is noise, cries of grief and confusion and conflicting instructions. The entire household is in motion yet Caesarion and I remain an island of stillness amid the chaos. He softens in my arms, snuggling into my neck, sensing the change in mood. We don't move as the shouts break around us, we're the rocks amid the crashing tide.

I told Caesar that he could be King of Rome, and I was the bellows to the fire of his ambition. I said aloud the whispers of his heart. I did not kill him. And yet, guilt noses at me, insistent as a wet dog. I push it away. It was his own desires, his longing. I only gave them voice. But he is dead all the same.

Caesarion does not know. And he will never know his father now. He is dead but there is no time for sadness. We can grieve later. Rome is not safe for us. We must run.

24

SERVILIA

We stood in the atrium, now thronging with slaves and several other senators, similarly spattered with blood. I ignored them, looking only at my son. I could not be with Caesar as he died nor share his pain, but I had to feel its echo. The pain brought me closer to him. I wanted it.

'Tell me again,' I repeated.

I listened, dry-eyed, to the account of the crime. I would cry later. Brutus stared at me. The blood on his toga had dried to brown. I could see a rind of blood beneath his nails and all the way up his arm. 'Continue,' I said, impatient.

He shook his head, pleading with me.

'Please, Mother, there is no more to tell. You've heard it all a dozen times. Every detail. Every drop of blood.'

'Tell me again. You owe me this much.'

I wanted to hear it repeated until it made sense to me, but of course it never could. Wincing, face pale except for the freckles of dried blood, he began once more.

'When Caesar entered the senate, we all stood up to show our respect to him.'

I made a sound in my throat, and spat, 'Your respect? Knowing what you were about to do to the man who saved you, pardoned you, loved you?'

Brutus did not answer, merely waited a moment and then continued again. 'And then some senators came about his chair—'

'And who led those senators? Don't leave any part out. Do not leave Brutus out.'

Now he cringed, but only for a moment, then straightened. 'It is true. Brutus was the leader of the small group who gathered about Caesar.'

I glanced about the room, where the household was now gathered with several more senators, and the co-conspirators, their togas similarly dowsed in blood.

'Brutus? Did you all hear? Brutus, my son. My son,' I said, gesturing to him.

The senators and slaves huddled alike, big-eyed with fear. None of them would meet my eye. I waved at Brutus to continue.

'We urged our petitions upon Caesar but he would not grant them. And then when Caesar was sat down, he refused to comply with our requests. We urged him again and again, until eventually he began to reproach us for our rudeness.'

'But this was a ruse, was it not? A meaningless provocation?' I said, my voice rising.

Brutus hesitated. 'His reaction was anticipated. And next, grabbing hold of his robe with both my hands, I pulled it down from his neck, which was the signal for the assault. Cassius gave the first cut.'

'In his neck?'

'Yes, madam. In his neck. It was not mortal or dangerous.'

I gave a short laugh, aware of the shrill note of grief in my voice. 'A cut to the neck sounds dangerous to me. But I was not there. I do not know. And he is dead, is he not? So it was both mortal and dangerous.'

'Yes, he is dead. But that was the first blow, madam. It did not kill him.'

Brutus swallowed and I saw that he was sweating, his face bathed in perspiration that coated his unnatural pallor. I did not offer him wine nor any other restorative. Merely waved for him to continue.

'Caesar immediately turned about and grasped the dagger and kept hold of it. He cried out.'

'And tell me what he said?'

Brutus sighed. 'He said, "This is violence!", his voice heavy with dismay and shock.'

'And what did the senators do? Did none help him?'

'Those who were not privy to the plot were astonished and looked on in shock. In their panic they did not fly to assist Caesar, nor so much as speak a word.'

I could not understand those cowards and their hesitation. Their guilt did not lie as heavily as Brutus's, but it was weighted all the same. I hated them all for their hesitation and cowardice. I would have rushed to Caesar and shielded his body with my own. Let them rain their blows upon my soft flesh, pierce my breast and thigh and stomach with their blades, my skin and muscle a mere cushion to soften the blows aiming for his. But these brave men, these senators, commanders of legions and conquerors, were too frightened and stood rooted there like children fearful of the dark.

Brutus hurried on with his account, as eager to have done with the telling as with the deed.

'But those of us who knew in advance about the business enclosed him on every side, daggers drawn in our hands. Which way soever he turned, he met with blows and blades, and saw our swords levelled at his face and eyes, and was trapped, like a wild beast, on every side. It was agreed we should all make a thrust at him and wet ourselves with his blood. All equal in this glorious act. For now, blighted Rome is rid of its tyrant.'

I was silent for moment and did not acknowledge his words of self-justification. Then I asked, 'And Brutus? What did Brutus do?'

'I stabbed him.'

'Just once?'

'Aye.'

'Where?'

'In the groin.'

Sickness rose in my throat. I forced it down. I'd heard the story repeated so many times now that I took over the final portion.

'Caesar fought and resisted, wrenching his body every which way to avoid the blows, and crying out for help, but when he saw Brutus's sword drawn, his own Brutus, the boy who'd been as a son to him, beloved and tender,

Julius covered his face with his robe and submitted, letting himself fall.'

'I loved him too,' said Brutus.

'Of course, my darling. Your actions speak of your devotion,' I spat. For a moment I could not look at him, then I inhaled slowly and continued. 'And whether it was by chance or fate or that he was shoved there by his murderers, he lay at the foot of Pompey's statue. The white marble of Pompey anointed wetly with Caesar's blood. And then Caesar lay there at his old enemy's feet, and breathed out his soul through his multitude of wounds. For this was not just murder, it was butchery.'

I turned on Brutus, my voice shrilling with fury and desperation. 'You all stabbed him so hard and so often that in your frenzy you sliced open your own hands and each other's. And then after he was dead and his soul flown this charnel house, you stabbed him as he lay stilled in the river of his own blood.'

Brutus remained motionless, saying nothing.

The gathered senators and slaves stared at me. No one spoke. The silence throbbed, a held breath. I edged closer to Brutus, took his hand, doused with the blood of my love, my Caesar, and I held it to my lips, and kissed it.

'And you too, Brutus?' I whispered. 'You, Brutus, my child? You killed us both with the same knife. Caesar is dead, free from this restless earth, but I still breathe and move and speak, though I am dead all the same and you killed me. My heart is no longer in my chest. It no longer fits.'

Brutus gazed at me, his eyes wet with tears. Then he said, his voice low, 'I am sorry for your pain but I am not ashamed. I acted for the good of Rome and the republic. I had to rid it of Caesar to save it.'

I stared at my son, so foolish and wretched and cruel. He made himself a murderer to save the republic, and yet was so short-sighted that he had no plan for Rome after his act. The streets were empty, silent. Everyone cowered inside their houses in terror. Brutus had torn down the sun without another lamp to hand. The silence and fear would not last. It would soon turn to rage, and maybe war. Caesar's allies would hunt down Brutus and the other plotters. I had no doubt that Antony would demand that they be killed for this treason. I started at my son, wondering if he knew what he'd unleashed.

He took my silence as an invitation to continue.

'My father was Brutus and my ancestor Brutus rid Rome of the tyrannicide. It was not merely my duty, but my fate, for I am Brutus.'

'You are Brutus,' I said, my voice little more than a whisper.

'Will you help me, madam? There are those who call for my blood, my death.'

My beloved foolish son, who started an uprising by committing murder and sacrilege and could not think to plan what might happen next. I could not breathe. I was done. And gone. I stared into the eyes of my lover's murderer. The face of the only man left alive whom I loved.

'Yes,' I said. 'I will help you.'

25

CLEOPATRA

Guards are stationed on every entrance, but beyond the gates Rome burns. A mob has taken to the streets, ransacking houses as they hunt for the assassins. The crowd is split between those who would tear the murderers limb from limb, and those who want to slaughter all those close to Caesar. I need to find a way to get my son home. We came here to further his position and clarify my power but now unless we can get back to Alexandria, it will melt away. At the far end of the hall, I hear my brother-husband, little Tol, talking anxiously to his nurse. He is old enough to be frightened, but not old enough to help me come up with a way to escape.

For the present we are safe behind the villa walls. But whose villa is this now that Caesar is dead? I don't know. His death was vicious and full of pain. He did not deserve such a death; it was not worthy of him. I do not miss him yet, for his departure is too recent, too raw, and I still half expect to see him striding along the path to find me.

Yet nothing is the same. The very air is altered. I am restless and can neither sit nor sleep nor eat. My hands shake as though I suffer from palsy. Above the city hovers a haze of smoke from fires burning in the streets. I pace through the villa gardens, for I cannot bear to be inside. Here, birds sing, unstilled. A bee investigates a clump of sunny narcissi beside a pool. For all the portents, now Caesar is dead nature does not care. The nursery slaves play with Caesarion beside a fountain of Venus, for I order him to be always in sight. Anxiety has taken lodging in my chest, and I feel the hurried beat of my heart. When I think of the danger to my boy I can't breathe, and my vision blanches bright, as though I'm looking directly at the sun.

There's a noise downstairs and for a moment I think that the house has been breached, the mob is here. There are footsteps on the stairs. I wait for the shout of the guards outside my chamber, but they are silent. The door opens, and I see her. Charmian stands in the doorway, dirty and travel-worn. Her feet are blistered and bleeding, her sandal flaps broken.

'You came back. You came back to me,' I say, doubting my eyes.

'You needed me. I had to come,' she says.

I run to her and she hugs me, holding me tight, and suddenly all the tears that I have not shed fall at once as she holds me and rubs my back and whispers that she has missed me, that she loves me. 'I'll never leave you again,' she says. I find that I cannot speak at all.

*

I know that the world is burning, and we must run, and Caesar is dead, and yet my sadness is leavened with joy. I stare at her in bewilderment. She is a freedwoman, able to make her own choices, and she chose me.

'What about Apollodorus?' I ask.

She is quiet for a moment, as though unable to speak. Her face is stricken, and when she speaks, it is in a whisper. 'I love him. But I love you more.'

I twist and ache for him. He was my friend and I tried to give him freedom and happiness, but it seems that we can't both be happy. There isn't room in the world for both of us to have what we want. The thought of him on the farm, lonely without Charmian, even as he's surrounded by his family, tugs at me. Guilt and sadness flare inside me. 'I am sorry, Apollodorus,' I murmur. I don't ask Charmian what she said to him when she left. I don't want to imagine his grief or pain at their parting, I already know what it is like. I pity him but I would not trade places.

She has come back to me and with her beside me, I know that we will escape, survive this, as we have all other dangers before. She might not have come with Apollodorus, but she has not come alone. She's carrying his child. I do not ask her if he knew that she was pregnant, it seems cruel. I will take care of her and the baby as if they were my own flesh. I keep her beside me, only letting her out of my sight to wash and find clean clothes. I insist she eats at my side. I watch her tear into bread and fruit.

'The slaves are readying the essentials for our journey. The rest will follow,' she says.

'How do we make our escape? We're hemmed in on every side. The mob will not let us leave,' I say.

Her face tight with worry, Charmian chews her nails, an old habit that used to get her beaten as a child. We need a plan, but I haven't found it yet. My fate is too closely tied to Caesar, even after his death. It is like being back in the palace at Alexandria with enemies on every side, only now we lack his power. I realise with a nudge of sadness that there is loneliness in his death. I did not expect that. I want his protection but also his company. Despite Charmian's return, there is a void and an echo. There isn't time to dwell, we must only think how to escape, survive.

'There are rioters on every street. Still, we must travel through them, fight our way out, before they try to reach us here,' I say.

'That is too dangerous,' says Charmian.

I think of the soothsayer in Alexandria on the evening Caesar and I met. They killed the tree and now they will come for the fruit.

'We are friendless here now Caesar is gone,' she says.

And then I wonder. A strange thought strikes me. I recall Servilia. We are sisters in sorrow. For a moment I consider her loss. If my love for Ceaser is a river, then hers was the ocean, wide and deep.

26

SERVILIA

I ordered Brutus to stay downstairs and posted guards on each of the doors. The city hummed with men hunting for him, eager to kill him for what he had done. He would be safe here in my house, for no one was closer to Caesar than me. And there was no one who felt his loss more keenly. Not the death of the statesman or dictator or general, but the loss of the man. Caesar the man with brown eyes slightly bloodshot with tiredness, who still always smiled when he saw me. He spoke to me in a voice that he used with no one else. No one would speak to me like that again, nor look at me with such tenderness.

I sat in my room, still in my night gown and shawl. The world was smashed and ended and yet I was cursed to see it still. I found that I spoke aloud as if to Caesar himself, and as I spoke, I saw a vision of him, hands clasped over his wounds, bleeding, beside my bed, the bed where we had talked and laughed and argued and fucked for thirty years. Without pausing to consider the unlikeliness of this apparition conjured from my unquiet mind, I talked to his ghost.

'I heard no portents. Nothing warned me of this, my love. I slept. Was I thinking about my roses as you lay dying?'

He gazed back at me in silence.

'I shall plant only bloody roses now. All the white and pink and yellow shall be torn up, and only Caesar's red dug into those beds. They will have the sharpest thorns that will make the finger of anyone who picks them bleed.'

The ghost did not answer, simply sat, watching me with sad eyes.

My grief became rage, and restless in my fury I spun around the room, hands clawing at my hair and scratching at my face. Brutus was bathed in guilt. It dripped from him. But where was Antony as Caesar lay dying? Where were those others who could have saved him? Where were the men who loved him? I swallowed the question. What did it matter? Brutus loved him and he butchered him anyway.

The slaves dressed me in a fine linen dress, combed my hair and bathed my hands and face, assembling me in an echo of Servilia. Then I was lifted into my litter. The streets were emptier now, and the danger less acute, but I almost longed for accident or danger, for then I would not have to do this. This most horrible of tasks.

For the next hours, I knocked on the doors of senators,

those friends of Caesar who were not party to the plot and were now filled with outrage and sorrow at the murder. I wanted to join them in their anger and their demands for vengeance. I wanted blood to assuage Caesar's, but instead, I went on my knees and pleaded for my son the killer. As I begged, my eyes bleary with grief, I placed the box containing Caesar's pearl at their feet. The symbol of his loyalty and love for me.

They listened to me with pity. None accused me of complicity. They knew my love for Caesar.

As I was carried home, I lay in the litter, feeling its rhythm, and I thrummed with humiliation and resentment and relief, for Brutus was safe. They would not demand his death.

My grief was doubled, Caesar was dead and my son had done it. I tried to put my heart back into my chest but it was too fat with sorrow. I protected my son, my enemy. His betrayal was absolute and yet I loved him still, even as Caesar's corpse burned.

When I returned home, I walked out into the garden, my head aching. I stood in the air for a long time, feeling the wind on my skin and wondering how it was possible to feel so much pain, so much betrayal and grief, and yet still live.

I found myself thinking of that other boy. Caesar's son. I hoped he would never have to pay for his father's sins. But this is the way of things. Children grow up to be men and kill or are killed for the acts of their fathers. Mothers try and protect them from their own misdeeds, and yet mostly their actions are not remembered. I would in all likelihood disappear from history, my own self erased. Perhaps I was only ever the people I tried to save and only the men I saved or failed to save will be recalled. They will not know that I was the pebble, they will just see the ripples as I slid away beneath the surface. They will not know how I grieved for my lover, or how I tried to save my son; the senate meetings to plead for him, the wranglings and hurt. They will leave me out of the story. Perhaps it is best. There is peace in silence.

I took a breath of cool fresh air and then I returned to the house. I wanted to retreat upstairs and crawl into bed and wait for the sleep that I knew would not come. I waved away the slaves and all offers of refreshment or comfort. But then, to my dismay, I saw there was a visitor waiting for me.

'I'm sorry, madam, she would not go,' said one of my slaves, full of apology. 'Charmian is come, Cleopatra's freedwoman.'

With a sigh, I turned to face the intruder. A young woman. Charmian. Cleopatra's servant. Fury hummed again in my veins. How dare she come here to plead for her mistress? Cleopatra did not kill Caesar but she handed the knife to those who did. But as I looked at her, I saw that it was not Charmian at all, but Cleopatra herself in her servant girl's clothes. In my exhaustion, anger clarified into hate.

'I am your sister in sorrow,' she said softly,

'How dare you claim kinship with me in my grief? Your love is for yourself and your own interests.'

She did not answer nor condemn me for my outspoken rudeness, only stared at me, her expression heavy with pity. I sat on the bench and put my head in my hands. And yet, before my eyes I saw our sons. Mine, foolish, covered in blood, and hers, the small boy with Caesar's curls and stubborn mouth. The child was the last piece of Caesar. I knew Caesar would want his son to live. I'd saved my own son, the murderer. Cleopatra's son was only a baby, an innocent. I detested Cleopatra the queen, but Cleopatra the mother, I understood. I turned to her.

'I hate you. I blame you for this.' I took a breath. 'And I will save you and your son.'

27

CLEOPATRA

Servilia comes to the villa and hurries inside, surrounded by guards. Outside the mob screams for my blood. A simple disguise would no longer be enough to fool them. There's no restraint in their rage: all they understand is that Caesar is dead and the world broken open. They will kill us if they find us. My fear is only for my boy. I do not care for my own flesh.

We huddle together, making our plans with Servilia.

'They will drink themselves into a stupor by dawn. It will be quieter then. The soldiers will patrol, and that is the safest time for you to leave. You'll take my litter, not your own. No one will molest you, if they believe you are me,' she says. 'They saw me enter, and they will not know that it is you who leaves in my stead.'

I turn quickly to Charmian. 'We leave everything behind. Nothing matters.'

I arrived here as queen with hundreds of slaves and a retinue of wagons and treasure, and I leave with nothing, I must shed it all to escape. Even my name. I will put it on again when we reach Egypt.

None of us sleeps. We wait, listening, watching till dawn. The first light sneaks across the sky, bleeding into the light of the fires in the streets. I rise from my seat and signal to the others. It's time. The villa is abandoned, half packed, ready to be picked through and pilfered after we flee. I care for none of it; not the inlaid furniture or jewels or carpets or rare wines. Only us. Charmian, and me and my boy. My brother Tol will ride in a separate litter with his own guard, all painted with Servilia's insignia. Caesarion is furious to be woken, in the night, plucked rudely from his cradle, but he settles again in the litter beside me, sleeping unaware of the danger. We are tucked up in Servilia's litter, and she sends us out surrounded by her slaves, all clearly wearing her insignia. Caesarion snuggles into my lap, and I play with the golden hoard of his curls.

'Take them out of the city, the shortest route. Be gone before dawn breaks,' she orders.

Charmian frowns, tries to argue with me again. 'My queen, you and Caesarion should not travel together, in one litter.'

I understand her fear – that if we are discovered, the mob will drag us out and kill us both. I shake my head in refusal. If we die, we die together.

As we are carried away, I sense Servilia watching us from an upper window. We shall not meet again.

*

The streets of Rome are mostly empty, the citizens huddle in their houses, afraid. Under the blankets in the litter, I echo their fear. I hardly breathe. It takes too long to pass through the city. We avoid the main thoroughfares, but we don't want the narrowest backstreets where we could be trapped, unmasked. I stroke Caesarion's hair, willing him to sleep. We travel to the rhythm of the jogging slaves. Terror nudges me until I can't see, and my vision is smudged. We stop suddenly and, thrust forward. Caesarion wakes and begins to cry. I hush him but he won't be quietened.

'Who is it that you carry?' demands a voice. 'Who ventures out now?'

I daren't look and see, not even a peep.

'Servilia of the Servilii, as you can see,' declares a guard, one of Servilia's own men. 'Move or we will walk over you.'

Caesarion begins to wail and tug at the curtain.

'Servilia has no babe in arms,' says the voice. 'Let me see who it is you carry.'

'Move away. You do not sully the litter of a matron of Rome with your unclean hands unless you want to lose them.'

I gesture to Charmian to hold Caesarion firmly, and, my hands shaking, I take a bottle from round my neck and, forcing Caesarion's mouth open with my fingers, I shake in a few drops from the bottle. In a few seconds he quietens, goes limp. I hope I have given him the right amount, only enough to make him sleep.

'Move aside!' yells the guard.

Clearly, the challenger has chosen to step aside, for I feel the pace pick up and we rush forward. I curl up around my boy. He whimpers in his sleep.

*

Time passes in spurts. It rushes then stills. We travel through the city gates. I exhale and Charmian smiles at me, squeezes my hand. My fear makes me impatient and snappish. I am cramped and sore and we are jostled and shaken. The light bleeds around the edges of the horizon, reds smeared across the sky. We are not safe. Not yet. We travel on and on. To my relief, Caesarion wakes, but relief is short-lived. Soon my head throbs with his crying and the effort of holding him, stopping him from grabbing the curtains and trying to climb out. Nausea builds in my stomach, acid and sour, and my legs and arms are numb. The slaves slow and stall some distance beyond the city gates, unable to carry us any further.

We are handed down from the litter, and now climb into a waiting cart. It's no luxurious wagon but a covered cart pulled by horses. Caesarion is scarlet with rage and tries to refuse to get inside, longing to run around and play, but is lifted up unceremoniously by a slave. I am sweaty and dry-mouthed. A pain twists low in my belly, I give a sudden cry.

'Are you well, my queen?' asks Charmian.

I wave away her concerns. The truth is that I cannot tell. I cannot see for fear, and there is a coldness deep within me.

We do not stop until we are hours away from the city. The light has changed to that of late afternoon. We stink of horses and sweat. The wagon pauses near the banks of a river, and the horses are unhitched to drink.

I wade out into the shallows. I need to wash, to cleanse myself. As the water tickles my ankles, I feel blood trickling down my thighs. There is a fist of pain. I double over and vomit into the river.

I sit in the shallows, ungainly, nesting on a crock of pebbles. Charmian comes and sits beside me, the water marbling pink with my blood.

'I didn't know,' she says. 'I'm sorry, I didn't know.'

I don't speak. I don't need to. We lie together side-by-side in the water, as the stream washes away this part of me and Caesar. The pain is acute, but I can bear it. I must bear it, for we have far to go. I bite my lip, clenching my fingers and toes.

'Tell me you won't leave me again,' I say.

'Never,' she replies. 'I'm yours.' She opens her arms. 'Lie back. Let me hold you,' she says.

I wriggle back and lie in her arms. I feel the small, hard curve of her own swelling belly. She strokes my face and my hair. I close my eyes and let myself cry.

She talks to me softly as she washes away my tears. 'I had a dream. Our children were playing together. My daughter, Caesarion and the spirit of this child. But there were other children too.'

'Yours?'

'No, yours. Not yet. But one day.'

I believe her. I consider everything she's given up to be with me. I gave her freedom but she chose me anyway. She came back to me for love. This pain in my belly isn't mine alone, for we are together. We will survive and find our way back to Alexandria.

The water sluices away the blood. I rest in her arms and do not move, allowing it to clean me. The coolness of the water soothes the pulsing ache. I don't know how long I lie there. Minutes. Hours. She just sits with me, holding me in her arms.

Some time later, I notice a little upstream Caesarion squatting in the water, peering at a fish. Love rises in me, a spinning coin. It's time. I rinse away the last of the blood from my thighs and stand, a little unsteady.

'Come,' I say, heading back to the wagon. 'We have far to go.'

Caesarion reaches for one hand and Charmian takes the other.

As we walk, I think of Servilia. I did not thank her. But I suspect she does not want my gratitude. Charmian stoops and picks up my son. We go back to the wagon together, my family.

Now I sit in the gardens of the palace. Home in Alexandria. In the distance the sea glints silver and green, above the gulls circle, sailing through the sky on great white wings. The air is perfumed with the scent of date palms and salt. The light here is blue, and heat rasps my skin, and I watch as Caesarion plays on a blanket with his nurse and Charmian, indulged by both. She is heavy with her child, he will be born any day now. Perhaps one day his father will visit. But I will be as a parent to the boy. I look at my friend and my son and smile, dazed with love. Charmian rises with some difficulty and, puffing, settles on the cushion beside me. I stroke her hair.

'I came back to you because I belong to you and also to this,' she says softly. 'The Nile flows through my blood. I am a creature of the court, not a farmer's wife. I cannot be other than I am.'

I kiss her forehead. 'And I love you as you are. Rest now,' I say.

She closes her eyes. And, as she sleeps, I take out my pen and resume my account. This is peace. Rome leaves us be, for now at least. The empire is too busy eating its own tail to bother with us at the far edges. Yet I know it hasn't forgotten me or Egypt, merely turned its head away for a moment. My sister is a prisoner in Rome, alive but safely far away from me. This calm is only a lull but I savour it all the same. Happiness is fleeting, and I grab it with my fingers as it slips through them like sand.

I know what they say about me in Rome. Already, my enemies chisel away my name where they find it. They want to erase all parts of me, have my body and my name sink back into the dust. Yet their words are more brutal than their tools for if it was up to them, they would seal me inside a history that never was. I worry that one day, their prattling, strumpet Cleopatra will step forward shrieking, my own self lost. Their voices are so loud that it seems even to me that my memories are only dreams and shadows. The world is stuffed with my enemies and rivals, who only see me through the veil of their own dislike and the misleading dazzle of their ambition. But I've told you my story and you know that I am not who they say. You hear my own history even as they race to erase and deface me. Don't listen to them, for who knows the truth better than me? For I am Cleopatra.

I heard that Brutus lives, and despite all he has done, the havoc and misery he has wreaked, I am glad for his mother's sake. I look at my son on the blanket, playing with his blocks, piling them up and shrieking with rage as they tumble, and I both feel it is impossible that he could ever grow into such a man, capable of such harm, and know that he could.

Servilia and I were joined for a moment, connected by our love for one man, and then by fear and loss. Without Caesar, there is no conduit between us. Yet, I think of her sometimes, the mother who saved her son and mine.

Charmian murmurs in her sleep beside me and I swat away a mosquito from her cheek. Rome might plot against me in deeds and whispers, but I have friends. I am loved, as a queen, a goddess and as a mother and friend. I will rule Egypt and defend my throne for all of us against the mighty tyranny of Rome. My voice is loud, I shout across the endless dunes and I will be heard.

Perhaps you are reading my account now in the great library at Alexandria, amongst the scrolls where I liked to sit as a girl. I don't know what happens next or how my part will end. I am only determined that my name will live on. And you know now the woman to whom it belonged. And, as you read, do not picture me crowded with jewels, bracelets jammed along my arms. I hope that you see me instead in the library seated on a low cushion, a scroll tucked in one hand, my finger twisting in my hair as I read, lips moving, a concentrated furrow on my brow, Charmian at my side. I will place this account there, waiting for those, like you, who want to find me.

AUTHOR'S NOTE

We all know Cleopatra, or we think we do. We certainly know her name – there is probably no-one more famous than Cleopatra. Most of us are familiar with the version of Cleopatra derived from Shakespeare, the aging seductress, caught up in the politics of love. Cleopatra is one of the greatest and most complex female characters Shakespeare ever created. Yet, why did he call his play *Anthony and Cleopatra* and not *Cleopatra and Anthony*? After all, it was Cleopatra who was Pharaoh and Queen of Egypt and the richest monarch in the world. Similarly, why did Shakespeare leave Cleopatra out of his play *Julius Caesar* entirely? She was living in Rome at the time, as Caesar's lover and the mother of his son, Caesarion. And yet, Shakespeare erases her from his history. I decided that it was time to put her back in and imagine her story from her own point of view.

Shakespeare created his vision of Cleopatra from Plutarch, Cicero and other Roman historians – the problem is not only

AUTHOR'S NOTE

that they were writing at a distance of at least a hundred years, but also that these Roman writers detested the very idea of her. They couldn't bear that a woman had come so close to beating them in battle, and since the Romans ultimately won, it was them who got to write the final account. So, the Cleopatra we're most familiar with was created by Shakespeare after the accounts of her hostile Roman enemies.

It's always a challenge when creating a fictional version of a historical figure, especially so when they are from ancient history. It's almost impossible to create with certainty a character from so long ago, especially one where the sources are so problematic – sometimes it can feel like guessing in the dark. I wanted to create Cleopatra as a woman with vulnerabilities and real human relationships – but who still feels like a Queen from an ancient world. I needed to both bring her to earth like lightening yet still keep that divine essence which makes her Cleopatra. She's both powerful and fragile, divine and human, a living goddess but also a mother who worries about her son – a woman who needs to trade her body and sexuality for her country.

I used Plutarch and Shakespeare as well as other sources – ancient and modern – and my own imagination. There's always a tension between history and fiction; while historical fact (as we can find it) is the bedrock for historical fiction, narrative dictates its own rhythm. Biography isn't always convenient for ideally paced drama. Here and there, I've needed to massage dates or places – for instance, the famous meeting between Cato and Cleopatra's father Auletes actually took place in Cyprus when the Pharoah was on his way to Rome. We don't know for sure that either a young Cleopatra or

AUTHOR'S NOTE

Servilia were there – but we also don't know that they weren't there: history often doesn't think women worth mentioning. I think they're worth mentioning over and over again and moving from the margins of the story to the very centre. For me, it's the stories about women that are the most interesting. I hope you enjoy meeting my Cleopatra.

ACKNOWLEDGEMENTS

This book was written amid turmoil and heartbreak. Looking back, it feels a bit of a marvel that it got written at all. It certainly wouldn't have been possible without the help of the following people: my parents, Carol and Clive Carsley, and my sister Joanna Garstang, who picked me up and put me back together again and again. My remarkable friends who are my support system and provide – in no particular order – hugs, perspective, tea, whisky, and kitchen dancing: Charmian Holcroft, Ros Chapman, Tracey Lewis, Rachel Borchard Lewis, Uri Baruchin and Georgina Howland who, despite everything she was going through, still had room in her heart for me. Thanks especially to Peter English who has driven up to Dorset again and again when we've needed him. Thank you to my lovely friends and neighbours in my Dorset village, you've appeared at all hours and helped out with such kindness whenever I've called on you; we're so lucky. I'm particularly grateful to Hannah Mckeand for reading draft after

ACKNOWLEDGEMENTS

draft – even when she was in the arctic – and to Edward Hall, for his unwavering faith in me as a writer.

Thanks to my agent Sue Armstrong – you are the absolute best. And, to her assistant Catriona Paget who has gone above and beyond again and again. Profound thanks to everyone at Bonnier for your patience and kindness as well as your indefatigable support for me and my books. Especially, my brilliant editor Sophie Orme as well as Zoe Yang, Ilaria Tarasconi, Ruth Logan, Stella Giatrakou, Tamara Douthwaite, Beth Whitelaw, Helen Reith, Laura Makela, Chelsea Graham, Jenny Richards, Nick Stearn, David Ettridge, Alex May and the Bonnier Books UK and international sales teams.

Last thanks go to my remarkable children, Luke and Lara. You've learned more than you wanted to about Cleopatra and the gang, putting up with me disappearing into my office and sometimes forgetting to make dinner until after bedtime. I am so proud of you and so grateful to you.

It takes a village to both raise a family to write a book, and it turns out with the help of mine, like Taylor Swift, I can do it with a broken heart.

About the Author

NATASHA SOLOMONS is the author of nine internationally bestselling novels, including *Mr Rosenblum's List*, *The Novel in the Viola*, which was chosen for the Richard & Judy Book Club, and *I, Mona Lisa*. Her work has been translated into seventeen languages. She lives in Dorset with her family.